THE
PRESIDENT'S
VAMPIRE

Also by Christopher Farnsworth

Blood Oath

THE
PRESIDENT'S
VAMPIRE

CHRISTOPHER FARNSWORTH

HODDER &
STOUGHTON

First published in Great Britain in 2011 by Hodder & Stoughton
An Hachette UK company

Published by permission of G.P. Putnam's Sons, a
member of Penguin Group (USA), Inc.

1

A CIP catalogue record for this title is available from the British Library

Hardback ISBN 978 0 340 99816 8
Trade Paperback ISBN 978 0 340 99817 5

Printed and bound in the UK by CPI Mackays, Chatham ME5 8TD

Hodder & Stoughton policy is to use papers that are natural, renewable
and recyclable products and made from wood grown in sustainable
forests. The logging and manufacturing processes are expected to
conform to the environmental regulations of the country of origin.

Hodder & Stoughton Ltd
338 Euston Road
London NW1 3BH

www.hodder.co.uk

To my grandparents, Ben and Dorothy,

who always protected us from the monsters

This world is a farm, and we are the crop.

—CHARLES HOY FORT

PROLOGUE

NOVEMBER 29, 2001, NEAR PARACHINAR, PAKISTAN

Nathaniel Cade watched the men from his hidden perch as they walked up the narrow mountain path.

One was clearly in pain. He stooped, despite his height, and a younger man helped him along, at times almost carrying him.

To the north, the bombing at Tora Bora continued. The 10,000-pound daisy cutters slammed into the caves, one after another, the impact felt more than heard as earth and sky shook with each explosion.

It would have been impossible to block all the treacherous, winding paths out of the area, but the Americans had not even tried. That job went to the Pakistani military and a few warlords who switched sides only weeks before the invasion.

At least, that was the cover story.

Cade recalled how the general swore when told to keep this escape route open. Cade had been around a long time, but the general managed to surprise him with the inventiveness of some of the obscenities.

The order came direct from the president. The general probably assumed it was a political deal with the Pakistani military—a chance to prove themselves in the War on Terror. And a chance to conveniently forget all the help they'd given to the bad guys in the past. The general could not imagine they were actually going to let the target leave.

And yet, Cade watched as the most wanted man in the world simply walked away. Stumbling and weak, but still walking.

Osama bin Laden was almost free.

IT HAD TAKEN SOME DOING to convince the president. Seventy-two hours earlier, in the Presidential Emergency Operations Center below the White House, Cade did not think it would happen.

"Gonna cost me the damn election," the president said, face pinched with anger. He'd already been stewing about reports that questioned his absence on September 11—fleeing from one secure location to the next, while the wreckage still burned in New York and D.C.

Griff, Cade's handler, sat across the table. He'd been on the receiving end of many presidential tantrums in his career. He was used to it.

"Sir," he said. "You want to use Cade. This is the only way we can do it."

"We can't at least, I dunno, bring back the sumbitch's head, or something?" the president asked.

"All missions related to Mr. Cade are above top secret. You know that," the vice president reminded the president.

The president gave him a look.

"Sir," the veep added.

"I just want people to see what we do to the bastards who do things like this to us," the president insisted.

"Believe me, so do I, sir," the veep said. He stood and placed a hand on the president's shoulder. "But there are things here . . ." He paused, looking for the right words. "Things here are complicated. Things it's better for you not to know."

The president squinted. "You mean that spooky shit, don't you? I don't like that."

"Which is why Mr. Cade will handle this."

The president appeared to waver. Then the vice president spoke again. "Besides, George—there might be advantages to always having Bin Laden out there. Nice to have a boogeyman whenever you need it."

"Yeah. All right," the president said. "Do it."

He walked to the door, still grumbling. "Gonna cost me the damn election."

At the door of the PEOC, he stopped and turned. He addressed Cade directly—something he rarely ever did. "Least you can do is make it messy, right? You make the sumbitch hurt."

Cade nodded. He could do that. It would be little enough payment for the wounds inflicted on the United States. He was still a patriot. Even if he was no longer human.

CADE LOOKED DOWN at the Arabs again. At this rate, they would take another fifteen minutes, at least, to reach him at the crest of the ridge.

Cade shifted, feeling the wound in his gut. It was healing, but it hurt. The only thing keeping his intestines inside his body was a heavy-duty neoprene sheath. Of course, anyone else would have been killed.

Cade had spent most of the day of 9/11 in an underground parking garage, pinned to a concrete pillar by a sword driven through his torso.

He was still annoyed by that. He decided he'd waited long enough.

With one leap, he was out into empty air. He fell the length of three football fields and landed on his feet without a sound, directly in front of the man in the lead.

The man's reaction time was admirable. He was one of the elite of al-Qaeda's fighters assigned as Bin Laden's personal bodyguards. He had been hardened by years of combat, first against the Soviets, then against other warring tribes. Now he had taken the most punishing bombardment the greatest military in the world could dish out—and lived.

Still, he barely touched his rifle before Cade pulled out his larynx.

The second man didn't waste time trying to unsling his rifle. He had a knife in his hand before his comrade fell, and he stabbed Cade in the side. It was a perfect strike—it should have driven up, between the ribs and into Cade's heart, ending him.

That is, if the knife's point had not skidded off Cade's skin, which was tougher than Kevlar weave.

Cade twisted the second man's head completely around. His body fell nerveless to the trail.

Now he faced Bin Laden himself, and his supporter. He shoved them to the ground, not wanting the man dead.

Not yet.

The fifth Arab used the clear shot at Cade to unload half a clip from his AK-47. Several of the rounds tore through Cade's wrapping, opening the wound again. He nearly doubled over from the pain.

But he didn't drop. The fifth Arab's eyes went wide as Cade took the rifle from him. He whispered the start of a prayer and choked on his own blood as Cade drove the rifle through his chest.

The man supporting Bin Laden was the youngest of the group—a boy, really, perhaps seventeen at the most. Despite what had happened to the combat veterans on each side of him, he did not hesitate to protect his leader. He reached for the grenades strung on the belt around his chest.

Cade snatched the belt away and tossed it to the ground before the boy could blink. Then Cade flung him into the abyss over the side of the trail. For a second, his arms scrabbled at the empty air as he began to drop. It would take a long time for him to hit the bottom.

Less than two minutes after it started, the fight was over.

Cade turned to Bin Laden.

The most feared and hated man alive did not look particularly scary, especially when compared to Cade. He had been injured in the bombing, it was obvious—one side of his robes had fresh patches of red blood, and he panted heavily, struggling for breath. Cade could smell disease in him as well. This weak, sickly creature had brought the whole world to a halt, if only for a little while.

Bin Laden seemed to know he was no match for Cade. He remained on his knees, glaring. Cade wasn't about to kill him. He had questions.

Due to a number of chemical and psychological causes, Cade's memory, like every member of his kind, was perfect. He did not forget. Time did not dim his recall of anything. He could play it back with perfect clarity, even reliving scents and feelings.

Touching the wound in his abdomen, he was there again.

LATE AT NIGHT on September 10, he followed a target into a parking garage. He'd been tracking the man for weeks—it should not have been so difficult, and that should have tipped him off. He was searching the lower levels of the underground garage. He saw nothing. Then the man appeared as if from nowhere, moving faster than even Cade could see, and impaled him with a sword, driving it into a concrete pillar.

It shouldn't have been possible. No one was supposed to be that fast, or that strong. No one human, at any rate. But Cade didn't waste shock on that. He was more concerned with the weapon that pinned him, like a moth to cardboard.

The sword was on fire.

Nobody believed him on this—not even Griff. But his memory was perfect.

The sword burned with a blue-white flame until he finally managed to pull it free from the pillar, and from himself. It had looked ordinary then, a piece of forged steel, but he knew: the blade was on fire when it stabbed him.

It turned out he'd deliberately been kept out of the action. Someone had wanted him out of the way so the hijackings could succeed and the planes could hit their targets.

Whoever had enough resources to know about Cade's existence—and then take him out of the game—was more dangerous than a hundred al-Qaeda fanatics with a backpack nuke each.

That meant Bin Laden had a great deal to answer for.

BIN LADEN STARED AT HIM, on his knees but his face still a mask of contempt.

"Who is the man with the sword?" Cade asked, voice perfectly level.

Bin Laden spat on the ground, replying to Cade's English with Arabic: "I will not foul my tongue with the language of the Great Satan. I am at peace with God. Do your worst. Know this, though: you are sending me to Paradise. I welcome death with open arms, for I am—"

Cade grabbed his face and squeezed. Bin Laden's voice died to a strangled little yelp.

"I do not believe you," Cade answered, in perfect Arabic this time. "I believe you know where you are going. And it is not to Paradise. I want answers. Who is the man with the sword?"

He released Bin Laden so the man could reply. "The sword is the sword of righteousness," he spat. "God's will is the fire in which it is forged, and your disgusting perverted nation will be split open . . ."

More gibberish. It appeared Bin Laden did not know any more than his own part in the operation. He thought himself to be the center.

Then Cade realized: Bin Laden had stopped talking. He looked at Cade, his eyes dancing with a hidden joke.

"I know what you are," he said. "I did not believe they would send you. But they did."

Cade grabbed him again, pulling him close. "Who told you this? How do you know me?"

"You are not the worst thing this world has to offer," he said, grinning. "I know the truth. The sheep cannot hear it, but I have known for years. There is no God. Mohammed was not His prophet. My master will show you. This world belongs to him."

Cade usually showed no emotion. He usually didn't feel any. His face was almost always an impassive mask, as still as the body in a funeral-home viewing.

But now his mouth narrowed to a thin line as he scowled.

"Belongs to who?" he demanded.

Bin Laden's grin only grew wider. Cade was ready to do whatever it took to get answers. But Bin Laden did know who—and what—Cade was.

He proved it by removing a small cross from inside his robes and jamming it against Cade's face. It felt like a railroad spike between his eyes.

Cade's lips peeled back as he screamed, and his fangs jutted out from his mouth. His human veneer dropped away. Cade already wore one cross around his neck as a ward against the thirst that constantly haunted him. The pain of another on his skin was almost unbearable.

"Vampire," Bin Laden laughed at him, shoving the cross forward again.

Cade recoiled involuntarily, giving another few feet of distance and another few seconds of time.

That was all Bin Laden needed.

The Saudi curled in on himself. Cade hesitated, not sure what was wrong with him. He wondered if Bin Laden's illness was about to claim him.

In a split second, Cade realized his mistake.

Bin Laden wasn't sick. He was *changing*.

His head and jaw jutted forward as black bile dribbled from his mouth. His skin shredded as muscle and bone moved beneath it like snakes under a tarp.

He locked eyes with Cade, and Cade saw his pupils had become diamond-slitted. His mouth gaped like a fish, revealing dozens of cruel, piranha-like teeth. The new flesh under his torn skin was dark green, almost black, and covered in scales.

Bin Laden's hands whipped out from under his robes, grabbing at Cade. But they weren't hands any longer.

Now they were long, yellow claws.

Cade barely had time to scramble away.

A harsh, snakelike hiss escaped Bin Laden's throat. To Cade it sounded like laughter.

Cade lost his footing as he nearly tumbled over the edge of the path. Bin Laden pressed his advantage and slashed again with his claws. He caught Cade's wound, tearing it open further. Cade began to lose blood.

Cade flung one leg out in a desperate kick, but Bin Laden had been walking these mountain trails for years. He was even nimbler now, scrambling around on reptilian feet. He dashed up the side of the cliff and came down behind Cade, claws darting, tagging Cade on the side, costing him more blood.

Cade spun, threw a punch, and missed. His momentum nearly took him over the edge again. He managed to avoid the fall, but only by landing in a belly flop on the path.

Bin Laden didn't let up. He leaped on Cade's back and began shredding him. Cade rolled over and tried to get his hands around the al-Qaeda leader's throat.

Bin Laden locked his claws around Cade's throat at the same time. His snakelike head darted forward, jaws snapping inches away from Cade's face. His neck seemed to extend like a spring. It took all Cade's strength just to hold him back.

The bleeding got worse. Cade could feel the power draining out of him. He didn't have much time.

He made a decision. He released Bin Laden with his left hand while still fending off the jaws and teeth with his right. He began scrabbling in the dirt with his free hand.

Bin Laden never looked away. He was enjoying Cade's humiliation. He let loose with the same hissing laughter as before.

Cade's fingers found what he'd been looking for—right where he'd dropped it on the trail.

The belt of grenades he'd taken from the boy.

He managed to pull one into his fingers.

His arm trembled. Bin Laden redoubled his efforts. He was nearly at Cade's throat now. His teeth clicked only a few millimeters away.

Bin Laden saw the desperation in Cade's eyes. The al-Qaeda leader spoke. "This world is his. But you will never see it, vampire."

Cade's arm bent, just a little more.

Bin Laden lunged, jaws wide, ready to latch down on Cade's neck.

And before Bin Laden could stop himself, Cade's left hand brought up the grenade and stuffed it in his mouth.

In the same moment, he kicked with both feet and sent Bin Laden flying.

The pin to the grenade stayed where it was, hooked around Cade's finger.

Bin Laden's body spun out into the empty air over the chasm. Then he exploded.

Green-black blood painted Cade and the rocks all around him. Bits of scales and skin fell in wet chunks to the ground.

Cade stood and tried not to think of the wasted opportunity. He'd had questions, and they would never be answered now. It was his own fault. His wound had slowed him down. And he'd underestimated his opponent. He'd failed.

Still, there was one small victory. He would be able to tell the president Bin Laden's death was, in fact, very messy.

ONE

Every culture in the world has a history of serpent people—reptilian or lizardlike humanoid creatures—in its folklore. The Yaqui of Mexico have their Snake Men. The Hopi have the Lizard People. The Chinese had the Dragon Kings. The Greeks had Glycon, a snake god with the head of a man, while the ancient Egyptians had Set, the serpent god. Early Judaism and Christianity put the serpent in the garden on his own two feet, and the Hindus had the Naga, a reptilian race that lived underground and warred with humanity. The Zulu in Africa have legends of a race of lizard people called Chitahuri or Chitauri who secretly rule the world. Nobody knows why this idea is universal across human history, or why snakes are so universally reviled as the source of all evil because of it.

—Cole Daniels, *Monsterpaedia*, entry "Lizard Men"

One Year Ago, Democratic Republic of the Congo, Near the Ugandan Border

In a better world, Joseph Kitambala would have been asleep in a warm bed with loving parents in the next room.

In this world, he was on his thirtieth hour awake, his eyes nearly closing despite all the brown-brown. He didn't think he could inhale any more of the noxious mixture of amphetamine and gunpowder without getting sick, but he knew better than to protest when it was offered to him. No one said no to the men of God's Army.

Joseph's brother, Daniel, had tried when they came to the village two months before. He stood his ground, chin up, defiant and proud, when they told him to get in line with the others.

A second later, Joseph saw his brother's head split open as the bullet tore through it.

The soldiers in God's Army beat him until he stopped screaming. They would not allow him to wipe Daniel's blood from his face or clothes. The dark brown stains still obscured the Nike swoosh on his T-shirt, a gift from a well-meaning church group overseas.

He never refused an order after that.

He was tied with a wire looped around his waist that linked him to every other child in his village. They were told to march. Anyone who fell from exhaustion or hunger was killed. By the time they reached other villages, they were half mad and starving, and they descended on the homes like plagues of locusts.

Many died. But it didn't matter to the men from God's Army. There were always more children to add to the line.

Today, God's Army was on the move toward the edge of the bush, where a unit of the government's soldiers camped. Many times, the God's Army soldiers told Joseph and the other children how the government soldiers were evil, how they were the minions of the Devil, and how they had to be stopped.

Joseph supposed some of the other children believed it, but he doubted anyone cared. They were barely alive. They would do what they were told. Believing took more resources than they had.

Not that Joseph particularly cared what happened to the government's soldiers, either. They were the ones who told him it was safe.

He'd been looking forward to his holiday trip home from the boarding school in Butembo. While he was away, he worried for his family. He remembered the sounds of gunfire, the times his mother would scoop him up and run with him into the bush to hide whenever the men came. But the government said the problems had been resolved. The rebels, like God's Army, had been sent back over the border to Uganda and Sudan. There would be no more raids or attacks.

He came home in December. Everyone was proud of him.

Then God's Army killed everyone he loved.

Since that day, Joseph had learned more than he ever wanted to know about the world.

The government troops were useless at best. The war was not over, as the government people had said. It had simply become quieter and more convenient. Refugees driven out of Sudan and Uganda had their own militias. Competing groups were hungry for fresh recruits. Even the government's soldiers were not above taking boys and girls and putting guns in their hands. All the armies needed bodies. Joseph and the other children were both soldiers and the spoils of war.

Joseph was a bright student. He'd absorbed knowledge like a sponge, picking up languages as if he'd been born to them. But his mind had shut down. Every one of his days had a distant, dreamlike quality. Too little food and too much horror. He barely knew his own name anymore.

So he was surprised when the talk of the soldiers at the head of the line shifted into something unfamiliar and yet recognizable. In a moment, long-ignored parts of Joseph's brain began to work.

English. The soldiers were speaking English.

They were talking to a man wearing all black. His clothes were neat and clean. He handed the men from God's Army a large bag of powder. It wasn't like the drugs that were usually mixed together before a battle. It seemed to have a bright green tinge to Joseph, even against the plants around them.

They were all given the powder and told to swallow it. Joseph and the other children complied. They were released from the long wire that held them together.

In a moment, Joseph knew, they would be told to run, screaming, out of the bush and into the clearing below. They would draw the fire of the government men, while God's Army would wait in the trees and watch to discover the enemy's positions.

But something was different this time. Somehow, Joseph found himself anxious to run. He felt stronger. Angrier. He was ready to tear the government's soldiers apart with his bare hands. He didn't care who they were or what they'd done. He just wanted them dead.

He noticed the other children on the line stamping with the same kind of impatience. Their mouths opened in wide grins.

"Go," one of the soldiers shouted, and they were off.

Joseph found himself running faster than he ever had before. Bullets sang into the air all around him, but for once, he was not scared. He simply wanted to rend, to tear, to bite, to kill.

He hit the first government man in the chest. The man's eyes were wide with terror. He was frightened—frightened of Joseph. It felt wonderful. To finally be able to strike back, to take revenge, to have someone scared of him for a change.

Joseph realized the man was screaming at the top of his lungs. He had not heard it until then. The pounding of his heartbeat in his ears had drowned it out.

He found he was up to his elbows in the man's viscera, pulling things from his chest one after another. Blood and gore slicked his hands and his face. He finally found something that made the screaming stop as he crushed it between his fingers.

The government man wore a look of pure terror on his dead face. Joseph looked at the thing he'd torn from the man's body. A wet, black and red lump of meat.

His heart.

It was almost up to his mouth when he realized what he was doing.

He dropped it, recoiling from the body. He almost shrieked, but nothing came out of his throat.

It was only when Joseph brought his hands to his face did he learn how he was able to reduce the man to bloody ribbons.

His hands were no longer his own. Instead, he looked at the talons of some kind of lizard. Sharp, yellow claws protruded from dark-green scales.

Joseph heard a hissing noise, and for an instant, he was back on his family's bicycle, the one with the constantly leaking inner tube.

The hissing came from his own throat. It was the only sound he could make now.

He turned and saw another soldier—this one wearing sunglasses that reflected the daylight back at Joseph.

In the tiny mirrors on the man's face, he saw a horrible creature: a fishlike head on a man's body, lizard skin and needle-sharp teeth and claws.

The fish-mouth gaped back at him, and he realized that when it moved, so did he.

He saw himself.

Joseph couldn't move. The soldier was equally horrified, but he had a gun. And with a simple pull of the trigger, he stitched a line of bullets across Joseph's chest.

They thudded heavily into him. He felt blood pour out of himself. He sat down on the grass.

But he didn't die.

The soldier ran away before finishing the job. The bullets alone were not enough, but Joseph knew he wouldn't be able to stand again. Cramps bent his legs. He felt bones cracking. Whatever had changed him wasn't done yet, but his body couldn't take any more.

All around, he saw the other children from the line. They were twisted and changed as well, but some had not transformed as fully as Joseph. Some were like large tadpoles, their bodies fusing at the legs and waist. Others collapsed into a heap, unable to take the strain. He saw scales and fangs like his own, claws and ridged backs, gill-like protrusions under snapping jaws. But he saw nothing remotely human. One by one, they all dropped. Even the ones still breathing, like Joseph, could not move.

The government men were long gone. They left their jeeps, their equipment, even their guns. Men from God's Army came down from the bush and began scavenging whatever they could find. They were careful to walk around Joseph and the rest of the lizardlike bodies.

Joseph heard the familiar and unfamiliar strains of English from behind him. His heart was beating slower now. There didn't seem to be enough blood to go through him anymore.

He recognized some of the words. It was almost a pleasure to recall learning the language.

"—how you have any right to complain," the first voice said.

"Every one of them died," the other responded. "Now we'll have to find more."

Joseph twisted his head around, despite the pain. He couldn't turn his neck as far as he did before.

But he saw the men who were talking. One was a commander in God's Army. He was speaking to the man in black, the one who brought them the powder.

"I'm sure you'll have no trouble filling the ranks," the man in black said. He kicked one of the bodies nearby. It squealed. He aimed a gun at the body and fired. It let out a hiss that trailed into nothing. He moved on.

"You didn't say it would kill all of them."

"That's the nature of science," he said, stepping closer to Joseph. "You keep on trying until you eliminate all the mistakes. That's how you learn."

Joseph wasn't scared. He realized how futile it was, waiting for salvation all this time. He understood now: he was dead. He must have died and gone to Hell a long time ago. He wondered how this could happen to him. What could he have done to deserve this? And now he knew: God had abandoned him. With that knowledge, a kind of peace settled over him. At the very least, he no longer hoped for anything better.

The commander scowled. "And what did you learn here?"

The man in black looked down at Joseph. For a moment, there seemed to be a dark mix of pity and amusement in his eyes.

"Enough," he said. "Enough for now."

He pointed the gun at the space between Joseph's eyes and fired.

TWO

If eyewitnesses and conspiracy theorists are to be believed, the Lizard People are still among us. Reports of reptilian humanoids range from Florida to as far north as Canada. There's the Gatorman of New Jersey, the Lizard Man of Scape Ore Swamp, the Loveland Frogman, and the Thetis Monster, to name a few. But these Bigfoot-like monsters are nowhere near as frightening as the alien-human Reptilians (or Reptoids) who allegedly control the world through a global secret society.

—Cole Daniels, *Monsterpaedia*

Two Days Ago, Gulf of Aden, Off the Coast of Somalia

Alex Howard sat in the bridge of the luxury yacht and listened to the sounds from the party below. It was past midnight and they were just getting started.

Howard drank coffee. The first part of the trip, from Miami to the Riviera, was pretty dull. His boss wasn't on board for the long haul across the Atlantic; he couldn't be away from his investments that long. He joined them when they reached the Riviera, bringing his entourage and a half dozen women who looked like strippers along.

At first, Howard joined the party at night. It was a huge mistake. Piles of cocaine and meth, bathtubs of liquor, a rainbow of pills, all from the boss's seemingly endless supply. Around day five, it began to seem like a grim endurance match. Even the women, longtime experts at faking delight, were strung out and snappish. He'd started to make mistakes. Piloting a 140-foot craft wasn't something you wanted to do hungover, even with the help of GPS and electronics.

But the real reason he was drinking coffee and not champagne was he nearly referred to his boss by his nickname, Moco.

Fortunately he caught himself in time. The last guy who'd called Jaime Carrillo by that name got a new nostril sliced into his face with a Tekna knife.

Howard didn't fool himself; he knew what he'd signed on for when he took the job. Carrillo loved to tell people he'd had the yacht custom-built, from its bronze sculpture in the main salon to the air-conditioned doghouse with marble flooring.

The truth was Carrillo had taken it for a fifth of its value when its previous owner, a real estate mogul, needed to liquidate his assets while facing the twin threats of a financial meltdown and a nasty divorce. The crew was given the choice of working for the new owner. Most of them left, but a few—including Howard—decided to stay.

Howard, who was first officer under the previous captain, wasn't entirely stupid. He would have known Carrillo was dirty even if his name didn't pop up on CNN every few months. The guy paid cash for everything, wore insanely expensive clothes and was guarded by enormous men with H&K MP5 machine guns slung under their arms.

But he wasn't currently under indictment for anything—rumor had it he owned several prominent Mexican politicians.

Carrillo was still living in the shadow of his father, a drug lord who belittled his son his entire life before dying, a casualty of cocaine and Viagra, in the arms of his nineteen-year-old girlfriend. He was the one who came up with the nickname "Moco" for his son's habit of picking his nose as a boy. End result: Carrillo had daddy issues, high-powered weaponry and limitless funds. Never a good combination.

Howard figured he could handle it. A job's a job, right?

He hadn't thought it through. Howard made it a point never to look in the hold, but he knew he was basically a smuggler now. As a fringe benefit, he spent long stretches of time in the middle of the ocean with a man who killed people for fun and profit.

But it wasn't like there were a lot of openings for yacht captains, and there were even fewer job opportunities for former Coast Guard officers in his landlocked Texas hometown.

Howard also had to admit Carrillo was pretty good at his job. As pressure had increased on the Mexican cartels over the past few years, he diversified. He reached out to the players who preferred their cargo not be examined by Homeland Security. He bought real estate. He recruited girls and women from the dirt-poor areas of Mexico and turned them into slaves in factories and brothels overseas. And he began smuggling guns—which were never in short supply in Mexico—to places that needed firepower.

Which was why they were anchored off the coast of Somalia now. Carrillo got a wild hair up his ass to see how his weapons were performing in the hands of some new clients, a loosely affiliated clan of pirates working out of Eyl.

Howard was skeptical about sailing the same waters as guys who carried RPGs on their speedboats, but he knew better than to argue. Carrillo said that his clients had guaranteed safe passage, and he wanted to see the pirates in action. All Howard could do was hope they wouldn't have to experience it firsthand.

So far, so good. Carrillo was charismatic, Howard gave him that.

Despite the language barrier, despite the mistrust and the haggling over money, he and the Somalis were becoming fast friends.

But Howard knew how quickly things could go bad. He spent more time on the bridge now. He warned the crew to stay sharp as well. He checked the radar and the surrounding waters. He kept people on watch around the clock, and kept the engines fueled and ready.

None of it would help.

NEARLY TWENTY THOUSAND FEET straight up, a crewman in an MC-130H military transport spoke to a young man through the radios of the helmets they both wore.

"FLIR showed the shipment going into those buildings," he said, pointing to a screen that showed a nearly indistinguishable dot on the coastline. "But there's been a lot of activity in the past couple of hours. They're getting ready for a raid."

On the screen, a smaller group of dots moved out into the great black field of the water.

The young man looked behind him, to the seats behind the system operator.

"Cade," he said, "it's confirmed. They're moving now. They're going to hit the yacht."

"I understand," Cade said, and unlatched himself from the seat. He took off his helmet. Unlike the others, he didn't need the oxygen. He walked through the cockpit door to the back of the plane.

The massive cargo door was open, with nothing but thin air between him and the ocean far below.

The wind began tearing at him and the plane lurched. Cade kept his feet. He narrowed his eyes and focused on a light on the black water as distant as a star in the night sky.

Then he dove headfirst out of the plane.

———

CARRILLO'S YACHT WAS SURROUNDED by an ever-shifting flotilla of pirate craft. The pirates buzzed back and forth from the shore in everything from speedboats to Zodiacs to Jet Skis. As the partying went on into the small hours, some of the Somalis and Carrillo's bodyguards began firing automatic weapons into the air.

That's probably why Howard didn't notice the new group of boats until it was right on top of them.

The blip hit the edge of the yacht's radar, moving fast toward the center of the screen. It somehow looked more purposeful than the usual traffic. Using night-vision binoculars—standard equipment on a drug lord's boat—he saw a small group of jetboats, holding in a fairly tight formation.

He swore to himself and tried to choose which was worse: interrupting Carrillo's festivities with a false alarm, or failing to alert him to an incoming threat.

The jetboats kept coming. They would be alongside the yacht in less than a minute.

Howard swore again and ran down the stairs to the main lounge. Carrillo was probably going to kill him no matter what. At least this way, he could pretend he was still doing his job.

CADE HAD REACHED TERMINAL VELOCITY—the point at which the pull of gravity was equaled by the resistance of the air against him. He fell toward the ocean at roughly four hundred miles per hour. His eyes were open. He blinked once and focused his gaze on the yacht. The small boats were pulling into a circle. He saw muzzle flashes in the dark.

Cade literally could not go any faster. He still had nearly twenty seconds of free fall left.

They were going to hit the boat first.

HOWARD REACHED THE SALON just as the gunfire erupted. He realized, too late once again, that wading into a room of drunk, armed men was not the smartest move. One of Carrillo's bodyguards struggled to get up from his place, shoving aside the woman giving him a lap dance. Carrillo's clients reached for their own weapons, and made a dash for the exits. Screaming and bellowing drowned out the gunfire.

It was an unholy mess. Howard was knocked to the floor and nearly trampled.

A strong hand pulled him to his feet again, then slammed him to the wall. He looked into the eyes of Carrillo.

"What the fuck is happening?" he demanded.

"Pirates," Howard said, and felt, for a moment, like he was in an old movie. "I think they're trying to board."

"Cocksucker," Carrillo screamed, and pulled out his ever-present sidearm. Unlike most of the men in the Mexican cartels, he didn't go for anything showy. No gold plating or pearl handles or laser sights. Carrillo favored an old Colt .45 of his father's, a World War II antique kept in pristine condition with a daily ritual of cleaning and maintenance.

It was old, but it worked fine. Howard had seen it in action several times.

For a moment, he looked down the barrel and thought Carrillo blamed him. Then the big gun swung away, to the head man of Carrillo's clients.

There was a deafening boom, and when Howard looked over at the Somali again, half his face was gone. Carrillo pumped another round into him for good measure, and the man's body went down onto the carpet.

"Double-crossing motherfucker," Carrillo said, before lapsing into gutter Spanish. He saw Howard staring and slapped him. "What are you waiting for? Get us the fuck out of here!"

Howard ran back up the stairs. The clients and crew ran around madly on deck, the bodyguards firing wildly at anything that moved, unsure who was on their side and who wasn't. Howard had to dive to avoid a spray of bullets and ended up near the deck railing.

He heard splashes and thought that people were jumping overboard. But when he looked, he realized that the invaders were leaping from their boats and swimming right to the sides of the yacht. He didn't understand. Without ropes, they'd never make it up the sides.

Then he saw it, shooting out of the water, coming straight at him.

It was the size of a man, and shaped more or less like one, but the head was narrowed down almost to a point in front, like a snake. Any nose it had was just a couple of slits in the skin. Rows of sharp teeth were visible behind the fishlike mouth, gaping open as if sucking in breath. Its skin was leathery and slick, dark as oil and shiny in the reflected light. The claws on its hands and feet dug into the Kevlar composite hull and it scrabbled up the side.

But its eyes were the worst. They were yellow, staring straight ahead, and cold, despite a luminous glow that highlighted their dark, diamond-shaped pupils.

Howard had been at sea for a while. He'd seen some things. He'd gone deep-sea fishing and pulled stuff out of the ocean that looked like it came from another planet.

But he'd never seen anything like this.

Its bulbous yellow eyes locked with his own, and it hissed.

Howard rolled over, got his feet under himself and ran as fast as he could.

There were more. They were coming over the railing, leaping onto the deck. They didn't carry guns. They didn't need to. One of Carrillo's bodyguards gaped at the snake-headed things, and it swung an arm past the man's gut. He saw a sudden gout of blood as the guard dropped his gun and tried to keep his entrails from falling to the deck.

The creature leaped on the guard, slashing with both hands and feet, snapping with its jaws. It tore away great strips of flesh.

Howard broke out of his frozen horror when another one of them nearly caught him. He dodged, but the thing tagged him on the arm. His whole side went numb and he ran.

He got to the foredeck before he realized his arm was laid open to the bone from shoulder to wrist. The cut was so clean it looked like it had been done with a scalpel.

Something blotted out the stars for a moment. It took him a second to realize it was a parachute. It wasn't drifting lazily, the way he'd seen other skydivers come in for landings. It was dropping like it was tied to a rock.

A second later, something hit the rear deck hard.

Howard grabbed his arm and tried to stop the bleeding as best he could. His hand was slick and red in seconds. He kept moving, back to the bridge. He had to get out of here. Start the engines, raise the anchor, move the boat. Get out of here. Get free.

By repeating that over and over, Howard thought he might stay sane.

CADE OPENED HIS CHUTE eight hundred feet above sea level. It was not nearly enough time to disperse all the momentum from the fall, but he was out of time.

Besides, he was a bit more durable than the average paratrooper.

He hit the deck at close to seventy-five miles an hour, cracking the hand-rubbed oak planks. He popped the release on his harness.

The chute billowed over the side and into the water. Cade took a second to survey the scene.

It was a small slice of Hell.

The Snakeheads were all over the deck, biting and slashing wildly at the human passengers. Some of the men had guns, and they emptied whole clips, trying to hit the reptilian creatures. A lot of bullets flew wide. Some hit the other people as the Snakeheads twisted and danced out of the way, impossibly sinuous and agile. Two of the things attacked each other, fighting over the carcass of a body with several hunks already bitten away.

Cade heard the skitter of claws on the deck behind him. He turned to see the Snakehead already leaping at him, all of its limbs out and claws up, ready to tear him to shreds.

It was very fast.

Cade was faster.

He stomped down harder on the plank under his foot, tearing it loose from the deck. The jagged edge came up into the air—right into the path of the creature.

The Snakehead tried to change direction in midair. It didn't work.

Gravity and momentum did the rest.

Cade moved before the thing stopped twitching. There was a whole boat of these creatures, and only one of him.

And he could not allow a single one to get away.

HOWARD WAS PRETTY SURE he was about to die. He was in an equipment locker just off the pilothouse. When he had tried to go inside, to get to the controls, one of the creatures had reared up through the broken window and spat at him. The spit—or venom or whatever it was—sprayed into his eyes, onto his skin and into his wound.

He heard more hissing from the Snakeheads, but fewer screams. There was no more gunfire. Occasionally, he would hear the sound of claws on the deck as one of the Snakeheads ran by his hiding place. He may have blacked out for a time. He wasn't sure.

It was quiet when he opened his eyes again. He could see. And he didn't feel as terrible. In fact, he was feeling strong enough to make a run for it. He listened closely, but heard nothing nearby. He decided to chance it.

He carefully opened the locker and crawled out. His arm still hung limply at his side, but other than that, he could move. He carefully walked toward the pilothouse. Maybe he could make it to the speedboat that the yacht carried with it for short trips to shore, or, failing that, he could try one of the survival rafts.

He saw a gun on the deck and picked it up. He didn't know if it was loaded, but it made him feel better.

Howard stepped over the body of one of his crew. The man looked like the carcass of a dog dragged under a car. But strangely, Howard didn't feel the urge to vomit.

It was weird, but he almost felt hungry.

Howard stopped in his tracks. A man stood in front of him, blocking his path. Despite all the carnage, he looked at Howard with an expression of perfect calm.

CADE FOUND THE LAST of the survivors on the upper deck. He'd been badly injured, but the bleeding had stopped. It hadn't yet occurred to him that he shouldn't be able to move, let alone walk.

Still. Cade had to be sure.

"Were you bitten?" he asked.

The man looked at him strangely. He blinked twice. Cade repeated the question.

The man looked down at his arm. "Oh. This. No. I was slashed. By one of those things. What happened to them?"

"I happened to them," Cade said. "This is important. Are you sure you weren't bitten?"

The man took a step back from Cade. "Isn't this enough?" he asked. "They nearly took my arm off, and then one of them spat this shit into my eyes—"

"It spat at you?"

The man stepped back again, suddenly wary. He looked at the gun in his own hand, as if trying to decide what it was for.

"Yeah. Are you going to tell me what the hell happened here? What were those things? And who are you?"

"How do you feel now?" Cade asked, ignoring the questions.

The man blinked again. "Uh . . . well . . . not bad, I guess. All things considered, I actually feel . . . pretty damned good."

Then he laughed. And blinked again. Cade saw his eyes. The pupils had already changed.

They were diamond-shaped.

Damnation, Cade thought. But he wasted no more time on regrets. He moved.

HOWARD REALIZED he wasn't just hungry. He was famished. A voice inside him was screaming at him, trying to tell him that there was something wrong with this intruder, that the man on deck was dangerous, but he didn't really care. He was feeling better every second. He felt pretty fucking invincible, in fact.

Above all, he felt hungry.

He realized, in a split second, that the man had decided something.

Howard dropped the gun. He didn't know if it was empty or loaded. At that moment, he couldn't have even told you what a gun was for.

With a snarl, he readied himself to fight. But it was already over. The man vanished in the time it took Howard to blink.

He stopped, confused. An instant later, he felt a crushing pressure around his neck from behind. The man somehow put him in a choke hold.

Howard thrashed. He used the new claws that were emerging from his fingers to tear at the man's arm, trying to escape.

Just before the very last of his human mind departed, before everything in his head became nothing but smells and heat and instinct and rage, he heard the man say something.

"I'm sorry," he said.

It meant nothing. It was noise. Aside from the sound of Cade snapping his neck, it was the last thing Howard—or the creature he'd become—would ever hear.

THREE

If it's secret, it's legal.

—President Richard M. Nixon

Today, the White House, Washington, D.C.

A year before, Zach Barrows would have laughed in your face if you told him vampires were real.

Now he sat next to one on a couch in the VIP waiting area of the West Wing.

Never let anyone tell you Washington, D.C., is dull, he thought.

Cade, as always, was perfectly still. Since Zach had become the liaison between the White House and Cade, he'd learned Cade was as motionless as a corpse in a casket most of the time. He had the unlined face of a college student, wearing a cheap suit with no tie. The only hint of anything unusual was the handmade metal cross on a knotted leather cord around his neck. It made him look like a rocker dressed up for a court hearing.

At his feet was a leather case, something GIs used to call their AWOL bag. The zippered top was closed.

Zach realized he was wringing his hands. He stopped. In the eleven

months Zach Barrows had been working with Nathaniel Cade, he'd faced
death more times than he could count. Less than twenty-four hours ago,
he'd been sitting in a Combat Talon transport, tracking the movements
of inhuman creatures off the coast of Somalia.

But this meeting made him feel like calling in sick.

It was late, but not so late that the West Wing was empty. People
walked by, faces serious, clothes wrinkled, papers in their hands. Zach
remembered doing the same walk himself when he worked here. Being
inside the White House could make someone getting coffee feel like he
was responsible for national security.

Most of the staffers were too intent to notice Zach or Cade. But
someone glanced at them, then did a double take. The staffer's momentum carried him a few more feet, then his face lit up with a grin as he
headed back to Zach.

"Barrows, man, how are you?"

Zach winced. He didn't want to be recognized. Blake Thomas. He'd
been an intern when Zach was still deputy director of White House
political affairs.

Zach was on his way up then. Or so he thought. He'd worked for the
president when Samuel Curtis was still a senator, and was one of the
tacticians who helped Curtis win the White House. But without warning, the president pulled him out of his job and partnered him with Cade.

Blake looked way too happy. This is going to be painful, Zach
thought.

He stood and offered his hand anyway, blocking Blake's view of Cade.
"Blake. How have you been?"

"Oh, terrific," he said, grin spreading even wider. "I'm on the health
care initiative now, spearheading the Medicare/Medicaid billing code
review. Really interesting stuff. You'd be amazed at what they're trying to
pull in the subcommittees."

Oh God, Zach thought. He'd made the mistake of showing interest. Everybody in D.C. was doing vital work. They were all this close to changing the way the country worked. Just ask them.

"That's great," he said. "Good seeing you."

"So what are you doing? You just totally vanished, man."

"Not much," Zach said. "A little consulting."

"Dude. That's so unfair. After all you did, to get fired like that."

Zach clenched his jaw. His cover story. As far as anyone in the daylight world was concerned, Zach was a non-entity.

"It's not that bad," he said.

Blake leaned close. "Look, if you want, I can make a few calls. Maybe get you in with a lobbying firm or something."

Zach caught Blake's joy at looking down on his former boss. The misery of others was always entertainment around here.

He thought for a second about telling Blake the truth:

Actually, I'm the latest in a long line of liaisons to a hundred-and-forty-year-old vampire who works for the President of the United States. See, there are things in this world much older than we are, and they don't like us very much. About every week, there's another attempt by them to break through and wipe out humanity like an ugly mildew stain in the shower. And my friend here? He's the vampire. I call him my friend, but that only means he hasn't tried to eat me. Yet.

It would have been a serious breach of national security. But it would have shut Blake up.

Blake finally noticed Cade.

"Hey," he said. "Blake Thomas. Nice to meet you."

Cade turned his full attention to Blake. Zach could feel it. He said nothing.

But Blake's expression went slack. His legs began to shake slightly.

Zach knew what he was feeling: panic. The inexplicable urge to run, as fast and as far as he could.

Cade had that effect on people. Mainly because he wasn't people.

"Um, well . . ." Blake said, struggling with the sudden onrush of anxiety as some vestigial part of his brain blared an alarm at him.

"Don't let me keep you, Blake," Zach said.

Blake trotted out of the room, fresh sweat staining the pits of his shirt.

Zach sat down again, feeling a little better.

An assistant wrapped in a short skirt emerged and told them, "He'll see you now."

Cade picked up the bag and stood.

Zach did the same. Too late to go home now, he thought.

WILL PRADOR, the new White House chief of staff, rose from behind his desk.

Prador was the guy Zach compared himself to when he really wanted to feel like a failure. He was only a couple of years older than Zach, but his résumé read like he'd been in politics for decades: coordinator of statewide campaigns before he was out of college; political director of a high-level think tank in the off-year; TV pundit; consultant; then a highly visible spot as the media director for Senator Samuel Curtis's run at the White House.

And now, chief of staff. The job Zach wanted before he became caretaker for the president's pet vampire.

Zach and Prador worked together on the same side of the same campaigns for years. But Zach had no idea who was sitting on the couch along the wall.

He didn't rise. He was dressed in a very expensive black suit with a blinding white shirt and red tie. He simply eyed Cade and Zach with a kind of bemused hostility.

Zach immediately went into information containment protocol,

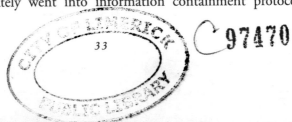

which was standard whenever they dealt with someone who wasn't in the loop.

"Nice to see you, Will," he said, before Prador could greet them. Then he extended his hand to the man on the couch.

"Peter Tork. This is my partner, Mike Nesmith. We're with the president's Internal Security Service Office."

The man didn't take Zach's hand. He just smiled a bit wider.

Up close, it was difficult to say how old he was. The suit was well tailored, but he was obviously fit underneath it. His hair, though white, was still full and thick. His face was a waxen mask, as if the years had polished it smooth. It seemed frozen in place, even as it moved.

But the man's most arresting feature was his eyes. They were pale, milked of any color except a dull, reflective silver.

He wasn't looking at Zach. His attention was focused on Cade.

Zach kept his hand out. "And you are . . . ?"

"You can cut the shit," Prador said to Zach. "This is Colonel Graves. He's inside the knowledge."

Zach was immediately concerned. That meant this guy, whoever he was, knew about Cade. And nobody was supposed to know about Cade.

Zach noticed neither Prador nor Graves appeared too nervous around Cade. That happened from time to time.

With Prador, Zach wasn't surprised. It was probably Prador's greatest gift—he was never rattled by anything. Photos of the candidate in a leather corset show up on the Internet? No problem. Down by twenty points in the latest poll? No problem. A supernatural war against the United States, and a bloodsucking fiend was America's only real weapon? No problem. If Prador had any emotions, he kept them in a secure vault controlled by a legal trust.

As for Graves, some people were simply so self-absorbed, so non-observant, that they couldn't feel the dread Cade regularly inspired in others. If they actually stopped and noticed the thing sharing their breathing space—

Then Graves got up and stood face-to-face with Cade.

He didn't move like an old man: no muffled groan, no levering himself off the cushions with his arms. He just stood, and crossed the rug to Cade.

"Mr. Barrows," he said. "Mr. Cade."

Cade and Graves continued to stare at each other. Cade appeared troubled. "Do I know you?"

"I thought vampires never forgot anything," Graves said. "I'm sure you'd remember me if we'd met."

Cade didn't say anything else. Zach was more alarmed than he wanted to show. He couldn't remember Cade losing a staring match before. He didn't even think it was possible.

Graves knew who they were. He knew *what* Cade was. And they'd walked in here without a clue.

Zach realized this meeting was going to be worse than he thought. He suddenly felt very conscious of the fact that he was wearing last year's shoes.

Prador got right to the unpleasantries.

"You've really fucked the dog now, Zach," he said in his usual, infuriatingly calm voice.

Cade sat down, placing the bag on the floor. Zach remained standing. Something was going on here, but Cade left this sort of thing to him. It was human politics, and it barely registered on Cade's radar.

Zach, however, was born to it. He could find a hidden agenda in any conversation, and felt double crosses and half-truths like seismic waves. This was the division of labor: Cade killed monsters, and Zach dealt with politicians.

"Look, Will, we just got off a plane from Somalia—"

"I managed to figure that out from the half dozen news reports that have been playing every hour. Did you see the Fox headline? 'Slaughter on the Water'? They're writing it off as piracy, thankfully. Is that what you call being discreet?"

"It was necessary," Cade said, his voice as dry and cold as winter air. Prador didn't appear impressed.

"That's not really your call, Mr. Cade," Prador said. "I thought you were supposed to follow orders. That's how it works, right? 'Bound for all the days he walks the earth' or something?"

"Something like that," Zach said.

Actually, the blood oath sworn by Cade went: *By this blood, you are bound: to the President of the United States; and the orders of the officers appointed by him; to support and defend the nation and its citizens against all enemies, foreign and domestic; and to serve it faithfully for all the days you walk the earth.*

The vodou priestess Marie Laveau had cinched those conditions tight around Cade back in 1867, shortly after he became a vampire. Cade's blood was mingled with the stains on the bullets that killed Lincoln, and this small fetish anchored the pact. To this day, the bullet was kept in a small leather pouch in a safe in the Oval Office. Zach wasn't sure why or how it worked—but it worked.

Still, it wasn't always as magical as it seemed. Cade was loyal. He was dedicated. He was even a patriot.

But he was still a vampire. Zach had learned from hard experience that Cade could find a lot of room to maneuver between the lines.

Prador would probably find that out himself.

Zach nodded at Graves. "Before we get into anything that's classified, you want to take a minute and explain who this guy is, and why he's here?"

Graves turned his pale eyes on Zach. "I am someone with whom you should not fuck. That's all you need to know."

Zach blinked. "Fair enough."

Prador continued as if there had been no interruption: "Forty-eight hours ago, we had a detachment of special CIA operatives tracking a compromised shipment going through Somalia," he said. "We believed the Somali pirates were working with al-Shabab, and we were very close to establishing a connection with a direct threat to the White House."

Zach looked over at Graves. "I'm going to assume that's where you come in. You're the CIA's guy on this?"

"I could tell you . . ." Graves let the punch line to the old joke just hang there.

Prador picked up the story again. "Just when it looked like we were making progress, our CIA squad had to pull back. Someone dropped out of the sky and began killing everything in sight. Any chance we had of learning who compromised our supply chain was gone. In just a few minutes, you destroyed an operation that's been in the works for months."

"Wait," Zach said. "That's the big deal? Because the CIA has to put another one in the loss column? You'd think they would be used to it by now—"

"Shut up, Barrows," Graves said, his voice flat. "The reasons don't matter, at least as far as you're concerned. This is need-to-know. And you are no longer among the needy."

Zach had to laugh. "Excuse me?"

"You heard me. You and Cade walk away from this. Right now."

"We don't answer to you," Zach said.

"But you do answer to me, Zach," Prador said. "And I am telling you: you're done with this."

Zach turned to him. "Don't you even want to know why we were there? What we found?"

"Judging by the impressive body count, I'm sure you and Cade thought it was important. But frankly, I don't care," Prador said. "Whatever it was, this operation takes precedence. I'm going to have to ask you to step back and allow Colonel Graves's team to take over."

Zach looked at Cade, whose mouth curled, just for a split second, at the corner. It was the only way anyone could tell the vampire was amused. Blink and you'd miss it.

Zach looked back at Prador. "No," he said.

"No? I think you misunderstand, Zach. This isn't a request. You've endangered an ongoing mission that has direct implications for national security. I can understand why you have a personal investment in this—"

"What he's trying to say is now the grown-ups are in charge," Graves said. "You can go back to chasing the boogeyman."

"He hasn't been spotted in over a year," Cade said.

"We can settle this right now," Zach said. "Let's get the president on the phone."

Prador shook his head, like he was almost sad at how badly Zach had read the situation. "He doesn't want that, Zach. And believe me, neither do you. The shipment—the one we were tracking—it came through Archer/Andrews. They were doing renditions for us."

And now Zach got it. He felt slow. He really had been out of politics too long.

Renditions. Such a clean and painless word, and for Archer/Andrews, an extremely profitable one. The military contractor charged millions of dollars to the U.S. government to make travel arrangements for a select group of unwilling passengers. The itineraries were always similar: a group of heavily armed men in black would board a Gulfstream jet in the U.S. and fly halfway across the world, then land at a private airfield in the dead of night. They would pile into a van and kick down the door of someone unlucky enough to be on their list: suspected terrorist, sympathizer, accomplice, or someone whose name was spelled the same as one of the above. The passenger would be bound and gagged, a black hood placed over his head, and taken back to the plane. Then he'd be delivered to another country, usually one where the authorities weren't so squeamish about the use of cattle prods during questioning.

Archer/Andrews hired ex-military to do the rougher parts of the job. Starting salary: $150K a year. The ex-soldiers called themselves Archers. Everyone else called them Archies—but never, never to their faces.

Zach had met a few Archer/Andrews security contractors. Scary guys. And this was the judgment of someone who worked with a vampire on a daily basis. Unlike Blackwater, A/A wasn't known for pulling the best of the best from the military. They hired from the disciplinary files—the guys who were benched, jailed, discharged or reprimanded for excessive force in places like Iraq and Afghanistan. The company's unofficial motto was "It's a mean world out there; we're meaner."

It was a multibillion-dollar private army, and a big part of the War on Terror. Zach was fairly sure there was a photo somewhere of the president shaking hands with the CEO.

Prador kept talking, of course. He always felt it necessary to ram the point home.

"When we came into office, we gave orders. Close the secret prisons. No more extraordinary renditions. But the prisoners didn't just stop existing because we said that. *Somebody* still had to transport them from place to place. Archer/Andrews stepped in."

Zach turned to Graves; he understood now. "I thought that suit was too expensive for a guy from the CIA. You're with Archer/Andrews."

Graves gave him a slight nod and smile. "We're assisting with the internal investigation. Anything more public could be damaging to both this administration and our shareholders."

Zach couldn't believe this guy. "Yeah, it would be a shame if anyone found out your kidnap-for-profit scheme was being misused."

Prador frowned at Zach.

"The president has decided we need a little more distance—a little more delicacy—when dealing with you and Mr. Cade," he said. "That's the reason Colonel Graves is here. He's going to make sure this is handled quietly."

Zach knew what that meant: deniability. The most important protection in politics. Whatever had happened, it would be better for the president if he could claim he didn't know anything about it.

Zach had known Will a long time. He'd never known him to bluff. If he said the president wanted this, he had to be pretty sure of the play he was making.

President Samuel Curtis was the most honorable, intelligent politician Zach had ever known. But he was still a politician. Zach realized that somehow, he and Cade had stumbled on something that made the White House look bad. He might even be turned into the fall guy, if necessary.

"This sucks," Zach said.

"It's an awkward position," Prador said. "If anyone found out about our involvement with Archer/Andrews . . ." He trailed off.

"What are you worried about, Will?" Zach said. "Afraid the president will have to give back the Peace Prize?"

Prador had the grace to at least look apologetic. "You know how it is."

Cade's patience, however, was at an end. Zach heard him growl softly in the back of his throat as he stood, lifting the bag from the floor.

"Perhaps Zach does," Cade said. "But I don't."

Prador started to speak: "Well, I'm sorry you feel that whao*ooollly fucking shit!*"

He almost fell over his chair backing away from his desk.

All through the conversation, the leather bag had sat unopened at Cade's feet. Now he unzipped the top and deposited the contents on Prador's desk.

"This is what was in your shipment," Cade said. "This is what makes it my responsibility."

It was a head. Definitely not human.

BULGING, REPTILIAN EYES STARED at Prador from dead-center on his desk blotter. Scales, not skin, sloughed off the bones where it had been severed from its body. Its teeth peeked behind its lipless mouth in a jagged parody of a smile.

Prador's nice, clean self-control was gone. He looked like he was about to have a stroke. His mouth opened and shut, but no words came out.

Graves handled it better. He flinched, but mainly looked annoyed.

"You always keep things like that in your luggage?" Graves asked, looking at Cade.

Cade didn't reply.

"He likes to keep trophies," Zach said.

Cade ignored them. He kept staring at Prador.

Prador closed his mouth. "What is that?"

"This is what's left of the pirates. This is what happened to their victims."

Prador looked baffled. "I don't understand."

"They were human. Until they were touched by something. Then they became these."

"How . . . ?"

"We don't know," Zach said.

"No, I meant: how many were there?"

"Thirteen," Cade said. "That is, when it began. It could have been as many as twenty-seven."

Graves scowled. "You don't have an exact count?"

"No," Cade said. "I mean there were thirteen at the start. They spread their infection to an additional fourteen people. I had to deal with all of them."

Prador blinked twice. "I'm sorry?"

"Whatever those pirates did to themselves—whatever was done to them—it spreads on contact," Zach explained. "Could be from the bites, or maybe even the scratches, but if you're attacked by one of these snake-headed things, and you live, then you're going to turn into one."

Prador looked down, as if the severed head might leap out and bite him.

"You can *catch it?*"

"Not from the corpses, as far as we know," Zach said. "Still, you might want to run some Windex over your desk just to be sure."

"Jesus Christ," Prador said.

Zach winced. Although Cade didn't show it, he was offended by any-one taking the name of the Lord in vain. Like the cross around his neck, it was just one of the vampire's little quirks. Zach doubted Prador knew or cared, but Zach hated it when Cade got angry. Nobody needed that, especially not right now. He was angry enough.

Prador struggled to get control of the meeting again. "Well, that's unusual, yes, I admit, but, uh, I don't see how—I mean, there are still proper procedures . . ."

He trailed off as he realized Cade was staring at him.

"You asked about my oath," Cade said. "Let me tell you what my oath requires. I swore to do whatever is necessary to protect this country. No matter what the cost. Failure to keep this oath is extraordinarily pain-ful to me. And yet, at this moment, there are two men here with infor-mation about something that could, literally, end this world. Information they refuse to share. At this moment, these two men are the greatest obstacle to keeping my oath."

It was nothing overt, nothing as blatant as throwing over the chair or slamming his fists on the desk. But his stillness was somehow worse, implying hideous violence barely restrained.

"*Whatever* is necessary," Cade said again.

There was a long moment of silence. Graves and Prador glanced back and forth, as if trying to communicate in blinks.

Prador folded.

"Jesus, it's just not that simple, all right?" he said.

Graves scowled. He buttoned it down quick, but Zach caught it. Prador was going off script.

Prador put his chair upright again. He almost managed to make it look like he had a lizard-man's head on his desk every day.

"Please put that back in the bag," he said to Cade. To his credit, his voice didn't tremble.

Cade put the head away. Prador took a deep breath.

"I apologize, Zach. To you and Mr. Cade. I should have been more forthcoming. If we could all just sit down?"

Cade and Zach took their chairs. Graves took his spot on the couch again.

Prador shot a guilty look at Graves. Graves shrugged, as if to say, *It's your show.*

"It's not just the renditions," Prador said. "There's something else. We think we know who has infiltrated A/A."

"Who?"

Again, that hesitation. Another glance between Prador and Graves, as if deciding who got to break the bad news.

Cade didn't say a word. He moved an inch toward Prador, though, and that was enough to break through the reluctance.

"You and Mr. Cade already know them, Zach," Prador said. "I believe you called them the Shadow Company."

ZACH WAS STILL UNDER the restrictions of information containment, so he could never reveal too many secrets if he was captured by an enemy, or if he went rogue. That meant there were a lot of things he didn't know yet. But he knew about the Shadow Company.

It was like the evil twin of the U.S. intelligence apparatus. Nestled like a tumor inside every government agency, but primarily working out of the CIA, the Shadow Company did the things that could never be brought out into the light of day. Assassinations, coups, plots, drug-running—all the stuff no one in elected office wanted to know about.

Since the Company operated in the same netherworld that Cade did, no one admitted it existed. There was no way to hold anyone account-able for its actions. Its members worked in cells, much like terrorists, with limited contact with their superiors. It ran its own operations, moved money through black accounts and answered to no one.

And while it claimed to work in the best interests of the United States, it was so good at keeping secrets that nobody could say who headed the organization, or even what its ultimate goal was—not even most of the people who worked for it.

One thing was certain: it had forged alliances with the things Cade was supposed to stop and kill. It had made a deal with the devil. Literally.

Zach had encountered the Company on his first assignment with Cade. A small cell of operatives, led by a sociopathic blonde named Helen Holt, tried to kill Cade with fifty pounds of C4 and, later, assas-sinate the president. They failed, but only just barely. Along the way, Zach had almost died in the bomb attempt before being tortured for hours by one of the Company's operatives.

So yeah, Zach had issues with anything involving the Company.

"WHAT DO WE DO NOW?" Zach said.

"No chance you'll let Colonel Graves handle this?" Prador asked.

Cade simply gave Prador a look. Zach, however, laughed out loud.

"You tell us there's an extinction-level threat in the hands of the Shadow Company, and you want us to go home and let the senior-citizen special handle it? Not a chance. It's his company that's involved. For all we know, he's working with them."

Graves spoke up. "I have a suggestion."

"Yeah, well, I don't want to hear it," Zach snapped.

"We work together."

"That's . . . surprisingly reasonable," Zach said.

"You'll need our assistance and resources. And frankly, we'll need Cade's experience at dealing with this kind of threat."

Zach hesitated. "You're asking us to trust you."

"At least as much as we're trusting you."

"We don't need your help," Cade said.

Prador sighed with impatience. "*Enough*," he said. "Almost a year ago, this organization very nearly killed the president. It knows things that no one outside the White House is supposed to know. And we still don't have the first clue about it. You're supposed to protect the president, Cade. So I'm telling you—I'm ordering you—to work with Colonel Graves on this. As far as you're concerned, an order from him is an order from me. Is that clear?" Prador glared at Cade.

Cade, however, looked at Zach. Again, the barest movement of his head. This time, a nod.

It had all the hallmarks of a good compromise: it didn't look like it was going to make anyone happy.

Zach nodded back.

Cade said to Prador, "I'll follow your orders."

IT ONLY TOOK THEM a moment to decide how to proceed. Cade and Graves would go into the field and investigate the trail of the shipment; they would try to find out where it originated. They'd also try to deal with any other outbreaks of Snakeheads—the name Zach had given them—before they could spread their infection.

Zach, meanwhile, would stay in D.C. and work with some of Graves's analysts, trying to figure out where the Shadow Company had managed to infiltrate Archer/Andrews, and find a cure for the Snakehead virus.

They were about to leave when Graves asked Zach a question.

"Just out of curiosity, what led you to the pirates in the first place?"

Maybe they were working together now, but for Zach, it wasn't even a close call. He wasn't about to reveal their sources on this one.

"We had a report of nonhuman activity in the area. It was related to something that happened on the Ugandan border a year or so back."

"What kind of a report?"

"Tracks," Zach said. "There were nonhuman tracks found and photographed."

Graves looked aghast.

"Tracks? You flew halfway across the planet and slaughtered a bunch of people on a boat for tracks? You know those can be faked by a ten-year-old with cardboard on his sneakers, right?"

"But they weren't, were they?"

Zach and Cade went to the door. Prador offered his hand to Zach before he left.

"Sorry about all this. Just goes to show we're all on the same side, right? Fighting the same battles."

Zach smiled at that. "You ought to catch the fight live sometime. It's a little different than the view from behind a desk."

Prador gave Zach a smile that was barely room temperature. "Always nice to see you, Zach."

PRADOR AND GRAVES didn't speak for several minutes after Cade and Zach left. They knew just how good the vampire's hearing was.

They also didn't have a lot to say to each other.

A moment later, the door opened and Vice President Lester Wyman entered.

Wyman hadn't been around the White House lately. Although he had an office in the West Wing, relations between the VP and the president had been strained ever since the terrorist attack on the White House. Once the remodeling was done, Wyman spent most of his time in his offices in the Eisenhower building, next door.

Nobody missed him much.

"You fucking idiots," Wyman said. He'd been listening the entire time on the White House's recording system.

"We did our best," Prador said. "You heard Cade. He's not going to leave it alone."

"Sloppy," Wyman said. "And disappointing. I expected better from you, Will."

A half dozen good replies went through Prador's head. *Maybe you should have told me what was happening in Africa. Maybe you should have kept me in the loop. Maybe you shouldn't come crying to me for help after things go down the toilet. Maybe you should stand in front of a* fucking vampire *who's threatening, not very subtly, to tear your heart out.*

Out loud, all he said was, "I didn't see any way around it. They already know too much."

"You weren't terribly impressive, either," Wyman said, turning on Graves. "I thought this was your specialty."

"Shut up," Graves said, his voice as stark as a slap across the face. "Take that tone with me again and you'll be pissing blood for a week."

Wyman's face flushed and he took a step back. "You said they'd never find out."

Graves sighed. "No. I said I'd handle them. And I will."

"Then what are you going to do about it?" Wyman demanded.

Graves stood, and Wyman cringed again. "I'm just curious. That's all."

The unamused little smile returned to Graves's face. "Think of it this way. We've got them close. We can monitor their investigation. Lead them where we want them to go. We would have had to deal with them sooner or later. Now we deal with them sooner. The end result is the same."

Wyman stewed in silence for a moment. Graves waited him out. Prador knew Graves would get what he wanted. He had them both by the short hairs.

"All right," Wyman said. "But I don't like this."

"I suppose we'll just have to live with that."

He crossed to the door, clearly done with this meeting.

"It's time to show some sack, boys," Graves said. "They came to us. When you think about it, it's almost a gift."

As soon as Graves was gone, Wyman stood up straight again. He pointed at Prador. "I want to make sure you understand what's at stake here. This isn't just your career. This isn't getting hauled in front of Congress to testify, then moving on to a book deal and a talk show. You screw this up, and the next time you see your name in print it'll be in an obituary."

Prador just nodded. Wyman glared a few more seconds, and then left as well.

Alone once more, Prador opened his desk drawer and grabbed the first bottle he found. He popped it open, but nothing came out. He checked the label. Out of refills on the Xanax. He'd have to call his doctor again. And while he was at it, he needed more Klonopin, and Ativan. He was almost out of Zoloft, too.

This job was getting more stressful every day.

FOUR

MYTH #8: There is a subterranean archive center underneath the National Mall.

FACT: The Smithsonian's storage facilities are mostly located in Suitland, Maryland.

BACKSTORY: The notion that a labyrinthine network of storage space exists beneath the Smithsonian museums, under the National Mall, may have started with Gore Vidal's novel *The Smithsonian Institution* and was most recently popularized by the movie *Night at the Museum: Battle of the Smithsonian*. Unfortunately, no such storage facility is to be found. . . . There is also a tunnel that connects the Castle with the Museum of Natural History. Built in 1909, it is technically large enough to walk through; however, a person has to contend with cramped spaces, rats and roaches.

—Jesse Rhodes, "Urban Legends about the Smithsonian,"
Smithsonian website, September 1, 2009

THE RELIQUARY, WASHINGTON, D.C.

Zach entered through the secret passage, into the brick-walled space under the Smithsonian's Castle. He passed the stuffed corpses of creatures seen only in amateur videos or horror movies, artifacts from incidents deliberately left out of the history books, and weapons and tools that weren't supposed to exist.

Cade paused to drop the Snakehead skull into a tank filled with genetically modified *Dermestes maculatus*, a flesh-eating beetle. The ordinary beetles grew to less than half an inch in length. These variants were three inches long, with sharp, clacking jaws. They went to work immediately, chewing away the skin from the skull so it could be preserved with all the other relics: an "alien" corpse from Dulce, a gremlin skin, a Yeti pelt, the jawbone of a werewolf.

That was the purpose of the Reliquary: to house all the evidence of the nation's hidden struggle against supernatural threats. That, and to provide a home for its biggest secret: Cade.

Zach used to be amazed by the things kept inside the hidden chamber. Now he walked in like he was going into a convenience store.

The *Allghoi Khorkhoi* hissed at him from behind its glass case. He opened the small fridge in the corner and took out a pack of hot dogs. Quickly, he dumped them into the worm's terrarium and slammed the lid shut.

Somehow, saving the world ought to be more glamorous than this, he thought.

"You think we should do this?"

"I don't think we have much choice," Cade said.

"Fucking Prador. He set us up. Wouldn't be surprised if this was exactly what he wanted."

"Why are you so afraid of him?"

Zach stopped. Cade could do that. See underneath what you were saying to what you meant. And he had no tact, which meant he didn't avoid saying it out loud.

"I'm not scared of him."

"You don't trust him."

"He's the president's chief of staff, Cade. I trust him as much as I trust anyone else in the White House."

"You didn't reveal our source to him. You told him about footprints instead."

"I wasn't lying about the footprints. I just omitted the rest. It never hurts to keep a couple things in reserve. Just in case."

"Then why did this meeting provoke you so much?"

Because that was supposed to be my job, Zach thought, aware of how whiny and childish it sounded, even inside his head. He'd started working in politics before he could vote, and in the last election, ran the campaigns in three states for the president. He was a young political operator with a bright future. Everyone said so.

Most of the time, he could tell himself he'd gotten over it. He knew that this job was more important. He'd learned there were forces in the world hostile to the very idea of human existence, and he helped Cade kill them. It was a lot more direct than his political career. He'd saved the nation a dozen times so far—or at least, he'd helped. That had to be more important.

But there were times he was reminded of what he'd left behind. Like tonight.

"I'm not scared of him," Zach said again. "But speaking of scared, why wasn't he afraid of you? You scare everyone."

"He's too geed up to notice. Got a skinful of mahoska in him."

Zach sighed. Cade had been around a long time. As a result, his slang spanned decades. Antiquated terms could come out of nowhere. It got to the point where civilians would notice, and Zach couldn't have Cade becoming too noticeable. So Zach had taken the rare measure (for him) of giving Cade a standing order.

"Cade, what have we said about using slang?"

Cade grimaced. He spoke mechanically, as if forced: "'It embarrasses both me and the person forced to hear it.'"

"And . . . ?"

Cade frowned at him, but continued: "'And we try to avoid that kind of humiliation whenever we can.'"

Zach smiled. It always cheered him up a little when he got to pierce Cade's cast-iron dignity.

"What did you mean by whatever you said there?"

"All I said was, I suspect it had something to do with medications he takes."

"Prador's on drugs?"

"Antidepressants, anti-anxiety drugs and tranquilizers," Cade said. "He's under a tremendous amount of pressure, and he's used drugs to cut off almost all of his body's signals. I could smell it in his sweat."

"I never get tired of hearing what you can smell."

"My point is, he is no threat," Cade said. "I thought you would want to know."

That was the way Cade saw the world, Zach knew. Threats and prey. The change wasn't just physical; it went deep into the brain as well, restructuring basic responses. It was the hardest thing to remember, working with Cade. He might look like we do, but he's nothing like us. Not anymore.

As powerful as Cade was, there were many things he couldn't do. For instance, he couldn't take a step outside at noon without burning to death. But that was only the most obvious handicap Cade faced in moving through the human world. On a fundamental level, people knew he didn't belong. Simple human interaction was often beyond him. He was a predator. He didn't know how to talk to prey.

That was where Zach came in. He relayed the president's orders and did the human things that Cade couldn't. Zach knew that emotions weren't exactly Cade's strong suit. When he became a vampire, he was changed on every level—including the way he saw humans. His long life had only separated him further from ordinary people. It was a constant struggle for him to remain in touch with what it meant to feel like one of the people he protected.

Sometimes, like now, it was as if he was running a human emulation program through that computer-quick mind. Zach reminded himself that Cade was trying his best to relate to him as an equal—even as a friend.

It didn't make him any less annoying, however.

"Thanks, Cade. That's a big help."

"You're welcome."

Zach began gathering papers into his bag. But Cade wasn't finished.

"Does your reaction to Prador have anything to do with your lack of sex?"

Zach was completely thrown for a moment. If he'd been drinking coffee, he would have done a spit-take, just like in a sitcom.

"We are not having this conversation," he said.

Cade didn't even have the decency to imitate a look of embarrassment. "Your frustration is affecting your work, Zach. It's been almost a year."

I could have gone into the Peace Corps, Zach thought. Or worked at the U.N. There was that internship with Greenpeace.

"Since you've had sex, I mean."

"I know what you meant," Zach snapped. "We don't all have vampire girlfriends who drop by every few weeks for a little late-night crypt-action. You want to talk about affecting the job? Isn't that a security risk?"

Cade's face was stonier than usual. Tania—a female vampire, one who shared a long history with him—was a sore spot. She still fed on humans, for starters.

Zach usually avoided the topic for fear of where that conversation would end. Now he was annoyed, so he jabbed without thinking.

Cade wouldn't take the bait. "Don't change the subject," he said. "You have a problem. We need to address it."

"Look, Cade. It's not exactly a babe magnet, this job. I don't meet many nice single girls. Flesh-eating zombies, yes. Girls, not so much."

Cade hesitated. He seemed to search for the right words. "I know this is hard for you to hear. But you cannot have a normal life. That's gone. The sooner you reconcile yourself to that fact, the better."

"No." Zach shook his head. "That was Griff's problem. Not mine. I'm not giving up on my life just because he gave up on his."

Agent William Hawley Griffin was Zach's immediate predecessor in the post of liaison. He'd been killed during Zach's first assignment, at the end of the assault on the White House.

As liaison, it became Zach's job to go to Griff's house and organize his effects for any next of kin. He found a nearly empty space with bare walls and thick layers of dust on the furniture. There was an open bottle of whiskey sitting by an easy chair.

Zach also found Griff's will. There was no next of kin. He'd left the house to whoever came after him in the liaison job.

It was a decent place in a pretty good part of town, but Zach still kept his apartment. He couldn't bring himself to sell the house, and yet, he couldn't move in, either. Too much like wearing a dead man's clothes.

"This is your life now," Cade said. "That's what I'm trying to help you understand."

"Look," he said. "I appreciate the advice. It's my problem. I'll deal with it."

"Griff used whores," Cade said.

Zach sighed. "Good to know." He grabbed his bag and headed for the secret exit to the surface, and the National Mall.

"You've got a long flight tomorrow. Get a full meal and some rest."

He left.

Cade said nothing.

ZACH WENT HOME. He barely even slept there anymore. Most nights, he was in the Reliquary. And if not there, he was traveling from one literally godforsaken spot to the next.

He cracked open his laptop. He needed a little more detail about Colonel Graves.

As the machine booted up, a red beam flashed from the camera mounted in the laptop's screen, lancing into his eye. At the same time, Zach pressed his index finger into a pad on the base.

He was prompted for a series of codes, and only then did the laptop allow him access.

Pain in the ass, Zach thought. Nobody would believe a word contained in the files, even if they did steal the computer.

Even with all his top-secret database-cracking software, Zach ran into one brick wall after another.

Archer/Andrews was a subsidiary of PKD Ltd., itself a subsidiary of Pickman-Derby, a corporation under so many umbrellas it never saw the sun. He finally gave up trying to track down its true owners.

Graves was another cipher. He was ex-CIA, Zach was pretty sure. The "Colonel" title was something CIA operatives gave themselves when they were on military operations. But Zach had spent a lot of time around real soldiers, and Graves didn't have the bearing exactly right. His hair was a little too neatly parted. He wore cologne. His grooming spoke of vanity, not discipline.

He found the CIA's file on Graves after running his name through the NOC list—the "non-official cover" list of all the operatives the Agency would never admit existed. These were the men and women who were buried in false identities as they carried out missions that would never be formally approved, even if the Agency paid all the bills. If they were captured or killed, operatives on the NOC list couldn't expect a hostage negotiation or a public funeral. At best, they might get a quiet moment of mourning over drinks, or, in rare cases, an anonymous star on the wall at Langley.

The photo with the NOC list matched Graves, but there was a long string of aliases attached to it. Whatever his real name was, it was buried under years of disinformation.

Even in the NOC list, Graves's bio was heavily redacted. Everything was so classified it hadn't even been transferred to computer, and any paper records were likely shredded and burned.

All Zach could access on his laptop was a list of assignments, ordered by date and location.

That was enough.

Graves—whatever his real name was—had been a part of every major covert operation the CIA pulled in the past four decades. His résumé read like the Agency's greatest hits.

Yale degree. Recruited right out of college.

Clandestine service. Attached to various domestic agencies. Again, classified. No big surprise, since the Agency wasn't supposed to operate on U.S. soil. Locations: Los Angeles, New Orleans, Las Vegas, Miami, with trips back to Langley.

Laos. Probably one of the Agency's advisers to the Hmong fighters, although there was something about Graves being assigned to a different tribe in the highlands on the Vietnam border, the T'Chok.

Thailand, from 1975 to 1980. Afghanistan and Pakistan in the early '80s, followed by Honduras, just in time for the Nicaraguan civil war to heat up.

After that, he simply disappeared from the official records. Cross-checking other government files, Zach found a few other entries. A blurry photograph from a Contra staging base in Honduras. A buried LAPD report from an officer who swore there were CIA men moving drugs in South Central. A reference in a classified section of the first draft of a Senate report on international money laundering. Then, for almost a decade, nothing.

Then 9/11 hit, and the Graves alias began appearing on the NOC list again. Afghanistan, Iraq, Egypt, Nigeria, Uganda.

Around 2003, there was an official waiver and notice of separation from the CIA. Graves was free to pursue a career outside of government. That was about the same time Archer/Andrews began receiving government contracts. Graves began starring in slick corporate brochures that hinted at much more than they actually said.

The weird part: Graves's age was never mentioned anywhere. Zach tried to do the math in his head, but it didn't add up. If Graves was twenty-one in 1960, at the start of his career, he was at least seventy-one now. And while he was well preserved, Zach could tell he was human. There was no way he should still be operating, unless he was some kind of real-life mix of Nick Fury and every character Clint Eastwood had ever played.

One other weird thing nagged at Zach. Aside from the work history, there was nothing personal. Usually, Zach could assemble a pretty decent model of a person from this much information. But Graves remained a flat collection of facts. There was no depth to him.

Zach wasn't a complete idiot. There was a very good chance that Archer/Andrews was itself a front for the Shadow Company, that Graves was involved, or one of his underlings, or maybe someone else inside the firm entirely.

But if that were the case, why would Prador be working with him?

Prador could be a prick, true, but he was utterly loyal to the Prez, always had been. And Zach, in all the time he'd watched him, would never have imagined Prador doing something truly evil. It would be like an Eagle Scout selling secrets to the North Koreans.

Maybe this related to the leak in the White House that nearly killed him. Maybe it was a coincidence. Or maybe it was something else entirely.

Zach felt a headache coming on. He hated all this double-triple-crossing stuff. And, as Cade had said back at the Reliquary, it didn't matter much. If they were going to do this job, they were stuck with Graves.

Zach scanned the files again, looking for anything he might have missed until his vision blurred.

Finally he switched off the laptop and turned out his overhead light. He couldn't get a handle on the guy. It was like trying to grab smoke.

Might as well get some sleep, Zach decided. After all, Cade would have plenty of face time with the man soon enough.

ZACH COULDN'T SLEEP. He tried to watch TV, but nothing was appealing. He couldn't watch reality shows because seeing people pretend to have a life made him even more aware of the lack of his own. Horror movies bored him now; once you've seen the real thing, even the best special effects look hopelessly cheesy. And that was all his five hundred channels seemed to offer.

He thought about it, put on his jacket, and got as far as the door of a strip club before he turned back around and went home again.

He was going to get a life. He wasn't going to end up like Griff. He wouldn't pay for someone to rub up against him, and he was damn sure not going to die alone.

———

CADE PUT ONE CHANGE of clothes into a bag. That was as close as he got to a normal human's preparations for a trip.

Then he went to the small fridge and removed a waxed-paper carton, about the size of a half-gallon container of milk.

It was filled with animal blood—a mixture of cow and pig.

He looked at the carton for a long moment. Then he put the container in the microwave on the counter and waited for the beep.

Cade didn't like feeding. Or rather, he liked it too much. And he didn't like being reminded of what he was.

But it was necessary. He had work to do. He needed his strength. He had every reason to feed.

He told himself that as he opened the carton, forcing his movements to be steady and deliberate and slow.

The steaming blood flooded into his system, flushing his pale skin briefly before settling into deep, capillary-rich beds of tissue inside his body.

Two long gulps, and it was all gone. Cade shuddered and grit his teeth to keep from breaking out in a smile.

He loved it. Even this pale, weak imitation of human blood. He loved every drop.

Cade shook himself and threw the empty carton across the room. Someone might have even said he looked disgusted.

"Did you enjoy watching that?" Cade asked, apparently to the empty room.

A figure emerged from the gloom at the back of the Reliquary. She appeared to be a young woman, barely out of her teens. Strawberry-blond hair and an irrepressible smile.

It just happened that her cute little grin had fangs.

"I always like watching you, Cade."

Tania. Cade's sometime ally, sometime lover, and constant reminder. He'd once promised to save her. He'd failed.

Since then, she had become strangely proprietary of him. She followed him, appearing in his life from time to time, even helping him on his missions. But she had no love of humanity. Unlike Cade, she embraced what she was.

She had been showing up more often in the past year. He always knew when she'd gotten into the Reliquary. Despite what Zach had said, Cade had not invited her in. In fact, he'd changed the codes on the locks. She always got past them.

She looked at the bag. "Oooh. A vacation. I could use some time away."

"You're not coming."

"I'm sure I could if we worked at it."

Cade tensed and spun on her. "I am not joking."

She stuck her tongue out at him. "You're no fun tonight."

"I can smell the kill on you, Tania."

"I never promised to be a martyr like you, Nathaniel. I get hungry."

Tania had never fed on an innocent in Cade's presence. But to come here, stinking of fresh blood, that was a deliberate provocation.

"Do you think I'll simply let you go on like this forever?"

That banished the mischief from her eyes. "Sweets," she said, "what makes you think you let me do anything?"

It had never come down to an actual physical confrontation between them. Maybe she was only biding her time until she could be sure who would win.

They stared at each other for a long moment. Then Tania smiled again.

"If you're going to be such a stiff, I might as well look elsewhere for my entertainment tonight."

She paused, waiting for his reply.

"Lock the door on your way out," Cade said.

She frowned at him, and then was gone.

Tania was right. He was troubled, although no one else could have ever noticed it. He knew this shouldn't be happening.

He looked at the sharp, jagged teeth on what looked like a man-sized piranha's head, floating in a jar of formaldehyde. It was remarkably similar to the skull emerging as the beetles chomped noisily on the severed head.

The plaque read SKELETAL REMAINS FROM INNSMOUTH, MASS., 1928.

Innsmouth.

As foolish as it was, he'd really hoped he'd killed them all.

The fires were mostly out, although they still smoldered along the wharf. Cade kept well clear of them as he searched for survivors in the ruined pilings sunk into the sand. Dawn was less than an hour away, but the tide would be in before then. He had to get to them before the water did.

Above him, the men from the Treasury Department stomped in their asbestos-lined uniforms, carrying large tanks of fuel on their backs. Occasionally, he heard a shout, and then the squalling as something wet and fleshy burned beneath their torches.

Cade hoped they'd be careful enough to avoid doing the same to him.

But it wasn't likely that any of the T-men would come down here. The three federal agents who'd tried to search the underside of the wharf had been found in pieces when the tide receded. This was why Cade was on this mission: he was much more comfortable in the dark.

Still, it wasn't as easy as he expected; his sensitivity to heat was no asset. The things he looked for were cold-blooded, and the nearby fires were only confusing. His enhanced sense of smell was clotted with stagnant water, the town's sewage and rotting fish.

He almost walked past the nest.

Cade's boot squished into something with a different texture than all the other dead things down here. Something springing with life, enough to burst and spew its contents all over.

He looked down. A clutch of fish eggs, each the size of a man's fist. The one he smashed held one of the creatures in its tadpole stage; its tail thrashed uselessly as it tried to breathe with unformed gills.

There should be more, Cade thought. But there were only a half dozen or so, caught in their own slime.

He looked up.

In the shade of what was left of a plank, a huge sac of the eggs clung to the top of a piling, quivering like jelly as the things inside squirmed.

Cade opened his mouth to summon one of the T-men.

Then something whipped from around the piling and attacked.

It moved almost as fast as Cade at his top speed, and he had been fighting and killing these things all night. It managed to get him down in the salty muck and slash at his face with its claws and long teeth.

Cade fended it off and clouted it in the skull, hard. The skull dented, but the thing kept snapping with its piranha-like jaws. Its eyes bugged out, yellow and mad. Although it wore the dress of one of the towns-people, there was nothing human left in it. Its transformation was complete. It had probably been down here for months. That's why they missed it when they firebombed the temple, and the old houses.

Cade kicked the thing away, sending it flying. It bounced off one of the big logs like it was rubber and scrambled to attack again. Cade girded himself to deliver the killing blow.

A tommy gun roared above him, and the thing went down, lead tearing through its gelatinous skin. It deflated more than bled, collapsing slowly to the dirty beach.

Cade looked up. The man in charge of this assignment looked back through one of the holes in the wharf. He was already more serious than his age would have indicated—barely into his twenties. Cade saw gray hair at his temple. A mission like this one would only add to it.

"Are you all right?" the T-man asked.

"Fine," Cade said.

"You seemed to be having some trouble."

Cade pointed to the spot where the egg sac still held. "Mothers tend to be vicious when guarding their young."

The T-man pursed his lips in distaste and called to some nearby men. "Let's get those flamethrowers over here. Nothing gets back into the sea. Nothing!"

He looked back at Cade. "Anything else down there?"

Cade shook his head. "I believe that's the last of them. For this town, anyway. Someone will need to track down the remaining members of the Marsh family."

For a split second, the young treasury agent's stone-faced veneer cracked, and Cade could see the fear and nausea well up in him. "There are more." It wasn't a question, but he seemed to hope Cade would contradict him.

"You'll probably never see any of them," Cade said. "This was an emergency. I don't know how it got this far. Usually, I will handle something like this alone."

The T-man shook his head. "I don't know how you do it. No. That's not it. I don't know why you do it. Aren't you more like them than us now?"

Cade was not insulted by the question. He was not human. He knew that under other circumstances, these men would be tempted to burn him into ash. Only the weirdness around them, and Cade's ability to fight it, made him an ally rather than another nightmare.

"I haven't completely lost sight of what it means to be human," Cade said.

"I'm not questioning your loyalty, Mr. Cade. You've saved our lives a dozen times tonight. Whatever happens, I'll remember that. But I want to know: what keeps you on our side?"

Cade considered the question. The other men, with the flamethrowers and gasoline, made their way carefully up the rotting wharf. The sun was coming up. He'd have to get out of here soon. But he could see from the look in the federal agent's eyes that he would not leave without an answer.

"Do you know what a blood oath is, Mr. Ness?" Cade asked.

The young treasury agent shook his head.

"I took one. And I keep my word."

Cade sloshed through the seawater, now around his ankles, as he searched for any more of the creatures. Above him, the wharf exploded into fire and smoke, and a hundred tiny abominations squealed as they burned.

FIVE

Deception is a state of mind and the mind of the State.

—James Jesus Angleton, CIA chief of counterintelligence
from 1954 to 1975

DULLES INTERNATIONAL AIRPORT, VIRGINIA

Cade and Zach were in a small, private hangar at Dulles before
sunup.

On paper, the facility was leased by Executive Transport, a
privately held charter flight company. Executive was owned, according
to the documents filed with the state, by a series of shell companies, their
officers and directors buried in mounds of paperwork.

In reality, the hangar was used exclusively to hold several Gulfstream
V jets for A/A's renditions.

"Nice ride," Zach said to Graves as the older man met them in the
waiting area. "I guess torture pays pretty good these days."

Graves, wearing another thousand-dollar suit, gave Zach his finest
patrician smile, the kind that takes years of practice. "We're not responsible for what happens after we drop off our packages. We're a delivery
service. Just doing our job."

Zach snorted. "Just following orders. Right. Where have I heard that one before?"

"Take it up with your boss. What I do might offend your squishy liberal sensibilities, but it's necessary. You know it."

"Yeah, it takes a real hero to sodomize a prisoner with a nightstick."

Graves looked bored. "I'm sure we could have this sort of intellectual discussion all day, but we have to get a move on."

"I'm ready," Cade said. "Where are the analysts who will assist Zach?"

Graves walked out into the main area of the hangar.

"I don't need any assistance," Zach grumbled, as they followed.

Three people waited by the plane. They were dressed in cheaper versions of Graves's business wear.

"These are my top analysts," Graves said. "Book, Candle and Bell. You don't need first names."

They faced one another by the open door of the jet. Nobody offered to shake hands. Cade could feel the fear coming off them in varying degrees. They'd been briefed about him, clearly, but they were all struggling with the actual experience of seeing him in the flesh.

Book, the first man, was older than Zach—late thirties or so. He wore his hair cropped military-short and regarded them with dark eyes and a scowl. He kept his weight forward, on the balls of his feet, and looked hard and lean. If he was a data analyst, Cade was a vegan.

The second man, Candle, fit the stereotype of an information junkie much better. Unlike Book, his hair was longer and messy, and he wore five-day stubble. He had the greasy self-assurance Cade noticed in most of the politicians and their employees in Washington, utterly sure they had all the answers.

The last in line was a young woman. Bell. She wore no makeup. Her dark brown hair was tied back in a bun. Her face was open, honest and quite lovely.

Zach finally noticed her. He dropped his sulk. He straightened up, standing taller.

"Then again, it might not be so bad, having some backup for a change," he muttered to Cade.

Cade could almost smell the hormones rising in Zach's blood.

He said a small curse, only to himself. This was going to complicate things. He just knew it.

FOR A MOMENT, no one spoke. Then Candle, shifting uncomfortably in the silence, smirked. "Hey, check out my tie," he told Zach.

Zach looked down. Candle grabbed the sides with his fingers and stretched it—and then the geometric pattern resolved itself into words.

EAT ME, it read.

Candle laughed like Carlin had returned from the dead. Book sniggered nastily with him.

Zach and Cade stared back. "You get that from the novelty section of Brooks Brothers?" Zach asked.

"Lighten up," Candle said. "It was just a joke."

"Right," Zach said. "Like your beard, then."

Bell might have sneezed, or it could have been a laugh. Candle's face turned red and he glared at Zach.

Book shifted forward. "Oh. A smart-ass, huh?"

"Sorry, it's been a while since I've operated on your level. Is this where you take my lunch money?"

Book reached for Zach's lapel, as if he was going to grab it, or maybe poke Zach in the chest.

A blur, like a snake striking. Book's face was ash-white and his wrist was locked in Cade's grip.

"Never touch him," Cade said quietly.

Book tried to pull away. His eyes widened when he realized he couldn't.

Nobody else moved.

"It takes approximately forty-two pounds of pressure to break the average human bone," Cade said to Book. "Some are more brittle. Some are more durable. Unless you want to find out the breaking point for each and every one of yours, you will never touch him. Understand?"

Graves let out a weary sigh. "That's enough, children," he said. "Book. You're out of line. You too, Candle. I expect you to treat Mr. Barrows with courtesy, and not just because Mr. Cade could turn you both into a stain on the carpet. Are we clear?"

Book nodded. Cade looked at Candle, who nodded also.

Only then did Cade release Book's wrist. He blinked away tears. "I apologize," he said, in a tone that sounded like knives being sharpened.

"Good. You're all friends now," Graves said. "Try to play nice while the grown-ups are out."

Graves turned his back on them and walked up the stairs into the plane. Cade pulled Zach a few steps away.

"Goodbye kiss, I guess . . ." Candle stage-whispered. Book muttered something, still massaging his wrist.

Cade ignored them. "Do not trust them," he said to Zach.

"You think you need to tell me that?"

Cade touched Zach's arm. He never did that. But he wanted to make sure Zach was listening.

"Listen to me. Don't trust them. *Any* of them."

Zach nodded, but his eyes darted over to Bell.

Cade felt some irritation. He'd warned him. He couldn't do any more.

He turned to go, but Zach opened his case. He removed a false bottom and revealed two plastic bags, nestled in a self-contained cooler system.

Blood.

"Your in-flight meal," he said. "I have a feeling you might need it before this is over."

He closed the lid on the case and handed it over.

Cade was almost touched. "I didn't realize you carried this."

Zach shrugged. "Hey. Who's got your back?"

Cade took the case with him and got on the plane.

The pilots were used to secrecy; the cockpit door was already closed and locked when Cade boarded. The shades of the windows were sealed shut. No one would see in, and more important to Cade, no light could enter.

The standard seats had been removed and replaced with couches that could fold into beds. A fully stocked fridge and galley kitchen took up much of the forward space, and a door separated a bedroom and full bath with shower in the back.

"Beats hell out of flying in the cargo hold, I bet," Graves said, his coffee cup now exchanged for a full tumbler of Scotch.

The luxury barely registered with Cade. What he really noticed was the scent, under the cleaning chemicals, of blood and bowels spilled on the deep-pile carpeting. Pain and desperation and fear, hidden but not gone.

"It's what I expected," Cade said.

He took his seat across the aisle. A few moments later, the jet rolled from the hangar and air traffic control cleared them a space in the line. The Gulfstream rose into the air like it was sliding on polished silver rails, and they were on their way across the Atlantic.

BACK IN THE HANGAR, Zach looked at his new coworkers.

Book glared. Candle did his best to imitate Book from behind his thick glasses.

Bell broke the silence. "Is the dick-swinging over, or do you guys need to wrestle?"

Zach couldn't help it; he laughed.

She offered her hand. "Look. We're going to be working together. Let's try to keep the casualties to a minimum."

Zach shook her hand. He tried not to notice the softness of her skin. "Fine by me," he said.

"Dickhead," Book muttered, not quite under his breath.

"Knock it off, Book," Bell snapped at him. And Book, remarkably, cringed at her tone.

"Sorry," he said, both to her and to Zach.

Zach realized she was the one in charge.

"All right," he said. "Where do we start?"

"We've got an office rented," she said. "Neutral ground. I didn't think you'd want to invite us to your secret headquarters. We didn't want you in ours, either."

Zach nodded. His attention was drawn by two big men entering the hangar from the outer door. Their heads were shaved so close that the stubble looked like the bluing on the barrel of a gun. They wore boxy suits that barely covered them and earpieces trailing down the back of their necks. Private security. The product that A/A specialized in. They looked as if they'd been pulled out of a life-sized blister pack of action figures.

Bell followed his glance and saw them.

"That's Hewitt and Reynolds," she said.

The big men joined them. They towered over Zach.

"They'll be our shadows for as long as we're on the job," she explained. Book and Candle smirked as if she'd said something funny. Zach didn't get it. "I doubt we'll need them," she continued, "but without Cade in town, I thought it might be safer."

Both Hewitt and Reynolds—he wasn't sure which was which, and neither man looked about to introduce himself—stared down at Zach.

Zach recognized the look immediately. They homed in on him. Bullies. And, contrary to the crap spouted by Zach's parents and teachers, bullies in this weight class were not scared of anyone who would stand up to them. They didn't pick on people who were smaller and weaker because they were cowards. They did it because they liked winning every fight.

And despite their size, they didn't seem all that healthy. Up close, Zach could see the acne dotting their faces, the greasy look of too little sleep and too few showers.

They smiled at him. Zach made a mental note never to be caught alone with those two.

Ever.

SIX

I toiled wholeheartedly in the vineyards because it was fun, fun, fun. Where else could a red-blooded American boy lie, kill, cheat, rape and pillage with the blessings of the All-Highest?

—CIA operative Colonel George H. White

CHANTILLY, VIRGINIA

The U.S government spends more than $50 billion annually on classified activities, ranging from secret aircraft to covert military units, all wrapped up in what insiders called "the black world." Zach figured that a pretty good chunk of that money was spent on rent in Chantilly alone.

Chantilly was filled with corporations that existed mostly in theory, anonymous blocks of generically named tenants—Excelsior Transport LLC, Tech Solutions Ltd., Performance Design Inc.—in the office parks located near Dulles Airport. If the CIA ever decided to relocate, there would be a lot of vacancies to fill.

Zach and his new colleagues parked their sharp black Humvees near one of these buildings, which looked exactly like its neighbors. A man was still putting the finishing touches on the new name on the glass door: BBC CONSULTING.

"Don't I rate a spot in the name?" Zach asked.

"Just pretend one of the B's stands for Barrows," Bell told him.

The offices were new, but plain: white-box workstations at every desk, freshly assembled from kits. Hewitt and Reynolds took up guard positions at the door. Zach and the others gathered in a conference room that had a table still covered in plastic wrap.

Bell tore it away with one hand, stuffing it into a nearby wastebasket.

"It's show-and-tell time," she said. "You share what you know, we'll do the same."

"Why don't you go first?" Zach said.

Bell rolled her eyes. "If it makes you feel better," she said.

She gave him an expanded version of the basic facts they'd heard from Prador. A prisoner transport, sent from A/A facilities, had been routed to a group of Somali pirates. Whatever was actually inside was a mystery, but about an hour after it arrived, the Snakeheads began attacking the yacht in the gulf. That's when Cade stepped in.

"How did you track the shipment?"

"We keep a comprehensive database," Bell said.

"What's in it?"

She shook her head. "Classified. We're not about to let you look at proprietary information."

"That's not a very cooperative attitude."

"We'll search the database. We'll relay what we find to you. Those are the terms. And before you go running off to tattle, Mr. Prador already agreed to them."

Thanks ever so much, Will, Zach thought. He thought about arguing, but it would be a waste of time. He'd have to rely on Bell and the others to get the info he'd need.

"All right. Then you tell me: where was it supposed to be from? What was the fake info on the records?"

"Routine transfer from Egypt," Bell said. "Pretainees on their way to another interrogation facility in Ukraine."

"Pretainees?"

"We're not allowed to call them prisoners, since they haven't been charged," Bell said. "And they're no longer 'detainees,' either. 'Enemy combatant' is a big no-no. So there's a new classification, called 'indefinite preventive detention.' Those are the pretainees."

Zach grimaced. "It's amazing we haven't won the War on Terror already."

Bell flushed a little. "If all you can do is make jokes—"

Zach wasn't done. "Who had access to this prisoner transport?"

"We don't know," Bell said.

"Where did it originate?"

"We don't know."

"Who was in charge of the prisoners?"

"We don't—"

"Right. You don't know much, do you?"

"Hey, genius, we're a covert operation," Book snapped. "You know what that means? It means we don't keep a lot of paperwork around."

Bell nodded. "He's got a point."

"Yeah, yeah, yeah," Zach said. "It's a dirty job, but someone has to do it. I never get tired of people telling me how important their job is as an excuse for screwing it up."

Candle and Book looked ready to explode, but Bell beat them to it. "You done with your little spasm of moral outrage? Because we don't have time for you to prove how spotless your conscience is. We need to focus on how our system got infiltrated by the Company. We need to figure out how they got in."

"Yeah," Zach said. "You're right."

That sucked a little anger out of her sails. "Your turn," she said.

"That's what we've got. You tell us how you and Cade ended up in Africa."

"Not much to tell. This is what we do." He repeated the same line they'd given Graves about the tracks. They all looked dubious, but Zach was a good liar. And turnabout is fair play: they were all keeping secrets from one another.

Bell sat down and took charge in the same smooth motion. "So if we're all up to speed, let's get to work," she said. "Book: I want you to talk to your Pentagon contacts. See if you can find anything with your buddies in black ops. Candle: check the A/A records. Maybe there's something in there we overlooked. We're behind already, and Graves is going to expect results as soon as he hits the ground."

They moved toward the cubicles in the office like they were heading onto a battlefield. Zach paused.

"I need to make a quick call," he said.

Bell's lips pursed in a little moue of irritation. "Knock yourself out."

Zach looked over his shoulder at Hewitt and Reynolds.

"It's private."

That caught Candle's attention. "What, you need to check in with your boyfriend?" Book provided a one-man laugh track.

A grown-up would have let that slide by. But in many ways, Zach had to admit, he was not a grown-up. "No," he said. "Your mom. She worries if I don't show up on time."

"Hey, fuck you."

"Sparkling comeback."

"Boys, boys, *boys*," Bell said, a warning tone in her voice. Candle sat down and looked pointedly away from Zach.

"Go wherever you want," Bell said. "We're not your babysitters."

But she called after him as he headed toward the front door.

"Is it your girlfriend?" Bell asked.

Zach stopped. "What?"

Bell looked a little sheepish. "It's none of my business."

"Uh, no," Zach said. "Definitely not my girlfriend. I mean, I don't have a girlfriend."

She didn't say anything else. But Zach thought she might have smiled.

ZACH WANDERED OUTSIDE the office complex. Satisfied that he was far enough away from the building, he brought out his phone.

It was the only high-tech gadget he'd been given, but it was undeniably cool. Android? Nexus One? Toys. Convenience-store specials compared to his phone. GPS, satellite capability, universal computer access, camera, even a built-in flashlight. If James Bond carried an iPhone, this would be it.

It also had a special function to defeat electronic surveillance. A tap on the touch screen and he set up a kind of dead zone around himself that baffled any attempt to listen in with bugs or microphones. It would even blur his image on a security camera.

He activated the safeguard, then dialed a number. He wondered if she was awake.

She answered on the second ring. "Well?"

"He's in the air now. You'll be able to trace him with the homing device I gave you. The tracker is in a briefcase with him."

"He doesn't know, does he?"

"Don't be ridiculous. He'd never approve of this."

"What would you do if I told him?" Her voice was mocking.

Zach didn't hesitate: "I'd order him to kill you."

Silence. Then: "You don't want to threaten me, Zachary."

He checked his watch. He didn't have time for this. "It's not a threat. You know this is the only way it works. Don't screw with a good deal."

More silence. He could almost see her pouting. "Don't take me for granted, Zachary."

"Believe me, I don't," he said. "You need to get moving. You've got to catch up with him."

The mocking tone came back into her voice. "Whatever you say, boss. You're so commanding and forceful."

Zach rolled his eyes. "Just do as you're told, Tania."

Zach ended the call and walked back into the building. He didn't notice the shadows moving in the doorway just over his shoulder. If anyone had been watching, they might have seen it as a trick of the light, as if part of the darkness peeled away from the wall. For a moment, the shadow of a man in a trench coat and old-fashioned fedora stood there.

But there was no one around to cast that shadow. And no one to see it.

A second later, it was gone.

SEVEN

IN THE COMPANY OF SHADOWS (2001, Drama/Supernatural)—Kevin Costner stars as Robert Westlake, a veteran CIA agent ordered to find any possible witnesses to the years of atrocities he's seen or committed in his long career. Each one of his targets has a piece of the answers to the big mysteries—the real killers of JFK, for example—and Westlake silences them to make sure no one can ever put all the puzzles together. But at the same time, someone is stalking Westlake. He sees figures in the shadows, hears voices where there are none, and keeps getting strange messages. Eventually, Westlake discovers that the Company doesn't let go, not even at death. Described as *Bourne Identity* meets *The Sixth Sense*, this movie was withdrawn by the distributor after appearing in a few test markets and never released in theaters. No records of the production can be found in any Internet databases, all materials for the promotional campaign were destroyed, and cast and crew deny they were ever involved. The official reason given was that after 9/11, audiences didn't want to see anything that put America in a bad light. However, the extreme paranoia about the production has led some to believe the real CIA found something in the script a little too close to reality. No prints survive, but a few bootleg copies are rumored to exist on DVD.

—Tucker Layne-Baker, *The Day the Clown Cried and Other Movies from Hollywood's Vaults*

42,000 Feet Above the Atlantic Ocean

Graves leaned his seat back and put his feet up. He was on his second Scotch.

"You don't seem particularly worried," Cade said.

"About what?"

Cade's mouth twitched. "The infiltration of your company. The existence of things like me. The threat to the nation and the human race."

Graves took another long sip of his drink and smacked his lips. "Taking those in order, I'm going to deal with the problem in my company when we find it. I'm confident in my abilities, so I have no need to worry about that. I've known about things like you for a long, long time, and I've made my peace with it. Likewise, there's always a threat to the future of the human race. I've made my peace with that, too. No reason to let any of that destroy the little moments of joy in life."

Cade didn't say anything at first. He decided to ask the most obvious question: "Who are you?"

Graves smiled. "I don't imagine many people ever have you at a disadvantage, Mr. Cade. Let's just say I'm a troubleshooter. I've been doing it for a long time. The government cannot fulfill all its duties—too many weak sisters worried about bad headlines on Al-Jazeera and what the rest of the world might think. So the private sector has stepped up. I still do my job, but now I make considerably more money. That's the way the system works. And it's what makes our country great."

"Is it?"

Graves laughed. "Don't pretend to be naïve, Cade. How do you think it's possible for a stoned college dropout behind the counter at Starbucks to live in more luxury than any Roman emperor? You think he works harder than the wetback who picked the beans for his vanilla latte? Hell, no. But he goes home to Internet porn and cable TV and more calories in a single meal than that bean-picker sees all week. Other countries struggle. We consume. America is the biggest, fattest kid at the party, gobbling all the candy. But someone has to break the piñata."

"Is that you?"

"I'm proud to do my part."

"Kidnapping people and delivering them to be tortured," Cade said.

"And what would you do with them? Terrorists. Traitors. Murderers. How would you handle them?"

Cade showed his teeth.

"I would kill them all," Cade said, his voice flat. "I would burn their cities until the desert fused to glass. I would tear the wombs from their mothers. I would poison their babies and dismember their children. And then I would drown the men in the blood of their families."

Graves stared back at him for a moment.

"But then, I'm not human," Cade said. "I don't need an excuse to act like a monster."

Graves nodded and chuckled, acknowledging the point scored. "Christ, you're a pain in the ass."

"Don't blaspheme. Not in my presence."

Graves looked at him, as if to gauge his seriousness, and laughed again. "Sorry, Cade. I'm not a religious man and I'm not scared of you. I'll take the name of the Lord in vain whenever I goddamn please."

Cade's eyes narrowed a fraction of an inch. "You don't believe?"

Graves cranked his seat back. "If they get you praying, they've already got you on your knees. I'm not looking for God to save me."

"I wouldn't worry about it if I were you," Cade said.

Graves snorted. "I've got my own exit strategy."

Silence again.

"I get the feeling you don't like me, Mr. Cade."

Cade said nothing.

"You don't get to judge me," Graves said. "I told you: I know about you. I know the things you've done. With all the blood on your hands, you expect me to believe you never once licked your fingers?"

Cade looked at him carefully. "You're certain we haven't met?" he asked.

"I'm sure you'd remember," Graves said. He put in a pair of earbuds and closed his eyes. Conversation over.

THE QUIET SUITED CADE. He needed a few moments to think.

He looked at the dark wood paneling of the ceiling and thought about the Shadow Company.

Before his encounter with Holt, he didn't know the Company existed. They'd been around at least as long as he had. That much was obvious. But Cade, like most of his kind, focused on the immediate threat. An enemy willing to wait, to plan over the long term, would be as hidden from him as an animal that could blend completely into the foliage in the background. Conspiracies didn't matter to him until they matured into a frontal assault. He was arrogant enough—and capable enough— to believe he could defeat anything that came at him directly. Until someone or something forced him to consider it, he didn't waste the time or energy. He focused on the present.

Still, looking back, he began to see a pattern emerge. What he had dismissed in the past as mere incompetence or random outbreaks of human greed, viciousness or malice began to connect with each other. Taken separately, they were simply incidents in his long and strange life.

But together, they pointed to an opponent he didn't even realize was on the other side of the board, watching him, making moves, countering him in some places and ignoring him in others. Above all, this opponent's moves were designed to keep itself a secret.

Cade realized he'd been closest to the Shadow Company when it tried to remove any hint of its existence. At those moments, it broke from cover. And revealed itself more openly than any of the evidence ever could. In hindsight, the pattern was almost painfully obvious. You simply had to know where to look, and it stood out against the landscape, never to be fully hidden again.

The January wind knocked against the wooden frame of the Grand Avenue Hotel like an insistent hand on a door. The old man limped down the hall to his room. The cold hurt his leg. The break had never healed properly.

He sighed heavily as he sat down in the armchair in the corner. The bottle was already there on the table, waiting for him. Like many drunks, he had his rituals, followed with precision to keep him from stumbling too far from the supply of his booze.

He looked up and saw Cade, standing by the window. He didn't seem surprised.

"I knew someone would come," he said.

His voice was still a rich baritone, deep and resonant from his years of theatrical training. Once this was the most famous actor in the nation. And then the most wanted man alive for twelve days in 1865.

But no one looked too hard for a man who was supposed to be dead.

He made no move to escape. Instead, he took another glass from the table.

"Drink, sir?" he asked.

"I don't drink . . . whiskey," Cade replied. "You know why I'm here."

"It has been a long time in coming," he said, putting the empty glass back on the table. "Which of them sent you?"

"The president sent me."

That, at least, gave the man a start. "I'm honored to be a topic of discussion in the White House again. What shall I call you?"

"My name is Nathaniel Cade. Which name do you prefer?"

That brought a smile under the old man's mustache. "John will be fine."

Cade stepped toward him. "I don't think we'll know each other long enough for me to use your first name."

"No, I imagine not," he said. He sipped his whiskey again. "I'm ready. As I said, it's been a long time."

Ordinarily, Cade would have eviscerated the man by then. He was more brutal in those days, more direct. But he felt an insistent prod of curiosity.

"Why did you begin talking?" Cade said.

"I'm sorry?" The man's eyes were bleary. The drink was working on him.

"You knew someone would come. You've been telling people who you are. Who you really are. Why?"

A long sigh. "Do you believe redemption is possible, Mr. Cade? I don't mean for breaking the covenant of marriage, or stealing a few coins here and there. I wonder if it's possible to be forgiven for a truly monstrous sin."

Cade almost smiled. Not the first time he'd considered that question. "It depends on the sinner, I suppose."

Sadness filled the man's eyes. "I don't know either. It's been the abiding preoccupation of my days. I suppose I was looking for some punishment. Perhaps that would expiate some of my guilt."

"You feel guilty?" Now Cade was surprised.

The man nodded and drank. "It has taken me some years to realize how mistaken I was. Everything seems too clear when you're young. You believe in the absolute rightness of your cause. You believe the end justifies the means. For the greater good. My confederates at the time were all too happy to use me to further their own ends. It was only much later I realized they were in league with our supposed enemies. Each for their own reasons, they wanted an American Messiah. At the time, I was sure we were blazing with the light of truth. Now I realize they were most comfortable in the shadows."

"Your former allies? You think they're still around, watching you?"

"Oh, they still exist," he said. "They change the name of their organizations, their public leaders come and go, but they never die. I knew they would have to silence me once I began confessing. But I had to admit it, even if I was too much of a coward to do so before old age caught up with me."

"And now you're ready to pay for your crimes."

The man gave a short, bitter laugh. "Whether I am or not, you're here now. I believed the others would find me before any federal man could cross the country, however."

Cade smiled, showing his fangs. "I'm not your typical federal man."

Again surprising Cade, the man didn't react with the usual terror or shock. "I've heard of things like you. I suppose it only proves I'm going to Hell, if you're here to claim me."

Cade felt something. He couldn't quite name it. Something in his blood sang in proximity to this man, the same man who fired the bullet that was part of the ritual binding him to the presidency. A bit of the "American Messiah"'s blood was on that bullet, and Cade swore he could feel it now. However small those drops, however little remained inside him, he could feel it.

Perhaps that was what motivated him to ask the next question.

"Do you really feel you did something wrong? Do you repent?"

The old man's eyes blazed with conviction. "I killed the best man who ever lived. I deserve whatever you have in store for me."

This was not acting, Cade knew. This was the truth.

He poured the old man another drink.

"You were right, actually," Cade said. "I wasn't the first here. Another man entered your room. The whiskey you've been drinking has been laced with cyanide."

The man considered this. "I thought it tasted a little bitter. But when you get to my age, you can't be too choosy with your spirits."

"It wouldn't have killed you. Not before I did," Cade said. "It certainly would have been less painful."

"My hard luck, then. Do what you must."

Cade pushed the glass toward the man's hand.

"One last drink," he said. "You have time."

The man tipped his head in thanks. He drained the glass in a single gulp.

Almost immediately, it fell from his hand. His breathing grew shallow. As Cade had figured, the last glass had been enough for a lethal dose. Within minutes, Cade heard his heart slow, then stop.

He didn't know why he let the assassin of President Lincoln die quietly, without the pain and fear Cade usually inflicted on his enemies.

Perhaps it was the last bit of that great man's blood, still flowing in him somewhere.

Perhaps that's where he found a drop of genuine mercy.

EIGHT

1928—Providence, Rhode Island—A series of "vampire murders" reported. Later, local authorities intercept a bootlegger's truck that contains the stolen corpse of Benjamin Franklin. Cade sent to investigate. Results inconclusive. Possibly related to the Innsmouth incident.

—BRIEFING BOOK: CODE NAME: NIGHTMARE PET
  (EYES ONLY/CLASSIFIED/ABOVE TOP SECRET),
  Partial Chronology, Unknown "Events" and Operations

EYL, PUNTLAND REGION OF SOMALIA

Business in the little coastal town was booming. Piracy had turned what was once a sleepy fishing village into a third-world amusement park: Pirateland. When the pirates came in from the sea, the village doubled or tripled in size, and dollars were dumped in piles amid the bone-grinding poverty. Restaurants on the coastline catered to the pirates and their prisoners as well. They offered menus, daily specials and delivery by boat. Rolls-Royces and Bentleys parked in the mud next to pens of livestock. Modern designer homes overlooked the gulf, paid for with ransoms and stolen goods. Pirated Internet cables were strung through the air, delivering wi-fi to the accountants who tallied the loot on their laptops.

Cade and Graves walked through the carnival smells and polyglot shouts unmolested, but not unnoticed. It was unusual for two white men to be here, but not unheard of. It was possible they were negotiators, or buyers. For some reason, no one wanted to approach Cade to find out.

"This is a waste of time," Cade said.

"It's all we have," Graves replied.

Graves had changed into a tropical-weight outfit while on the plane—linen suit and shirt, khaki tie. He kept his shades on, even though it was now full dark. He looked like colonialism's ghost on a tour of its old home. The only concessions he made to the setting were the waffle-stomper boots on his feet and the heavy N-frame, 8-shot Smith & Wesson .357 Magnum holstered in plain view on his belt.

They'd arrived at an airstrip—basically a long, flat section of dirt—about ninety miles east of Eyl. Over the intercom, the pilot said landing would be impossible; "a jet-fuel cremation," was how he put it. Graves stepped into the cockpit, and a moment later, they came in for a landing that felt like going over class IV rapids.

The pilots stayed at the plane, trying to figure out how to turn the Gulfstream for takeoff, as Graves and Cade transferred into a black Range Rover. They left behind a couple of Archies with full-body armor and automatic weapons to stand guard.

By the time they arrived, it was past midnight, but no one was sleeping. As long as the pirates were in port, Eyl was a twenty-four-hour operation.

Still, they'd found nothing. The pirates who'd been infected with the Snakehead virus were already dead, killed by Cade. Their boats were gone, wrecked or scavenged. Their names brought only blank stares from the few people willing to talk.

"A waste of time," Cade said again.

Graves shrugged. "If you have any other ideas, I'd be happy to—"

Cade had already turned away from him and activated his phone. He called Zach.

"Give me something I can use," he said.

"AND HELLO to you too, Cade," Zach replied.

It was past six in the offices, and nothing seemed nearly as fresh as it had this morning. They'd all been up since before dawn, with nothing to show for it.

Bell and her colleagues were frozen with some combination of humiliation, fear and ass-covering. They refused to call Graves without any fresh intel.

They were stuck. They knew it. They'd even sent Hewitt and Reynolds out for pizza. The stink of failure was starting to fill the air.

Bell looked up from her screen. "Is that Cade?"

Candle didn't stop popping M&Ms into his mouth. "Tell him we say hello."

"Well?" Cade asked.

"We've got exactly dick," Zach admitted. "Sorry."

"Look harder," Cade said.

Zach allowed himself a little sigh of impatience. Zach actually liked talking to Cade on the phone. The nerve-rending effect of his presence was neutered. Even Cade was incapable of reaching through the telephone to tear out your throat long-distance. Sure, his voice still had that creepy, cold flatness, but Zach could handle that. It made him a little bolder, a little more likely to give Cade a direct order.

Of course, Cade always came back. Always. You could send him out against the worst possible nightmares, things that handed out death and destruction like business cards, things that had extinction encoded into their DNA—and Zach *had*—and he'd still come back.

Which meant Zach could act as tough as he liked on the phone, but there would be a price to pay. Eventually.

Still, Zach figured, you have to enjoy yourself when you can.

"Hey, fire me," he said. "We've done our best. I've run names of all the pirates through our covert databases, with no contacts to any of the known players. No activity at all in that part of Africa. The Archies looked at their database. No employees match the authorization for the original Somali shipment."

"That's what they did, is it?" Cade left that hanging for him.

Zach didn't pick it up. "Well . . . yeah."

"And what did *you* see when you looked through their records?"

Son of a bitch, thought Zach. Of course he should have checked their findings. Old habits. He'd actually started to think of them as coworkers, like they were all on the same side. He chipped in for the *pizza*, for Christ's sake. Stupid, stupid, stupid . . .

"Call you back in five."

He hung up and moved around the desk to sit at Book's workstation.

Book, who was lying on a couch across the room, flipping pages of documents, began to rise. "Just what do you think you're doing?"

"This is your shipping and freight database, correct?" Zach clicked around, getting a feel for the interface.

"You don't have clearance—"

"Nice. Very intuitive. Almost like a Mac." He quickly found the shipment number. Book had left it up on the screen. He was over Zach's shoulder now.

"I'm not going to tell you again, Barrows."

"He's right, Zach," Bell piped up. "There's a protocol we have to follow. We're talking about trade secrets as well as national security—"

Zach talked over her. "You couldn't find any record of this guy here who authorized the shipment, right?"

"That's right, genius," Book said. "No such employee. Fake ID number, fake clearance level, all planted in our records. Otherwise the shipment never would have gone out. But no way to find out who did it, either. We've been over this."

"Right," Zach said. "A/A employee: Stephens, Justin. A transport engineer, whatever the hell that means."

"He doesn't exist," Book snapped. "We explained this."

"Yeah?" Zach spun in the chair and faced all three of them. "Well, he sent another shipment twelve hours after the first one."

Silence. Zach pushed back from the screen to show them what their own computer database had pulled up a few seconds before.

"Maybe we ought to figure out where that's going, you think?"

NINE

Cade's speed is perhaps his most formidable attribute, even more than his strength or resistance to damage. Cade's running speed is nearly three times that of the fastest recorded human, at 75 mph. However, what is more impressive (and more useful, from Cade's perspective as a predator) are his "short burst" movements— i.e., moving across a room or another limited distance. These have been clocked at over 50 mph *from a standing start*. This speed is on par with the action of the pistol shrimp, which attacks its prey so quickly that even the highest-speed cameras have trouble catching the movement.

Cade is able to accomplish this due to his altered physiology. His tightly coiled, highly dense muscle tissue is almost always in the "potential" state to release energy (excepting, of course, when he is in his coma-like state for rest during the day). His neural transmission is much faster than human as well, so his nervous system delivers commands nearly instantaneously—thought and action are almost simultaneous. The potential energy is released explosively and Cade is effectively hurled into motion.

The mean human response time to visual stimuli is approximately 180–200 milliseconds. In that amount of time, Cade could move 13.1 feet. In a confined space or in the dark, this is nearly impossible to track visually. In these circumstances, Cade is, for all practical purposes, faster than the eye can see. This is probably what gives rise to the myths of vampires being able to disperse into mist or even fly.

—BRIEFING BOOK: CODE NAME: NIGHTMARE PET

CAMP LEMONNIER, DJIBOUTI, NORTHERN AFRICA

P FC Tom Gangwer was working the midnight-to-0800 shift with Lewis, both of them inside the guard station at the front gate.

Lemonnier was the only U.S. military installation in Africa. What was once a collection of double-wide trailers and air-conditioned tents—basically an afterthought in the defense budget—received a serious upgrade for the ongoing War on Terror. Over the past few years, they'd added an airstrip capable of landing a C-130, dorms for personnel, a drone launch facility and a new rec center. The number of soldiers and sailors had doubled to more than three thousand.

Even though the Navy was in charge of the site, the Army helped out with security. Gangwer didn't mind. Security was a pretty easy detail, all things considered. Yeah, they had to watch out for any local who decided that a car bomb was an e-ticket ride to Heaven. But most of the locals were actually pretty cool here. And the soldiers were assisted greatly by the fact that the camp was in the middle of BFE. Sentries could see anyone coming on the main road, and anyone who wasn't on the main road had to cross open space—miles and miles of flat, dusty ground.

Tonight, the only thing on the schedule was a prisoner transfer. Archer/Andrews was bringing in human cargo. Soldiers were, in fact, encouraged to look the other way from these special deliveries. The less you knew, the better.

That was fine by Gangwer. This wasn't Iraq, where everyone and his brother wore a suicide belt under his robes. He'd been happy to get the transfer order here, and he wasn't about to screw it up.

"You know, in my hometown, there was a theater called the Baghdad when I was a kid?" he told Lewis.

"No shit?" Lewis was only mildly interested, but it beat staring at the planes coming in and out of the airport.

"Yeah," Gangwer said. "They changed it right before Gulf War One—"

"Hah. I bet."

"—but my dad said it had been around since the twenties. It was a big old place, with all this fancy gold stuff on it. I mean, it was pretty run-down by the time I saw it, and it was in a part of town we usually didn't go. I think they were running porn movies there, actually."

"We had a theater like that downtown," Johnson said. "Not porn movies. But it used to be a silent movie theater. Lots of gold decorations. Statues of King Tut. The Egyptian."

Gangwer nodded. "Exactly. The Baghdad, even when it was a shit-hole, you could see it had been something once. Lots of fake palm trees and all kinds of Middle Eastern stuff, all crammed together. It made me think, you know, once upon a time, our grandparents, all they knew about Baghdad was it was a cool name. They thought it was exotic. Like dancing girls and all that."

Lewis laughed. "Not exactly accurate."

"Right. You think they ever would have thought their grandkids would end up fighting in Baghdad? Probably seemed like going to the moon to them."

"Sure. If the moon was a hundred-twenty-degree toilet filled with people trying to kill you."

Gangwer sighed. He wasn't sure what he was trying to say, but he knew Lewis wasn't getting it.

Then he noticed the truck. "Hey," he said, pointing. Lewis turned and looked.

A big panel transport; a new truck with no markings. The Archies were here. But the truck was moving slowly, barely idling along.

It slowed even more, as if the driver somehow noticed their attention.

Finally, roughly three hundred yards from the camp perimeter, it chugged to a halt on the road.

Not good. They both knew it. Maybe something happened to the Archies. Maybe the prisoners got control of the truck. Or maybe it had been hijacked and turned into a bomb.

But those were all just maybes. It would suck balls to call out the cavalry for nothing more than engine trouble.

"Check it out?" Gangwer asked.

Lewis nodded. "I'll go."

Lewis jogged to the truck while Gangwer made the call. So far, nothing too far out of the ordinary. Just a truck . . .

Then, when Lewis was about twenty yards from the truck, the driver door opened and a man sprinted away.

He was gone, out of sight into the dark, in seconds.

Oh shit, Gangwer thought. He and Lewis shared the same thought, separated by distance: bomb. They both hit the deck.

A moment later, they both got back up. Nothing. Just the truck, still idling.

Lewis looked back, shrugged. He hand-signaled that he was going to check it out.

Gangwer began to get a bad feeling about this. A truck bomb would make sense. But a guy running away in the middle of the night? That was just weird. Even weirder, Gangwer was pretty sure that the guy was wearing A/A fatigues. He could recognize the corporate logo. And the Archies were so damn proud of their slick uniforms.

Lewis wasn't being stupid. He had his rifle up and ready. Gangwer wished he'd called for backup already. He picked up the phone.

Lewis went to the back doors of the truck. He tested them, carefully, using the butt of his rifle to flip the latch.

Gangwer was tensed for another explosion. Again, nothing. Then the door swung wide, and Lewis disappeared behind it.

Then gunshots burst out—stuttering, hesitant, and over almost before they began.

The screaming just kept on going, however.

Lewis was a veteran. He'd been in firefights and transports hit by IEDs and pinned down by insurgents with heavy artillery. But Gangwer had never heard that kind of fear in his voice before.

Lewis broke from around the truck and sprinted toward the gate-house, as fast as he could, something black covering half his face.

Not black. Red. It was blood. Half his face was simply torn away. Peeled open like a banana. Lewis's rifle was gone. His helmet was gone.

Something was right behind him.

It hopped almost playfully, jumping at Lewis's heels, springing along in his wake with an ease that said it could take the soldier at any time.

Gangwer thought it was a big cat, maybe—they don't have tigers in Africa, do they?—but then it moved into the perimeter light, and he got a look at the green-black scales.

Some kind of big . . . lizard? But it walked on two legs. It stood up like a man.

Gangwer realized Lewis was screaming his name. Over and over. And a single plea: "Shoot! Gangwer! Shoot!"

Gangwer broke from his daze of shock. He dropped the phone. Picked up the rifle, aimed and fired.

"Son of a bitch," Gangwer said. He tagged the fucker—he knew he did—but it just stumbled and then kept going. What was that thing?

It leaped on top of Lewis with one long, loping stride.

"Please," he shrieked as he went down. "Please, Gangwer! Just shoot!"

Gangwer wanted to cover his ears. He realized Lewis wasn't asking him to shoot the creature. He was asking for a bullet himself.

Gangwer dropped the rifle. His hands felt clumsy and thick on the phone. He wasn't sure how to call it in, but he knew the other guard stations had to be alerted.

"This is main gate to all points, we have an unknown on the base, repeat, an unknown on the base—"

The phone dropped from him. He looked at it, wondering why he'd done that.

Then he realized he hadn't done it himself. His hand was still around the phone. It was just no longer attached to his body.

Gangwer looked up, blood dropping out of him so fast that everything seemed to be happening in a dream.

There was another one. Tall as a man, blazing yellow eyes and sharp teeth. And claws; claws so sharp they could reach out and sever limbs faster than an industrial saw.

In the distance, more of the things came sprinting out of the dark. He could see them now. Hear them hissing.

He realized Lewis wasn't screaming anymore. The thing next to him moved, too quick. He couldn't process it.

His brain vainly tried to send signals down to his body, and nothing was coming back.

In that nanosecond, Gangwer had the strangest flash of memory—of being upside-down on a roller coaster at the state fair. Then he felt nothing.

His head bounced twice on the ground, right at the feet of the other Snakeheads going through the gate.

TEN

Meeting with C. tonight at the Gayety. Hard to enjoy the fan dance with that thing sitting beside me in the box. He showed me a copy of a magazine he said had been taken from the stands due to its strange and unsettling content. (Thankfully, he did not make me read it.) It was related to a supposed creature or animal in a house in Massachusetts, and requested permission to investigate. I gave him free rein, knowing it would get him out of my sight that much faster. I know that what C. does is vital, but I am a simple man of limited talents from a small town. The less I have to deal with him the better for us all.

Had I known this would be part of the cost, I would have stayed in Marion and told the Duchess to go to hell. May God help me, for I need it.

—President Warren G. Harding, private diary (classified)

Cade knew it, even as he calculated time and distance, listening to Zach's hurried, stuttering information over the phone. He knew it even when he picked Graves up bodily, despite the old man's shouted protests, and ran them back to the plane. He did everything he could short of picking up the Gulfstream and hurling it into the air.

They were only a few hours away.

But they would never make it in time.

———

MOST OF IT WAS OVER by the time the plane touched down. The air was thick with the smell of cordite and blood, and the cleanup had already begun.

Cade walked.

Cade had witnessed too many disasters at military bases, and the response was almost always the same. Men and women put aside their shock and horror. They didn't ask anything but relevant questions, such as "Where?" and "When?" and "How many?" Abstract concepts like "Why?" they saved for later, along with their mourning or panic. Soldiers and sailors swarmed to the source of the problem, and each one found an angle they could approach, a role to play in staunching the bleeding, whatever small effort they could make.

Cade crossed half the camp in three seconds when he heard the hissing.

Buried amid the piles of dead bodies, he found one Snakehead, disoriented, newly transformed. It still wore some of its human clothing—remnants of a Marine uniform.

Everyone nearby turned and stared as it kicked and tore its way out of the corpses. It was looking for fresher meat.

It turned to see Cade coming, but was in no way ready. It almost split open on impact. He didn't allow that to stop him from beating it down into the dirt.

He didn't care about the witnesses. They were military, and they could be shut up later. Most would want to forget what they'd seen. Others simply wouldn't believe it, would rather disavow the knowledge from their own eyes than live in a world where things like this were real.

None of that mattered to Cade.

All that mattered to him, at that moment, was that he was too late.

———

GRAVES WALKED THROUGH the camp's medical center, surveying the wounded—the ones who had not been bitten or clawed, the ones suffering from merely human injuries.

Graves moved with authority, as if he belonged, so people assumed he must belong. No one stopped him or even questioned him. It was as if the entire camp was still in shock, stunned into a kind of mute acceptance. Many soldiers and sailors hadn't even seen the Snakeheads. There were rumors, but they were muted by the threat of court-martial or worse. Anyone who had actually seen the creatures didn't want to talk about it. They were too busy with grief or struggling to hold on to their sanity.

The only certain thing was that whatever had happened tonight *didn't happen*.

In this kind of atmosphere, Graves might as well have been invisible.

The critically wounded had already been moved to the nearby French army hospital, which had better facilities for the men hit by shrapnel or caught in the cross fire of their own forces. But a few dozen were still on the base, recovering from minor injuries.

In one of the patient areas, Graves found a young Marine sleeping. The young man had a clean bullet wound through the meat of his right leg. He was on IV fluids, and according to his chart, would be up and walking in days.

Perfect.

Graves took a small hypo from a pocket of his vest. It contained a clear solution, indistinguishable from the saline and plasma the Marine was already receiving.

He poked the needle into the tube, emptying the fluid into it. It flowed into the young man's IV, and from there, slid into his veins.

He didn't even shift in his sleep. Graves noted the time, then walked out.

On his way to the front door, he put the needle into a sharps container marked CAUTION—BIOHAZARD.

CADE FOUND GRAVES overseeing the extraction of a young Marine at the helipad. An Archer/Andrews transport chopper idled, its rotors starting to spin.

"What are you doing?" he demanded.

Graves looked up. "Kid needs medical attention."

"Then take him to the hospital. Or bring the doctors here."

Graves shook his head. "Nothing they can do for him here. There's a carrier out in the gulf, on its way to Kuwait. They're better equipped."

Cade turned away from him. The Marine was about to be lifted onto the chopper. He didn't look good. His skin was flushed and sweat poured out of him. Dark rings circled his eyes. He certainly looked as if he was about to die.

Cade didn't care.

"Stop," Cade barked at the men holding the stretcher. There was no reason they should have listened to someone in civilian clothes. But they heard something in Cade's voice, and they froze in their tracks.

"Belay that," Graves shouted angrily. "Get him out of here!"

Cade spun on him. "You know why we can't allow him to leave here."

Graves eyed him coolly. "I won't let a good young man die. Not if I can help it."

"If he's infected—"

"He's not. He's shown no symptoms. I'll take responsibility."

Cade looked at Graves, who held his stare. "You can't."

He turned back to the crew and the stretcher. The blades were spinning up now. He had no choice. He'd stop this himself.

"Cade, don't interfere! That's an order!" Graves shouted above the rotors.

Cade froze. He felt the oath, like chains across his mind, holding him fast. A lawful order, given by a designated representative of the president. He could try to resist, but bad things would happen. Seizures. And then worse.

Reluctantly, he watched the crew back away from the helicopter, the Marine strapped inside. It lifted off like a fat, ungainly seabird, and then churned its way out toward the gulf.

Graves watched it leave as well.

"You did the wrong thing," Cade said.

"Sorry, Cade," Graves said. "Did you want to drink his blood yourself?"

Cade didn't reply. Graves stomped away from him.

"Come on," Graves called over his shoulder. He almost sounded apologetic. "Let's try to keep this from happening again."

Cade kept watching the copter until it dwindled to a small dot in the sky.

REAR ADMIRAL VERNON PARRISH, the base CO, had a great don't-fuck-with-me stare. It had probably helped him get to his rank, commander of the Horn of Africa Joint Task Force. He was anxious to reassert his authority over these two interlopers who'd shown up with demands but no answers.

But when he turned his stare on Cade, Cade had simply invoked priority code RED RUM. Parrish blanched and left without another word. A few moments later, an aide returned to tell them they had full access to everything on the base.

Now the sun was an hour from rising. Cade and Graves sat in the camp CO's office, looking at a speakerphone.

Cade stood, his clothes still stiff with the blood of the Snakehead he'd killed. Graves sat behind the desk.

They had all the data on the incident—no one was sure what else to call it right now—laid out in front of them.

One hundred fifty-seven personnel dead. Most of them in the first twenty minutes, due to sheer surprise, not any numerical advantage. Eyewitness reports put the number of "unknown creatures" at less than a dozen. Small-arms fire was useless. Unlike the creatures Cade had faced just twenty-four hours earlier, these Snakeheads were impervious to anything less than .50 cal rounds. It required either a grenade launcher or mounted machine gun to kill them.

Then there were the infections. Another forty-three were killed by their own comrades in arms. As soon as the first symptoms appeared, the military personnel had responded quickly, despite their shock, and turned their weapons on the wounded. Some small amount of good news there: no one froze up. These were kids raised with zombie movies after all, although some would probably need counseling for the rest of their lives after killing their friends, bunkmates and officers.

The Snakeheads went on the run as soon as the heavy artillery was unleashed. They scurried toward the coastline with a strange, froglike gait, the surviving witnesses reported. It made sense to Cade; they were still enough like the Innsmouth breed in that way.

The military had learned the first rule of dealing with monsters: if it's trying to kill you, it doesn't matter if it's impossible.

As a result, they shot first and saved their nightmares for later. Many people survived. You could almost call it a victory.

But all Cade could think was: it never should have come to this.

"So, angels," Graves said to the speakerphone. "Anyone want to explain to me how this happened?"

Nothing but static on the line.

"Anyone? Don't be shy, kids."

Book tried to mount a defense. "Look, how were we supposed to know the same alias was used elsewhere in the system?"

"Yes," Graves said. "That was pretty damned stupid. Someone who did that, I'd be surprised if he doesn't walk around with his dick hanging out because he's too dumb to zip up."

"Come on, Colonel." It was Candle. "You know the problem here. We're stuck with these hitchhikers. Sorry, but someone's got to say it. Barrows and Cade are only in the way."

"Yeah," Zach snorted. "*I'm* the one who missed the clues here."

"If we didn't have to explain everything to you every five minutes—"

"Let me explain something to you—"

There was the sound of a chair sliding back, a mumble of raised voices and shoving.

"Enough," Cade shouted. Even across an ocean, it stopped all movement on the other end.

"We failed," he said. "Every one of us. And people died."

A moment of embarrassed silence. Then, Bell: "You're right, Mr. Cade. I apologize. It was our screwup. Zach came in and found the link. If we'd shared info earlier . . ."

"I don't care," Cade said. "The attacks are escalating. Clearly, there will be another, and soon. Find out why. Find out where. Above all, stop wasting my time."

He left to search for a place to go to ground for the day.

Graves waited until the door had swung shut. "All of you clear enough now?" he said to the speaker. "Need any more motivation? Because I'm pretty sure you don't want Mr. Cade coming back to provide it. Get your goddamn heads in the game."

He hit a button, ending the call.

CADE WENT OUTSIDE. He walked to the grave site, not far from the airport, just outside the camp's official borders. The cover story had already been decided. These men and women would not get the honor of a military burial. As far as the outside world was concerned, they had all been blown to pieces by a truck bomb. Their relatives back home would receive only ceremonial flags.

Their remains were to be buried here in the soft African soil, where quicklime and the wet earth, rich with insects, would turn them into unidentifiable mulch.

Morning was just below the horizon, but Cade still picked up a shovel. The burial detail watched in openmouthed horror as he completed the pit single-handedly.

As they began loading bodies, and pieces of bodies, Cade dug another hole, a short distance off, for himself.

He lay down and burrowed into the soil. He would sleep here for the day, alongside the victims he had failed, and try to guard them, in some hopeless way, on the first of all the days they had lost because of him.

Because he was too late.

ELEVEN

The CIA's most effective line of defense against exposure of their mind-control operations (or any of their operations, for that matter) has always been self-effacement. The agency portrays its agents as incompetent stooges, encouraging the public to laugh at their wacky attempts to formulate cancer potions and knock off foreign leaders.

—Jonathan Vankin and John Whalen,
The 80 Greatest Conspiracies of All Time

CHANTILLY, VIRGINIA

The quiet in the office lasted long after the call ended.

Zach and Candle were at opposite ends of a table, a temporary DMZ between them. Bell looked beaten. Book was just pissed.

"You didn't have to take all the blame," Zach said to Bell.

"Or any of it," Candle said.

Zach stood up, ready to start the shoving match again. "That's it, jackass—"

"Stop it," Bell ordered. They both sat down again. "Colonel's right. We have a job to do. We missed the obvious before. Let's start again. Up from the ground floor. Go."

"It's late," Book said, looking at his watch. "Shouldn't we get some rack time? Start fresh in the morning?"

"It's morning over there already," Bell said, an edge in her voice. "But hey, if you're too tired, go ahead. Take a nap."

Book scowled and stayed where he was.

"Ideas?" Bell asked. "Anyone?"

"What about that mad scientist guy? He could do something like this?" Candle asked.

"Konrad?" Zach was surprised these people knew about him. His whole existence, like Cade's, was classified far above the usual definition of top secret. "We already ruled him out."

"Well, rule him back in."

"No," Zach said. "Konrad prefers things that have his signature on them. He'd want to make sure Cade knew he was involved. It's very personal with him."

"That's not much of a reason to eliminate him, Zach." Bell sounded apologetic.

"Konrad also hates working with anything related to Innsmouth. Finds it disgusting and beneath him. And frankly, the Snakeheads aren't half as tough as anything Konrad could put together in his spare time."

"Fine. Moving on."

They went in circles like that. Zach learned they knew a few things about the Other Side and its incursions into our world—some things that surprised even him.

But none of it got them any closer to an answer.

After another hour or two, they sat, resentment filling the quiet spaces between them.

There was another lead, Zach knew. But it was firmly under NIGHT-MARE PET, and he'd be breaking about a dozen conditions of his clearance to let anyone else in on it.

Hell with it, he decided. "I know someone who can help us with this," he told Bell. "Let's go."

Book and Candle began to get up from their chairs, moving like someone had just told them they were being sent to the dentist.

"Not you," Zach said.

"Why not?" Candle demanded.

"Because it's not a tour group, all right? I'm taking enough of a chance here."

Hewitt stirred from his post at the door. Bell shook her head. "It's okay," she said. "We'll do this Zach's way."

They looked like they were about to protest, then thought better of it.

"All right," Candle said. "For what it's worth, Barrows, I'm sorry about before. We're on the same side. I just . . . I missed it. You know? Embarrassing."

Zach was taken off guard. It must have shown on his face.

"Same here," Book said. "You caught the error. Credit where it's due. Now let's get these fuckers, all right?"

"Yeah. Sure," Zach said. "Thanks." He didn't know what else to say.

Hewitt and Reynolds didn't pay any attention to this little warm and fuzzy exchange. They remained slumped in their chairs. Reynolds was asleep; Hewitt was downing snacks from the vending machines.

That made Zach feel better somehow. He didn't know what he'd do if they wanted to hug it out.

He and Bell left the office.

BOOK DIDN'T EVEN WAIT for them to get to the car. "Well?" he said to Hewitt.

Hewitt looked up, crème filling dotting the corners of his mouth.

"Follow them, jackass."

Hewitt gave Book a scowl, but stood, crumpling a Twinkie wrapper. He turned toward the door and suddenly, without warning, he was simply—gone.

A dark shadow fell across the floor, and then that vanished as well.

Candle shuddered. "Man, that creeps me out every—"

Book took two steps across the room and slapped him. It sounded like a racquetball hitting a wall.

"You fucking moron," he said. "How goddamn lazy are you? The same fake ID? You couldn't even find a different name?"

Candle rubbed the fresh red welt on his face. "You were the one who let him at your terminal," he whined.

Book raised his hand again. Candle flinched. "Don't," Book warned. "Don't even try to shift this. You screwed up. We could have kept them running in circles for days. Weeks even."

"How was I supposed to know someone else would be checking the database?"

Book considered hitting him again, but knew it was a waste of time. That was the trouble with all these double games and cover identities. You had to work with who you were given.

"Never mind. You think you can fix it now?"

Candle nodded furiously. "Not a problem. Take me five minutes. I swear."

He sat down at his terminal and began clacking keys, staring hard at the screen: a picture of the model employee.

Book decided to throw him a bone. "That was good, what you did there with Barrows. Keep him unbalanced. Make him think we're his buddies now."

Candle shrugged, but Book could see the pride. "He's a political hack. They all want to be loved."

In the corner, Reynolds was still snoring softly. None of this had even made him stir. Candle kept typing for a moment. Then: "You think Bell is into him?"

"Who, Barrows? Don't worry about it. You didn't have a chance anyway. She likes men."

Candle pulled on his tie, which showed the message again: EAT ME.

"You know what I mean. It could complicate things. If she's not on board."

Candle rummaged through Hewitt's pile of snacks. He held out a package to Book. "Want to split a Twinkie?"

"No," he said, and kicked Reynolds in the foot, waking him. "Come on," he said. "We have someplace to be."

"Where are you going?" Candle said, like a kid left out of a class trip.

"Just going to make sure everyone stays frosty," Book said. "Get to work. We'll be back soon."

Reynolds followed Book to the door in a kind of sleepwalk. They got into one of the Humvees and began driving for D.C.

TWELVE

In Colorado during the Depression, a number of witnesses claimed to have seen man-sized, bipedal, dinosaur-like lizards. One was supposedly exhibited in a farmer's barn for several days after it was shot and killed. Whether or not this is related to the "serpent people" legends of the local Hopi Indian tribes is unknown.

—Cole Daniels, *Monsterpaedia*

Zach thought about blindfolding Bell, but he had no idea how to ask a woman something like that. A girlfriend had once tried handcuffing him in bed and he'd laughed so hard it completely spoiled the mood.

Besides, Zach realized, if he trusted her enough to share one secret, then she might as well know the rest of them.

He drove the black A/A Humvee down into a service tunnel for the Metro and waved his phone at a panel on the ceiling. A radio receiver picked up, and a gate opened in another side passage. A few sharp turns later, and they were down a ramp into a much older series of tunnels—ones that had been around since Washington, D.C., was built.

He parked the Humvee. Bell was trying to look nonchalant, but she was still staring at the walls around them. It was like an eighteenth-century street, paved with stones, under a brick ceiling.

"I had no idea," she said.

"Not many people do," Zach said, trying not to sound like he was bragging. "Cade's been using these tunnels for years. You can even reach the White House from here."

"Is that where we're going?" she asked.

"No," he said, and pointed to an exit in the wall, just large enough for them to walk through. "This is a lot less glamorous. Believe me."

"It's really a remarkable accomplishment," Dr. Carl Everett said. "Sophisticated, but actually quite elegant. Even beautiful."

They were in the basement laboratories below the NIH, where a series of fallout shelters had been rebuilt to house a variety of classified experiments.

Everett was speaking of the body. He stood by a steel table laid out with a Snakehead from the raid on the yacht, partially dissected. Crusted blood and gore leaked from the wound Cade had punched in its torso, and its eyes stared blankly at the ceiling.

Zach suppressed a shudder, but not because of the creature on the slab. Everett creeped him out.

Zach and Cade did not work completely alone. There was an entire support structure of specialized personnel, men and women who had been drawn in because of their own contacts with the Other Side, or because they simply didn't flinch as much as regular civilians when faced with soul-rending horror. He didn't even know how many there were. They were all a little weird—they had to be, to keep a job where a hostile work environment meant occasional zombie outbreaks—but Everett won the prize for grand high freak.

It wasn't his appearance or demeanor. Everything about him was mild. He wore a warm cardigan sweater under his lab coat. He always made Zach think of Mr. Rogers.

Except Mr. Rogers probably never looked so calm while up to his elbows in a monster's guts.

Perhaps all his time dealing with death had made him callous, but Everett's composure faltered only when he confronted something new and hideous. And then he'd break into a smile, as if he was watching a child receive a new puppy at a birthday party.

Bell, however, looked like she was barely holding on to her lunch. And Everett's placid manner seemed to have the same effect on her that it did on Zach. He decided to hurry this along.

"Aside from the aesthetics, what can you tell us about the Snakeheads?" Zach asked him.

"I've mentioned before, your nickname for them is not very accurate. The creature contains reptilian, aquatic and amphibian traits—"

"Doctor," Zach said. "Cut me some slack, okay? Just the high points."

Everett grimaced, but nodded. He pointed at the body.

"What you have here is a human being who's essentially been re-engineered by a very powerful infectious agent. He was hit with what appears to be a retrovirus that rebuilt him from the cell level up. And from what you tell me, onset of the change was nearly instantaneous after infection. Truly remarkable."

"You're sure it's a virus?" Zach asked. "Cade has fought things like these before."

Everett shook his head. "This is related to Innsmouth, but it's not the same thing. The transformation in Innsmouth was triggered by years of interbreeding, as well as occult ritual and environmental factors. Basically, you had to live there and be related to the Marshes. A very shallow gene pool. Bin Laden was clearly infected with an earlier variant of this strain, but again, it wasn't contagious, and probably required months of treatments in near-total isolation. Probably some ritual as well."

Bell furrowed her brow. "I'm sorry, did you just say Bin Laden?"

Zach made a face. "One security breach at a time, okay?" He turned back to Everett. "So if this isn't the same as the earlier outbreaks, what is it?"

"Someone has taken the Innsmouth DNA and turned it into a disease," Everett said. "They've loaded it into a fast-spreading viral carrier that spreads in body fluids. It doesn't require ritual, or any weakening of the usual barriers between our world and the next. It will infect people who've had no previous contact with the Other Side."

"So, like demonic possession, but on a cellular level," Bell said.

"Exactly right," Everett said, as if he hadn't heard the sarcasm in her voice. "Put simply, it appears that the virus is a carrier for a package of RNA that immediately transcribes itself into the host DNA of the cells. Each infected cell is then repurposed, and the host organism made into an optimal carrier for continued proliferation of the virus itself."

Zach and Bell exchanged glances. She shrugged. "Try putting it a little more simply," he said.

Everett shrugged. "The virus changes humans into the shape the virus wants."

"How can a virus want something?"

Everett blinked at them. "A figure of speech. The virus has the goal of reproducing. That's all it does. And this body is the best way for the virus to do that. It's like someone decided to take humans all the way back down the evolutionary process and start again at the ground level."

He looked at Bell and Zach, who stared back.

"Look," Everett said impatiently, as he pointed at the corpse. "The skin. Transformed into scale-like layers. Denser and tougher, like a reptile's. The cells receive a boost of keratin and osteopontin that's leached from the bones, causing them to thicken and harden. At the same time, the skeleton becomes more flexible and resilient, like that of a fish or amphibian. It's capable of taking much greater force without breakage. It flexes under pressure. Which is necessary, as the muscle tissues have also been augmented. The fibers of the skeletal muscle are replaced by fibers that are much closer to Type Two muscles—which contract faster, and with much greater strength. It also requires less oxygen and is capable of greater endurance in anaerobic conditions. And this, of course, is of direct benefit because of the blood."

That caught Zach's attention. "What about the blood?"

Everett was smiling now. "The blood cells have nuclei."

Zach looked at him blankly. So did Bell.

Everett kept smiling. "Human red blood cells don't have a nucleus," he said. "But reptile blood cells do. Partially, this is because the lower metabolism of reptiles enables them to transfer blood without the same metabolic cost."

Zach was starting to lose patience now. "Still not following you, Doctor."

"Don't you see? They are turned from warm-blooded to cold-blooded in a matter of minutes. That frees a massive amount of metabolic energy, which is all consumed by the change. This is the key factor—there's no way the human body could undergo this transformation otherwise. It would burn out all the blood sugar available to the host in seconds. Their bodies would simply drop dead. But with this little tweak, the virus keeps them alive long enough to become self-sustaining engines for reproduction."

Everett paused, and a troubled look flashed across his face. "Of course, they'd be spent. Even in a tropical environment, where you found this one, they would require an immediate infusion of energy to sustain themselves. They would need to feed very quickly. A lot of protein, fast."

Then his smile returned. "But that, of course—oh, yes, that explains it."

He went over to a wall where MRI screen shots were displayed. "The brain. The changes in the brain. This is why."

Zach and Bell followed him. Everett pointed to a section of brain, outlined in high-contrast colors.

"The frontal lobe," he said. "It's shrunken. It's a quarter of the size it should be. But the forebrain—especially the basal ganglia—has actually swelled. It's as if the frontal lobe shed neurons, while the forebrain gained them. The frontal lobe controls our impulses. It's where we reason and learn. The ganglia, however, are sometimes called the reptile brain. It's the most primitive structure in our heads—the one that evolved before all the others. It controls motivation. It controls appetite."

Zach got it now. "The human part shrinks, and the lizard part gets bigger."

Everett smiled again. "And they have almost no capability to govern their needs. This maximizes selection of new infectious targets for the virus. They will attack and feed on whatever is warm and closest."

"They wake up from the change hungry," Zach said.

Bell nodded. She understood now, too. "And the virus spreads in the bites."

"Yes. Exactly," Everett said. "It is the quickest way to ensure the virus finds a new host."

Zach noticed that Everett's face was animated now. He was enjoying this. No, not just enjoying it. He was in awe. He had the same rapt look of attention that a nun might have in prayer. His voice quavered as he looked back at the reptilian corpse on the slab. "It truly is admirable."

"Admirable?" Zach asked.

"This is an amazing accomplishment. Someone has created a hardier version of the basic humanoid form. It's better equipped to survive on this planet than any previous version of *Homo sapiens*. This is a triumph."

"They eat people? And you think it's a triumph?" Bell asked. She didn't look well. If anything, she looked even sicker.

But Zach couldn't worry about that now. Something else bothered him. "I thought you just finished telling us how these things have no real brains."

"Brains are overrated," Everett said, with a wave of his hand. "Believe me. I've had the crap kicked out of me by muscular idiots all my life. When it comes to survival traits, you want to look to the reptile species. They require less food, less water, even less oxygen than mammals. They don't have our need to maintain body heat, so most of their metabolic energy doesn't go to waste just staying alive. Some reptiles have been found alive inside stones—did you know they can hibernate in mud so long it will actually petrify? And they go on living, just the same, once they are broken out. They're much tougher than we are. They can regenerate lost limbs and heal from all but the most debilitating injuries. If not for the fluke of a meteor hitting this planet, the dinosaurs would still rule the Earth. You could even call these beings a way of correcting nature's mistake."

There was a long silence. Everett looked up. From the looks on their faces, he seemed to realize he might have gone too far.

"I don't mean to imply that I approve of this," he said quickly. "I'm speaking metaphorically, of course."

"Right," Zach said.

Everett turned back to the X-rays and other images on the wall. "There was one more thing I wanted you to know," he said. "This specimen—when it was still human, I mean—had undergone reconstructive surgery. Steel pins were placed in the femur, just above the knee, to repair a fracture . . ."

"Zach," Bell said. She looked pale. "The smell is really getting to me. I can't—"

"As you can see from the X-ray here . . ."

Zach wasn't paying attention. His focus was on Bell. She swallowed, and put out a hand to steady herself. Unfortunately, she gripped the side of the autopsy table. Her fingers dipped into something from the body with an audible squish.

That did it. Bell began gagging.

Zach interrupted the doctor. "Can you make a cure? Or a vaccine? Something to stop it or prevent it?"

Everett blinked, taken aback. "That's not really my area. I gather the data, and then my findings—"

Bell gagged again, loudly.

"Great. Call me when you have a cure," Zach said. He took Bell by the arm and hustled her to the door.

"But you really should see—"

"Send me an e-mail," Zach snapped, and the door clicked shut behind them.

Everett shrugged. He never understood how some people could look at these things and react with disgust. Fear, yes. Everything he took apart in this lab was a threat, and he'd seen too many of them that could end all human life on earth if left unchecked.

But he'd never understand how other people could not see the intricacy, the design and the beauty of the strange wonders under his scalpel.

Everett looked at the body and marveled all over again. Whoever did this was an artist.

THIRTEEN

Facing the 2010 midterm elections, the president seemed distracted and distant. Many observers in the media, and even members of his own staff, said he didn't seem to take his party's imminent losses seriously. "He just sort of went through the motions, but you could tell he had something else on his mind. It was like he was waiting for some other shoe to drop," said one staffer of his meetings with Curtis during this period. "I mean, what could be more important than the elections?"

—Bob Woodward, *The Curtis Doctrine*

WASHINGTON, D.C.

Prador was exhausted. He thought he'd worked long hours before he became chief of staff, but this verged on surreal. The president seemed like he'd been hit with some sort of curse; everything was going to shit on a daily basis. There was that goddamn oil spill all summer, then the tanking poll numbers, an economy that couldn't get out of second gear, and the flying monkeys of the media, all ready to stick a fork in President Samuel Curtis and declare him done.

That's why so much piled up on Prador now. He had to run the White House while the president rallied the troops for the midterm elections. The problem was, Curtis was the world's greatest micromanager:

everything had to go through him. It was like the man didn't trust anyone.

All things considered, Prador supposed that wasn't unreasonable.

Prador was so tired and preoccupied that he didn't even notice the shadow on the wall inside his Georgetown condo. The one that stayed in place even after he'd turned on the lights.

He felt a cold breeze pass over him. It woke him enough to notice Book, standing in the living room.

"You look like hammered crap," Book said.

Prador didn't need this. Not now.

"What are you doing here? If someone saw you—"

"Nobody sees us until it's too late," Book said. "Wanted to check in. Had a little problem in Djibouti."

"Yeah, no shit," Prador said. "Thanks for the warning on the biggest terrorist attack in Africa since the embassy bombings."

Book shrugged. "Couldn't be helped. How's the cover story holding?"

"It would hold a lot better if I knew about these things before they happened."

Book exhaled heavily and punched Prador in the stomach. There was almost no swing behind his fist, but it hit with extraordinary force. Prador went to his knees and puked up coffee and bile.

Book waited calmly while Prador finished sputtering and coughing.

The dry heaves finally stopped. Prador shifted into a sitting position and began to get his color back.

"So," Book said brightly. "How is that cover story holding?"

Prador glared at him, then decided not to waste the energy. He'd chosen this path, or had it chosen for him, all the way back at Yale. Maybe even before. Like his father and grandfather, he'd joined the Order. The perks were obvious—money, success, an outwardly charmed life. But nothing was free. And before he knew it, they owned him absolutely.

Sometimes, at the holidays, he'd see something like an apology in his father's eyes after the old man had one too many drinks. No, not an apology, really. More like resignation. This was how their family had risen. Struggling against it was useless. When the time came, Prador knew he'd offer his own son, too.

Provided he lived that long.

"So far, we've had no reports of anything unusual," he told Book. "As far as Curtis knows, this is just more proof the political gods hate him. He's too wrapped up in the elections to ask for details now. But he will."

"I'm sure you can deal with it," Book said, starting to fidget. He always got bored easily. "Graves also wants you to revoke RED RUM."

"Cade's clearance? But that will—"

"Yes." Book sighed. "We know. Do it."

"How much longer will this go on? If Curtis doesn't hear about some deep weirdness soon, he'll start to wonder where Cade is. It's already been too quiet. He'll get suspicious."

"Relax. A week. Maybe two at most. Then he'll have more nightmares than he can handle."

Book carefully stepped over Prador and his puddle of vomit and walked out of the condo, shutting the door behind him.

The shadow flexed and lengthened, and slid neatly out under the threshold, thinner than a sheet of paper.

Prador stayed on the floor for a long time after that.

BOOK WALKED THROUGH the double doors into the parking lot. Someone facing him would have noticed a striking resemblance to a police sketch released in the first panicked hours after the Oklahoma City bombing of a man known only as "John Doe #2." Of course, the authorities later decided that John Doe #2 didn't exist.

He got into the Humvee and waited for Reynolds.

Book was a remarkable find for the Shadow Company. He'd been through the best psychological tests devised, including some that would never see the light of day in the civilian world. The Company had trigger questions hidden in every entrance exam, ASVAB, police academy application and federal government aptitude test. It was a fine net stretched out across the country, and it caught every variety of sociopathic behavior. The Company reeled in the most promising candidates based on their scores, and then kept testing until they found the right spot for them.

Book had come to their attention when he'd tried to enlist in the military, straight out of high school. He also filled out applications for the CIA, the FBI and several police departments in Florida.

The evaluators, hidden in their anonymous office buildings in Iowa, ran Book's scores through the computer twice. Then they tallied up the results by hand. They'd never seen anything like him before.

He couldn't be called a sociopath, not by the traditional definition of someone lacking the usual ability to feel empathy and understand human emotion. Book felt emotion; he simply didn't care. He knew the difference between right and wrong. He knew which of his actions were most likely to hurt other people.

Without fail, in every hypothetical, he chose to do the wrong thing. And it wasn't even out of some twisted selfishness, or the thought of future gain, which is how most sociopaths were wired. He didn't even get any pleasure out of another person's pain, if the MMPI could be trusted.

Book was plucked from the selection process and brought directly into the Company. The tests continued. He was hooked up to a polygraph, an EEG and an MRI while he answered questions. He was asked to imagine detailed scenarios.

The results were always the same.

He wasn't a sadist. He just had an unerring instinct for malice. It was almost a talent, like a virtuoso who plays the violin beautifully the first time it's placed in his hands. Book could find a person's weakness within moments of meeting him, and would gouge away at it. He was blunt and he was crude, but the evaluators watched as he reduced several interviewers—including one longtime CIA interrogator—to tears.

"Oh, we have to put this kid to work," one evaluator said. And Book's career began.

After infiltrating the militia movement and white supremacist groups in the early '90s, Book was sent to Seattle, where he joined up with anarchist protesters and antiglobalization groups. Some of the other members of the groups disappeared not long after the WTO riots. They were always surprised to find Book on the other side of the table from them in the interrogation rooms. He knew them inside and out. He broke them into pieces; some of them went back out into the world, filled with nothing but the desire to fulfill the agenda of the Company.

Book didn't seem to take a lot of pleasure in this. He was a hollow man, nothing but surfaces. He existed only in his impact on the world around him.

He moved back to Florida in time for the 2000 elections. Then he was abruptly transferred to snip some loose ends related to 9/11. After that, Book was sent to Archer/Andrews to work with Graves.

He thought again about what Candle had said about Bell. Maybe she was running a game of her own. Anything was possible. That was the problem with being so deep inside like this. You never knew who was playing whom; if the person you thought was working with you was actually watching you for your boss, or for the other team, or maybe both.

Graves was the one who'd brought Bell into this. Which didn't mean anything. Maybe it was just cover, a way to throw any observers off the track. Or maybe she really was one of them.

But if she wasn't, then she'd have to be handled. And that sort of thing usually fell to Book, because he was good at it. You don't keep LeBron James on the team without letting him play.

A darkness coalesced and pooled in the passenger seat. In a moment, Reynolds sat there uncomfortably, shifting as if his skin was too tight.

He waited for Book to start the engine. "So, we going back to the office or what?" he grumbled.

But Book was far away, wet fantasies dancing behind his eyes, thinking about what he'd get to do to Bell if she turned out to be on the wrong team after all.

FOURTEEN

We were waiting in the hallway outside the rally when I got The Fear. I thought it was the speed coming up on top of the ether, but my molars weren't grinding the way they usually do. Something was different. I saw one of Nixon's flunkies nearby, a young guy in a cheap suit, giving me the eye. I'll rack any lawyer with a quick shot to the nuts if I think it's necessary, but this one was different. Just a kid, but with that Hitlerian air of certainty so many of the Nixon youth carry. The way he looked at me made me think he was genuinely dangerous. It could have been the drugs, but I swear the bad mojo rose off this guy like smoke. I turned away to wipe the sweat out of my eyes, and when I looked back, he was gone. Maybe he'd never been there at all.

Jesus. I needed whiskey. I went in search of the bar.

—Hunter S. Thompson, *Fear and Loathing: On the Campaign Trail '72*
  (redacted in later editions)

Bell looked embarrassed, but she was getting her color back.

"Sorry," she said, smiling weakly. "I'm really not such a girl most of the time. Would you believe I was top of my class at the Farm?"

They were at a bar located near the closest Metro station. Zach offered to get her a coffee when they left the morgue. She said she needed something a little stronger.

They both sat, Bell with a half-empty glass of Scotch, Zach with a beer.

"It's normal to be freaked out by this stuff. Believe me," he said. "The day it stops being weird, then you start to worry."

"You seem to handle it pretty well."

"Hey, the first time I met Cade I peed my pants," Zach said, then immediately wished he hadn't.

"You know, I was a little surprised to see you with Cade," she said.

"Me?" Zach was mildly offended, even if he wasn't sure why. "Why would you be surprised?"

"You're not as secret as you think. There are all kinds of rumors. Cade is sort of a scary story in the intel world. Like an urban legend. Or a joke. You know, 'Better watch out or the vampire will get you.' Then you showed up with him. I knew Cade had a human . . ."

Please don't say sidekick, Zach thought.

". . . handler. But I expected some kind of thick-skulled FBI burnout, some guy who's more afraid of retirement than death."

"That was the old guy," Zach said.

"What?"

"Nothing. So I didn't look like what you expected."

"Yeah. I thought someone like you would have something to live for."

He wasn't sure what to say to that. "What about you? You said you were CIA before you were an Arch—before you joined Archer/Andrews?"

She grimaced at him. "I've heard the nickname. Don't worry. I don't mind. Don't repeat that to Hewitt or Reynolds, though."

"Really? They seemed as cuddly as a room full of kittens."

She rolled her eyes. "You know what we do for a living, right? Love and kindness aren't high on the job requirements."

"Then why did you get into this?" He was genuinely curious.

"Oh, I probably started with the usual ideals," she said. "Patriotism. Nine-eleven. Saving the world from the forces of evil. That's why I joined the CIA. My talents pointed in that direction, so I thought it was the best way to serve."

"But you quit and joined Archer/Andrews."

"It's not that complicated, really. Every morning they tell you you're saving the world. But there are only so many nights you can come home to a cheap apartment on the corner of Crackwhore and Homicide, deciding which bills to pay this month, before you say, screw it. Sometimes saving the world isn't enough."

She saw the look on his face. "You disapprove, I take it."

"Not my place," he said carefully. "I was shanghaied into this. If I had the chance, I'd probably bolt, too."

"Would you really?"

"No," he admitted. "If saving the world's not enough, then nothing else is, either."

"Don't judge me," she warned. "I'm just doing what I can to survive. A/A is a necessary evil. You worked in politics. You of all people should know there are shades of gray."

"Not for me," Zach said. "Not anymore. Trust me. Those are human ideas. But good and evil—they're not just human. They don't belong solely to us. They're real. They're solid. And sometimes, they've got teeth."

"And you're going to stand on the ramparts and hold the line," she said, smiling at him in a strange way. "I never would have pegged you for a crusader, Zach."

Zach was suddenly uncomfortable. He'd shared national secrets with Bell, but this felt like actually revealing something. "Yeah, well. You take enough blows to the head, anything can happen."

She gave him a what-the-hell smile. Her glass was empty. There was no trace of nausea or fear now. She was nothing but the competent operative again.

"I can't afford to get too philosophical," she said. "I'm one of the only women in a company full of spooks and soldiers. Worse, I'm in a command position. Ninety percent of the guys think I've fucked my way into my job, and the other ten percent think I'm a dyke. Who's fucked her way into her job. I cannot let my guard down for a second. Because I can't have any of these men seeing me as a target. I have to remain totally untouchable. Or I become a victim, waiting to happen."

Zach felt like he'd skipped a page somehow. She looked right at him.

"So I don't get much of a chance to date, if you understand what I'm saying."

Zach didn't. But he said, "I think so."

She stood up. Zach looked puzzled. She rolled her eyes at him again.

"Let's go."

Zach finally caught on.

"This might not be a good idea," he said.

She laughed. "No shit. It's a terrible idea. I know there's a time and place, but. You're a pretty decent guy. So. Well. Tomorrow we may die and all that."

She waited.

"Probably lots of reasons why we shouldn't do this."

"Dozens," she said.

For some reason, Zach couldn't think of a single one.

He got up and followed her out the door.

IT HAD BEEN A WHILE. Inside his apartment, it took all his control to keep from mauling Bell as he tore off her shirt. His fingers fumbled as he tried to work the buttons on her pants.

She shoved him off, smiling. Barefoot, she pulled down her pants and underwear, shimmying her hips a little.

Zach stared at her.

There was always something unreal, something impossibly compelling, about seeing a woman naked. Zach figured it must be coded into the straight male's DNA. It didn't matter who the man was, if a woman bent over, revealing a flash of cleavage, the cup of a bra—he'd look. Greedily searching with his eyes, reduced to a kid in junior high again. Just needing to see that little bit of flesh, that uncharted, unknown expanse of skin.

Bell's eyes laughed at him. But she didn't move. She watched him watching her.

Her skin was gorgeous. Flawless. Like something out of the description of a heroine in a Victorian novel. Her breasts moved slightly as her breath came faster. His eyes traveled up and down her body.

She stood there, very still, giving him a better look. He knew he shouldn't stare; it was juvenile, it was stupid and unimpressive. And yet he kept looking.

Bell stepped over to him and peeled off his shirt, one button at a time. She traced the line of his jaw, his neck, with one finger, drawing it down his chest, her eyes locked to his the entire time.

Zach was so hard it hurt. He couldn't take it anymore. He grabbed Bell and fell with her onto the bed.

His pants were down, and he was stumbling over them, trying to get them off over his shoes.

She began laughing openly at him then, pure and happy. He didn't care.

He slid into her like they'd been designed for each other. He was barely hanging on. He rose up above her—*Shit. Condom? Fuck it.*—and looked again into her eyes. They were wild, the grin on her face something animal now.

He found control he didn't think existed inside himself. She pumped her hips, pulling him deeper, locking her ankles at the small of his back.

Before he knew it, they were both slick with sweat. His mouth found hers. He felt her teeth against his own, his tongue and hers, tangled and darting back and forth.

He could not possibly hold back any longer. His body was pushing on its own now, his mind only on her skin, on the feel of her, on her taste.

Their bodies clapped together like applause, faster and faster.

He came first. It felt like his spine snapped clean, his mind emptied and he felt some great tide lifting him.

She wasn't done. She didn't unlock her legs, and she slammed into him, as if ordering him to stay hard. He still felt stiff as a board. He went along for the ride.

She tipped her head back, sucked in a deep breath, then opened her mouth, showing those lovely white teeth again, and laughed as she came.

Or maybe she was laughing the whole time.

FIFTEEN

Summer 1981—Boston, Massachusetts, and elsewhere—A wave of sightings of clowns who terrorize children and attempt to kidnap them reported in several cities and states. Sightings continue to the present day.

—BRIEFING BOOK: CODE NAME: NIGHTMARE PET

ABOVE THE GULF OF ADEN, OFF THE COAST OF DJIBOUTI

Corpsman Trevor Noonan was in way over his head, and he knew it. The Marine on the stretcher was dying. They were still a good hundred miles from the aircraft carrier with doctors who could save him. And Noonan didn't have the first damned clue what was wrong with him.

It was supposed to be a simple gunshot wound. That's why they didn't waste a doctor on the trip. He could keep the Marine stable.

He wasn't really sure why they'd decided to send an armed guard with him, but he gathered it had something to do with the terrorist attack the night before. He was lucky. He'd been off-base on a twenty-four-hour pass. He came back to the blood and the bodies, and nobody would talk to him. Partly out of guilt, partly out of shame, he volunteered to baby-sit the Marine when the Archer/Andrews guy offered a ride.

The guard was getting even more worried than Noonan. The Marine thrashed in his stretcher, and his skin looked shiny and tight.

"Can't you do something?" he demanded.

Noonan shook his head. He was scraping the limit of his knowledge.

He went to the cockpit, to ask the pilot to hurry again. Maybe it was just because he was an Archie—he was probably earning more in a month than Noonan saw all year—but the pilot didn't seem particularly sympathetic. Noonan picked up the passenger headphones so he could talk.

Then he saw the answer to his prayers out the starboard windscreen, practically glowing like a beacon in the morning light.

A hospital ship. There was no missing the bright white hull and the massive red crosses painted on its top. Noonan remembered something from the base bulletin about a humanitarian mission passing through the gulf.

In his joy, he whapped the pilot on the side of the helmet. "There! Dude, right there! Set us down! They can help!"

The pilot looked at him, eyes cold. "Not my orders. Colonel Graves said the carrier."

"Are you nuts?" Noonan shouted. "We won't make it to the carrier. He's circling the drain right now! You've got to—"

The pilot turned in his seat and shoved Noonan back. Noonan stumbled and landed on his ass.

"I told you: not my orders," he said. "Now sit down and shut the hell up."

Noonan noticed the pilot had the holster of his sidearm unsnapped and ready. Bewildered, he took off his headphones and headed into the back.

Noonan, as a corpsman who went into the field with a red cross on his back, could not carry a weapon on active duty. One of the burdens of being the good guys, playing by the rules.

As soon as he explained what the pilot had said, the guard was ready to back him up.

He stepped into the cockpit again, put on the headphones once more. He heard the pilot growl in frustration.

"Look," Noonan said. "I'm not threatening you. I can't. It's the first thing they teach us. 'Do no harm.' I swore an oath to preserve all life."

The pilot turned, opened his mouth to say something, but didn't speak.

Behind Noonan, the guard had his pistol aimed right between the pilot's eyes.

"But here's the thing," Noonan said, "*he* didn't."

The pilot closed his mouth.

"What do you say, Archie?" Noonan asked with a grin. "Want to land this bird?"

IT WAS SUPPOSED to be her day off. The USNS *Virtue* had assisted with emergency relief operations after a massive quake in India. Dr. Nina Prentice had been working around the clock for two weeks on victims pried from dirt and rubble. Now they were supposed to be headed home to Virginia by way of the Suez.

But her pager sounded and Prentice ran for the casualty reception area. Someone outside gave her the bare-bones details. A chopper carrying a Marine from Lemonnier, hit by a stray bullet. He started to go into convulsions and they were still a long way from their destination. *Virtue* was closer. Just a stroke of luck.

Nobody could tell her what exactly was wrong with the kid. Basic facts: nineteen, in good health and dying from a minor GSW. Great. Nothing like flying blind.

The Marine had already been off-loaded and a nurse and two orderlies were trying to get him prepped. At first glance, just another day at work. But she could already feel it. Things were sliding out of control. This wasn't the amplified rush of an ordinary trauma. The edge in the room felt uncomfortably close to panic.

Unlike most of her colleagues, Prentice wasn't on board because she owed the government for her tuition and fees. In fact, her student loans were accruing interest at a truly impressive rate, while she worked as a civilian trauma specialist with the Navy. She was here because she'd seen the devastation in New Orleans, Haiti and in the Middle East on TV. She'd decided these were the places that needed a doctor the most, and the *Virtue* would get her there.

There wasn't a day that went by that she didn't wonder what the hell she'd been thinking.

But she didn't have many moments for reflection. She got called for the worst cases: victims delivered by helicopter with burns over 60 percent of their skin; people nearly bisected by flying blades of shrapnel; others so mangled by war or disaster they resembled bags of meat holding broken bones.

Prentice's job was to keep them alive and stable until others could do the more delicate work. Everything was critical; everything was an emergency. She had to freeze her emotions, because if she stopped to think about the small child stuck on the length of rebar she was trying to remove, she would never be able to do it.

She assumed she was numb to horror by now. But when she saw the Marine, she discovered she could still be shocked.

"What the fuck—?" she said.

(Prentice had learned that the cliché "swearing like a sailor" wasn't at all true. The sailors on board had better manners than a Southern deb. But after the twentieth time some jackass had called her "Nurse," she began using "fuck" as her all-purpose noun, verb and adjective. Somehow, that convinced people she was a doctor. Or at least someone with authority.)

"I thought this was a gunshot wound."

"That's what they said."

This was no gunshot. The kid looked shredded as he thrashed on the table. If Prentice had to name what was happening to him, she'd say "skin failure." His flesh was splitting and peeling in great strips, and he was swelling like a Ball Park frank on the grill.

Despite all that, it took two orderlies to hold him. They couldn't even get an IV line.

"Haldol—" she snapped.

"Five and two Ativan already," the nurse shot back.

Seriously? Prentice thought. That was enough to knock most people cold. "Hit him again," she said. "Ten and two this time."

The nurse gave her a look but had the syringe ready to go. She spiked it into his arm. The orderlies managed to strap him into four-point restraints, which allowed Prentice and the nurse to finally get the instruments on him.

The nurse slipped the heart monitor on the Marine's finger. It began screeching as soon as she turned it on.

"That can't be right. Seriously, what is *going on* with this equipment?"

"I'm just telling you what it says. Heart rate two-fifty BPM."

"Temperature—what the fuck, what's with the readouts? Temperature one-forty? BP *three-twenty?*"

"Hey, I just work here," the nurse said. She slapped a couple of X-rays onto a nearby display. "He was near comatose when they brought him in. I don't know what happened—"

"Fine, whatever, let's just get it down before he strokes." Prentice ordered her to run sodium nitroprusside and examined the film. Hard to tell, but it looked like the bones were intact, just . . . bent. Like something was inside the Marine, pressing out.

"We need a CAT scan. I've got no idea what's going on in there."

One orderly laughed. "Good luck with that." Despite the restraints, he was still twitching like a third-grader without Ritalin.

Before she could look at the X-rays again, he opened his mouth. It sounded like he was choking.

"O_2's dropping," the nurse said.

"Intubate," Prentice ordered.

The nurse had the kit out of its sterile wrapping in a second. Prentice tried to slide it down the Marine's throat. No good. It stuck. No time for another try, not with his blood pressure that high and his heart running like a jackhammer.

"Got an obstruction. Trach kit."

She put the scalpel to his throat. Then she noticed something. The Marine's eyes were open.

That happened, even when people were under heavy sedation. But she couldn't escape the feeling he was looking at her. Tears were gathered at the corners of his eyes.

She saw the blood vessels in his sclera as they began to burst, popping one after another.

He was still choking, but it sounded to her like he was trying to talk.

She hesitated before she put the scalpel to his flesh.

It could have been her imagination, but she was sure he tried to say something.

She thought he tried to say, "No."

And then he erupted, skin bursting, bones shattering, his body exploding into a fountain of blood and meat.

SIXTEEN

Many authors—John Keel, Loren Coleman, Jim Keith—have noted that the so-called "Men in Black" who claim to work on behalf of some mysterious government agency share many traits in common with folk tales of witches and other satanic emissaries walking the earth. The Salem witch trials mentioned a mysterious man in black, as did many of the witch hunts of Europe. Legends in Ireland and England refer to strangers wearing all black who either threaten the people they meet, or offer them wealth and power. Some tales claim these earlier versions of the Men in Black are representatives of a lost and ancient culture that predates humanity by millennia.

—Cole Daniels, *Black Ops: The Occult-CIA Connection*

Bell walked into her own apartment near three A.M. She'd left Zach sleeping at his place. She'd never used her clandestine training to sneak out of a man's apartment before. But she doubted Zach would have woken even if she'd slammed the door behind her. He was exhausted. Frankly, so was she. The boy clearly had some tensions to work out.

She stretched and yawned.

She didn't notice the shadows lengthening behind her on the walls. She went into the kitchen of her tiny apartment and thought about making coffee, or possibly some eggs. She was starving.

The dark shadows stretched from the wall, moving through the empty air, reaching out toward her.

She turned, gasped and nearly dropped the carton of eggs in her hand.

"You *morons*," Bell spat. "Knock it off, right now."

The Shadowmen folded and shrank. The darkness melted away, and suddenly Hewitt and Reynolds stood in the middle of the room.

"Sorry," Hewitt mumbled, looking at his feet.

"You're just lucky Graves isn't here," Bell said. "He'd toss you in the Red Room for a week."

They both cringed. "Sorry," Hewitt said again.

Bell sighed as they kept staring at their feet, sullen and blinking in the light.

It was getting worse, she thought. It took more and more effort to drag them into the light, and there was less and less of them when they got here.

They were even starting to look alike, out in the real world. Skin pitted with zits, bodies they no longer bothered to wash. Not too surprising: they rarely ate, and when they did, they preferred candy bars and Cokes from the vending machines.

She would have to keep an eye on them. They still had time, but pretty soon . . .

"Never mind," she said. "Just tell me how Book and Candle managed to do tonight."

THIS IS A MATTER of public record: in 1981, the U.S. Army, at the direction of General Albert Stubblebine, then the head of Army Intelligence, tried to tap psychic abilities for use in warfare.

Code-named "Project Stargate," it was considered a laughable failure. No real evidence of ESP was ever found in any of the recruits. Stubblebine retired. The psychics were all let go, their budget allowed to lapse.

For some reason, the CIA took over Project Stargate in 1995. That's where the public record ends.

No one heard much about Project Stargate again, which was just the way the Shadow Company wanted it. Since the end of World War II, the Company had hired a long list of occultists, psychics, hoaxers, magicians and even a few lunatics. The Company knew Stubblebine was on to something. And it wasn't about to let anyone else reap the benefits.

But it wasn't until the Company assumed control of Stargate that it finally saw a result.

The details were classified above Bell's pay grade, but she'd heard rumors.

The experiment, carried out in a condemned building at the edge of Fort Meade, Maryland, was a standard parapsychological test. Two psychics sat on either side of a soundproofed divider. One would try to send pictures of what he saw in a book. The other would try to draw those same pictures by extracting them from the other man's mind.

They were observed by a third man, who tallied the results.

The rumors varied a little here. Some of them said the observer was bored. Others said he was desperate. They said he tried adding some occult symbols to the experiment, and they randomly fell into an order that turned out to be a summoning spell from an old book by Aleister Crowley. The other rumors said the observer added LSD and other chemicals to the mix, like the Company did for its MK-ULTRA mind-control experiments in the '50s.

Whatever actually happened, the rumors were all consistent on how the experiment ended. When other Company operatives finally broke down the door, they found three bodies.

Both psychics were turned inside out. The observer had used his sidearm on both men before he put it in his own mouth and pulled the trigger.

There was something else, too. According to Bell's most reliable source, it was as if something tried to use the psychics' bodies as handholds into our world, on a climb from someplace else, someplace deep. It *fed* on them, using them as raw material to build itself a body to live in our world.

But it only got as far as the skin before the observer killed them and slammed the door shut.

The Shadow Company immediately doubled the budget, trying to reproduce whatever happened in that little room. As far as Bell knew, they had never succeeded.

But the skin remained. After a while, the Shadowmen started working with every Company unit.

When Bell first joined, the Shadowmen were only rumors. Occasionally, while on assignment, other members of the Company smirked and talked about the "invisibility cloak." They were shut up by hard glances from more senior officers before Bell could ask for details.

She accepted that. Information was tightly controlled in the Company. All she knew for sure was what she saw on her missions. Secure buildings, armed guards, gated mansions—none of that was a problem. Shadow Company operatives could follow anyone, anywhere. They could get inside any location. She never knew how, in those early days. All she got were the reports, the intel. She only saw the results.

But when Graves moved her up to a field team, he gave her Hewitt and Reynolds as Shadowmen. But they didn't start out that way.

They were warm bodies, culled from the hundreds of thousands of people drawing a government paycheck for wearing a badge. They could have been bought in bulk from a federal warehouse. Both were former law enforcement who saw their chance to move up the ladder after 9/11. They were on the right side of the IQ curve. "Bright but unimaginative," their psych profiles said. Both divorced, wives and families forgotten back in whatever jurisdictions they came from.

Reynolds used to wear a mustache. That was how Bell told them apart back then.

Graves made her watch when they put on the skins. They were in a white room—completely white, even the table and chairs—in a subbasement of a facility paid for out of a classified section of the federal budget.

Bell was behind mirrored glass, along with Graves, looking into the room.

Reynolds and Hewitt entered, confident, swaggering. They didn't seem to feel any of the unease that crept up Bell's spine.

On the table were what looked like stereotypical spy costumes, right out of a grocery store aisle at Halloween: slouch-brimmed hats and trench coats, in pure black. Next to those, black sunglasses.

They seemed to eat the light as it hit the table.

At first, Reynolds and Hewitt looked at the outfits, then back at each other, then at the mirror.

Bright, but not imaginative, Bell remembered.

Graves sighed and pressed a button on the intercom.

"Pick up the coats," he ordered. "Put them on."

They smirked, made faces at each other. But they did as instructed. Coats, hats, then glasses.

Reynolds said something. Hewitt laughed. Without the intercom, Bell couldn't hear the joke.

Then the clothing started moving, rippling over them like black water.

"Hey," Reynolds said, loud enough to hear. *"Hey."*

Graves hit the intercom button again. "Just relax," he said. "Breathe deep."

Hewitt was way ahead on that. He was hyperventilating as the dark substance crawled its way up his face.

He turned away, just as the first tendrils reached into his mouth and nose.

They both started screaming. They didn't sound like men. Any age, any gender, had been stripped right out of their throats by terror. It sounded like the shrieks of children gripped by fear of the dark, completely uninhibited by maturity or restraint, completely void of the knowledge that daylight will ever come or that Mommy will return to kiss it all better.

They curled into fetal balls on the floor, the dark skins constricting around them, seeming to get smaller, tighter.

Bell looked at Graves. He was completely unperturbed.

When she looked back inside the room, she couldn't find them.

It shouldn't have been that tough. They were black outlines, dead-center in an all-white room.

But even with the fluorescent lighting, she couldn't seem to focus on them. They somehow kept shifting, just out of her range of vision. Sliding to the corner of her eye.

She caught a glimpse of men in hats and coats, but that was only their shadows.

Somehow she knew they were in there, moving around. But she couldn't really see them anymore.

She swallowed, and made her voice sound as normal as she could. "Impressive," she said.

"Isn't it?" Graves replied. "Don't worry," he added. "You get used to it after a while. Pretty soon, it seems as normal as your morning coffee."

Bell nodded, but she didn't believe him. Because it wasn't her sudden inability to see Hewitt and Reynolds that disturbed her most.

It wasn't the screaming, because that had stopped.

She heard a new sound, from nowhere and everywhere inside the room at the same time.

They were laughing.

They *liked* it.

BELL HADN'T BEEN lying to Zach. Not a lot, anyway. Much of what she'd told him was true. She just skipped some parts, especially

CHRISTOPHER FARNSWORTH

about her decision to join Archer/Andrews, and eventually the Shadow Company.

Bell might have been the first Shadow Company recruit in years to actively seek out the organization, if anyone kept track of that sort of thing. There was no denying she was a genius at research. It enabled her to put together all the disparate, contradictory evidence that led her to the real player behind the scenes.

She had joined the CIA for all the right reasons. Altruism, patriotism, War on Terror, everything she'd said. But then she ran into the facts on the ground, and the facts were, there was no war. A war requires a strategy, and leadership, and an identifiable enemy. Every assignment Bell took, every place she visited, was just chaos. There were thousands of hours of recordings from intercepted al-Qaeda cell phones, and no one who spoke Arabic. Their informants would point a finger at anyone for the right amount of money, so they ended up with genuine terrorists next to a guy who'd only pissed off his brother-in-law. She couldn't say for sure her work saved lives, or took them.

The only certainty was the money.

Government funds washed over agencies like floodwaters swamping small towns. Over nine billion dollars was missing from the reconstruction of Iraq alone. Bell knew that stacks of bills were simply absorbed by contractors like Archer/Andrews. She knew a guy who'd quit the CIA, spent a mere six months in the Green Zone, and was now retired and building a twelve-room house on a lake.

In Switzerland.

The opportunity was there. She'd have been an idiot not to take it.

It wasn't that she'd ever been poor. Her parents had always given her everything she needed.

But moving around in the secret world, she discovered she'd been incapable of imagining all the things it was *possible* to want. It wasn't just the flights in private jets, with Black AmEx shopping privileges at designer shops in Europe as part of her cover. It wasn't the government salary and the cheap apartment in her real life.

Rather, it was the power and ease that slid around her when she was in the field. It was addictive, living that life, because it was so much *more*, in every single way.

When she would go home to her parents' little two-bedroom ranch for the holidays, listening to them talk about the great bargains at Wal-Mart this year, all the while pretending to be a dull bureaucrat whose job was nowhere near as interesting as Bobby selling cars at the dealership— well, it embarrassed her, somehow. Not for herself, but for them. How small they were. How little they actually knew. And the idea of having to return to that ordinary, yard-sale version of life wasn't so much repugnant as it was simply unnecessary.

She had the skills to move on. Archer/Andrews offered her a ticket to the greater world. If she was smart enough, she'd earn a passport and live there forever, not as a citizen, bound not by mere loyalty, but as something a little more tangible—an asset, something far too valuable to ever trade or sell.

First, of course, she had to get the job.

She collected a paper trail that would have been invisible to most people. She secured the data in hard drives and mailed them to dead-drop sites all over the world. If she vanished, the information would go into button-down mode, and automatically be sent along to newspapers and several congressional committees.

Bell had been naïve enough to think that was enough to protect her. As if the Company didn't have ways of shutting down those kinds of inquiries.

But she didn't know that, so she felt secure enough to make a phone call to a man in an office in the Pentagon who didn't exist.

She spoke the code words no one else was supposed to know: "MOR-DRED, ALADDIN, CONNECTICUT-HULU."

"I'm listening," replied the man on the other end.

"I want in," she said.

They were impressed. They liked her audacity. They brought her on board and gave her a new name. She became Bell.

She hadn't looked back for a moment, until she met Zach. It wasn't that she was in love with him—God, no—but he reminded her of things she'd rather forget. Her college-girl idealism, back when she started—and the more disquieting fact that if they were going to make this op work, she was going to have to kill him.

She thought about that after Hewitt and Reynolds left—using the door, thankfully.

She wasn't sure she could do it. Maybe, if she was smart enough, she could find another way.

Maybe it was time to find another job.

SEVENTEEN

KINGSTON FALLS, INDIANA—Governor Robert Orr declared this small town a statewide disaster area today, sending National Guard troops to restore order and basic services. At least a dozen people are dead, and hundreds more injured, in what some are calling the "Christmas Invasion." Although what exactly invaded the town is still not clear, as everything from aliens to mass hallucinations have been blamed for the chaos. . . .

—Indianapolis *Post*, December 26, 1984

Everett sat alone in the mortuary, typing his report into an e-mail. Aside from the clatter of his fingers on the keys, it was quiet.

He liked the quiet. It was the main reason he liked his work.

Everett wasn't good with people. He knew that. He'd begin talking about something that fascinated him, and then look up at the horror on the faces of the other people in the room. He knew he'd said too much to Barrows and the woman, but he got carried away. He couldn't help it. The reptilian—what Barrows insisted on inaccurately calling a "Snakehead"—was remarkable. He was just being honest.

He'd always been enthralled with the insides of bodies, the blood, the guts, the squirm-inducing bits and chunks. It was one reason he went into medicine. He thought that his taste for the grotesque would be tolerated, even shared, by other people in his field.

That wasn't how it really worked. Other doctors found him unsettling and strange. During his training, he once had to be reprimanded when his description of a tumor reduced a patient to a sobbing wreck; apparently the man didn't share Everett's admiration for the thing that was going to kill him. "Problems with bedside manner and working with others," was how one of his attending physicians put it in Everett's evaluation.

He was gently steered toward a career in pathology. As brilliant as he was, Everett was only at home when surrounded by dead bodies.

Even there, however, Everett didn't fit in. Determining cause of death was ridiculously easy for someone with his intellect and inclinations. He might have left medicine altogether if the government hadn't found him. He was put through a security check and then assigned to his own lab, where he got to carve up things that rightfully belonged only in nightmares.

He'd completed his autopsy hours ago and placed the reptilian corpse in one of the cold-storage drawers lining the far wall. As soon as his report was completed, an anonymous group of janitorial workers—all with security clearances even higher than his own—would come to the lab and take the body away. He never saw any of his specimens after he was finished examining them, and didn't really care by that point. Once he'd unlocked their secrets, he was done with them.

He had to admit, he'd been stalling on the report. He didn't like the way Barrows had spoken to him. Hustling the woman out of the room, like Everett had upset her. Even in this job, he was considered the freak.

I'm not the one who works with a vampire on a daily basis, Everett thought. He'd met Cade several times, and despite his comfort level with the macabre, he was always left shuddering by the experience.

Although he wouldn't mind having Cade on the slab sometime. It had been years since anyone working in the government had Cade under the knife. There were all kinds of new discoveries waiting to be made . . .

A loud bang made Everett jump in his chair. He nearly knocked his wireless keyboard to the ground.

He looked around. No one was in the morgue with him. He would have heard. The place echoed. Every footstep was like a bass drum beat on the tiled walls and concrete floor.

Another loud bang. The unmistakable sound of flesh against metal.

He looked around. Nobody there. The autopsy tables were empty. Everett looked at the wall with the drawers, lined up in a perfect checkerboard.

He reached for his phone, ready to call security. The banging noise stopped him cold.

There was no mistaking it. The sound was coming from one of the drawers.

The drawers were airtight, kept at a constant thirty-six degrees to retard decomposition. Each one locked from the outside. Because why would a corpse need a sudden exit?

He wanted to laugh. This was the kind of juvenile prank he would have expected back in med school. As if he'd fall for something so stupid.

Everett didn't fear the dead. He'd spent countless late nights in the morgue. He'd seen everything that could be done to a human body.

Other people didn't have his experience, so they were still afraid. Fear of dying wasn't irrational, but fear of the dead was idiotic. It wasn't like you could catch death from a corpse (excluding some very nasty pathogens and viruses, of course). But people still didn't realize: it was the living you had to watch. The dead were reliable. They were quiet.

The loud banging started to beat steadily now. He could even see the metal door shake on its hinges.

Sneaking into a morgue, getting into one of the drawers might seem like a really scary idea in theory. But in practice, it wasn't that bright.

Because now the idiot inside the chamber realized he was about to run out of air.

Well, Everett didn't want another corpse on his hands. He decided to open the drawer. Although it would serve the joker right.

The banging stopped.

Uh-oh.

Everett hustled over to the wall. He hadn't anticipated this. Without the noise, he wasn't sure which drawer was occupied. He didn't know where to look.

He assumed the joker had passed out. He had to hurry. He started throwing open drawers. First, the one he thought had rattled.

Nobody there. He slammed it shut and started on the ones nearby.

Nothing.

After two minutes, he was sweating. He knew he was opening drawers he'd already checked, but he hadn't found anyone, and he was starting to panic. He began leaving the drawers open. Then he started ducking down and peering inside each one.

Still nothing.

He realized only one drawer was left. The one holding the body of the reptilian.

He walked over to it, hand out for the lever.

He stopped. He'd just told Barrows: reptiles and amphibians could hibernate, remain in a near-death coma for months, even years.

He had not done a full autopsy on the corpse. He had simply examined the hole that he assumed was the cause of death.

No, he had to be kidding himself. There was no way. Then he thought of the things he'd seen in this room, on these tables. He decided it would be better to call security first. He didn't care if they laughed at him.

He turned away from the metal door just as it burst outward, torn off its hinges.

The door tagged him on the shoulder, knocking him to the floor. His mind was flooded with pain, and he was surprised to learn you really did see stars when you were hit hard enough.

Another loud bang echoed in his ears. The rack shot out of the drawer. The creature sprang to its feet and hissed. It didn't sound happy.

Everett wanted to run, but he couldn't move.

As the reptilian leaned over him, claws and fangs out, he could not escape an overwhelming sense of betrayal. The dead were not supposed to do this. The dead were supposed to be quiet. They were supposed to be safe.

EIGHTEEN

1931—Antarctica—The Pabodie Expedition, sponsored in part by the Nathaniel Derby Pickman Foundation, is wiped out, except for two survivors, after discovering unusual fossils and perfectly preserved corpses of previously unknown animals from millions of years in the past.

—BRIEFING BOOK: CODE NAME: NIGHTMARE PET

CAMP LEMONNIER, DJIBOUTI

Cade woke one second after the sun dipped below the horizon. He rose to the surface, soil streaming off him, walking straight out of the ground.

He took out his phone, shook off the dirt and dialed Zach.

"I need answers," he said.

"Someone got up on the wrong side of the grave this morning," Zach said. An old joke between them now.

"What do you have?"

"Not much." Zach explained what he'd heard from Everett. No way to trace the virus to its maker, no cure yet. Related to Innsmouth; but not exactly the same as the outbreak there. The virus looked like it contained Marsh family DNA, but modified.

"Speaking of the Marshes, is there any chance we could talk to them?"

"I've been looking for the last of them for eighty-two years," Cade said. "If you think you will have better luck in the next twenty-four hours . . ."

"Yeah, yeah, I get it," Zach said. "The reason I asked, Bell had an idea about the Marsh connection—"

"How does she know about it?"

Zach paused, looking for a way to sugarcoat the answer that Cade already knew.

"What did you tell her?"

"Hey. We're working together. Prador said so. She's smart. She's dedicated. And she might be able to give us more inside information on A/A if we show her some trust."

Cade listened carefully as Zach spoke. He sounded more relaxed. His throat was less constricted by stress, and his breathing was more even. Or, to put it another way, he seemed almost happy.

Cade knew this would have to be handled delicately. "You're being an idiot," he said.

"Excuse me?"

"You know exactly what I'm talking about."

Zach sputtered for a moment. Then: "You can tell just from talking on the *phone*?"

"Did you really think I wouldn't know?"

"Wow. You sound exactly like a girl I dated in eighth grade."

"This isn't a joke, Zach." Cade's voice was tight. "You're risking yourself, and the mission."

"Prador vouched for her."

"Which means nothing," Cade said. "She has her own agenda. We don't know what it is. She might even be Shadow Company herself."

"So what if she is?"

Cade was actually stunned by that. No one could be that shortsighted, that stupid, that *selfish*.

"She's not," Zach said quickly. "But I'm a little offended. I've been threatened, beaten, tortured and almost eaten since I started working with you. And you think I couldn't handle myself if a girl turned out to be a snitch for the bad guys?"

"You're only human, Zach."

"So is she. That's my point. I know people. I can read them. And you should trust me enough to let me make my own decisions and take the consequences if I'm wrong."

Cade forced himself to relax his grip on the phone before he cracked it open. "The consequences aren't yours alone. The Other Side wants the end of all things. The things we fight are not supposed to exist. The human world cannot accommodate them. If there are people who have chosen to side with them, they have forfeited their human rights. You know what that means: we can never take anyone we encounter to trial. If she's involved, she has to die."

Zach didn't reply. Cade listened to the static for a moment.

"Zach. You know how this works."

"Maybe you need to explain it again," Zach said. "What gives you the right to decide who lives and who dies?"

Cade's mouth twitched. "You've been working with me a year, and you're still unclear on my job description?"

"I know what you do," Zach said. "You want to kill things that go bump in the night? Fine. You kill people who summon them or help them? Hey, no problem. As far as I'm concerned, that's written on the warning label when you make a deal with the forces of evil. But when you start talking about killing Bell, someone who's help—"

Cade cut him off. "Just because she's helping us doesn't mean she's on our side," he said.

"How do you know?"

"Because *no one* is on our side. If you can't understand that, hard cheese."

"Hard *cheese*? No. Don't explain." Zach let out a long, angry breath. When he spoke again, it was the tone of someone giving his final answer. "I decided to bring her inside the loop. I'm not your Tonto, Kemo Sabe. Occasionally, I make my own calls. Deal with it."

Zach hung up on him.

Cade switched off his phone and scowled. At least the whores would have been safer.

IN THE CO'S OFFICE, he found Parrish, Graves and a few others huddled around a ship-to-shore radio. Parrish and Graves stood close together. The body language was unmistakable. The two men had been bonding. Parrish gave him a hostile look.

"What?" Cade asked.

Graves shrugged. "It's probably nothing."

"What happened?"

"The Marine never made it to the carrier," Parrish said. "We called in, and heard the chopper made a detour. It dropped the kid off at the USNS *Virtue*."

"Hospital ship," Graves explained. "I would have expected them back by now. We need the chopper."

"Where are they?"

"That's the problem," Parrish said. "We can't raise the *Virtue*. Nobody's answering."

"They might be busy," Graves said. "It's a hospital ship, remember?"

Cade ignored him. "When was the last time the *Virtue* made contact?"

The men exchanged glances. Cade knew the sight he must present; covered in dirt and blood. He used it to full advantage.

"When?" he asked again.

The naval officer gulped. "It's been almost six hours."

Cade turned to Parrish. "Get me out there."

Parrish looked like he was tired of taking orders. "It's my man out there. I'm sending my own team."

"No. You're not."

Parrish's face turned red, and he began to build up steam for a bellowing lecture.

Cade didn't let him: "You send more men out there and they will die. They have no chance. And they will only spread the same disease that nearly took your camp last night. Listen to me: you do not know what you're dealing with. Don't be stupid. Don't sacrifice any more men. This is inhuman."

Parrish huffed through his nose, apparently trying to calm down. He looked to Graves for guidance.

"He would know," Graves said.

Parrish nodded. "You better bring my boy back alive," he said to Cade. "Don't make me regret trusting you."

Cade wanted to tell him this was not a rescue mission. But he'd wasted enough time arguing already. He needed transport to the ship, and Parrish could provide it.

"I'll do my best," he said.

In truth, Cade wondered if there was anyone left on the ship to save.

THE MARINE'S BLOOD and gore had soaked everyone in the casualty ward. Prentice got the worst of it. She began to change almost immediately. Her colleagues, admirably, tried to save her. They put her on a gurney and treated what looked like a massive, full-body infection.

She tore out the throat of the nearest orderly with her teeth, and used her claws to eviscerate a nurse and two corpsmen.

Still driven by an immense, mindless hunger, she ran through the nearest doorway and into the recovery ward. The patients on their beds never had a chance.

By the time she'd finished, she was fully changed. The few victims she'd left alive began to shed skin and hair, teeth dropping like seeds on the floor, to be replaced by scales and fangs.

By the time anyone thought to organize a defense, it was too late. As a hospital ship, *Virtue* was forbidden from carrying any weapons whatsoever. Some blockaded themselves into cabins. Others fought with fire axes, scalpels, bone saws, whatever they could find. They blocked sections of the ship, barricaded themselves into a smaller and smaller area. Inevitably, someone on the barricade side would turn out to be infected, and they would turn.

By sunset, the ship was boiling with the creatures. Hundreds of them. The humans on board could be counted in double digits.

NINETEEN

THE CHAIRMAN: Mr. Colby, I'd like to turn your attention to a budget item under the document, "BLACK CHAMBER, Goals and Accomplishments."

MR. COLBY: Mr. Chairman, as I stated, I cannot verify the authenticity of that document.

THE CHAIRMAN: It was my understanding that the Black Chamber was an intelligence group abandoned during the Hoover administration.

MR. COLBY: That was my understanding as well.

THE CHAIRMAN: Then how do you explain the continued payments under this budget in the amount of several hundred thousand dollars?

MR. COLBY: I'm at a loss, Mr. Chairman.

THE CHAIRMAN: Sir, you're the director of the Central Intelligence Agency. If you don't know, who does?

COUNSEL: Mr. Chairman, if I may, I believe this can be explained, but we should move to closed session.

THE CHAIRMAN: I have to warn you, counselor, I'm running out of patience. The goal of these hearings is to shed more light on these subjects, not push them back into the dark.

COUNSEL: **Yes, sir. And we are doing everything we can to cooperate.**

THE CHAIRMAN: **Very well. Clear the room, please.**

—Transcript, Senate Select Committee to Study Governmental
Operations with Respect to Intelligence Activities, also known
as the Church Committee, 1975

CHANTILLY, VIRGINIA

This is what I get for showing up early in the morning, Candle thought.

No one else was there. Not Bell, not Book, not even Barrows. He was alone in the office.

He was surfing for Internet porn, bored out of his skull, when Hewitt reappeared.

He nearly jumped out of his skin. He'd never get used to that.

"Where's Book?" Hewitt asked.

"Out," Candle said. "What's up?"

Hewitt looked unhappy. "I need Book. I found the place where Barrows took Bell."

"Why don't you handle it?"

"Not supposed to engage. Graves's orders."

Candle knew better than to argue. The Shadowmen were for surveillance, not combat. He'd asked why once. "You don't want them getting a taste for blood" was all Graves had said.

Candle stood up. "Well, he's not here. Let's go."

Hewitt looked at him. He didn't say anything.

Candle puffed up his chest. "Dude. I said let's go."

Hewitt wavered. "It could be messy."

Candle opened his desk drawer and took out a government-issue SIG Sauer. He racked the slide and leered.

"I hope so. I'm ready to do some damage."

Hewitt just looked at him again.

"What?" Candle said. "What? You think I'm some kind of pussy? I've done things, man."

Hewitt still didn't speak. He just turned around and headed for the door.

"Well, I have," Candle said, jamming the gun into his belt at the small of his back, then hurrying to catch up.

CANDLE NEVER REALLY FELT like a secret agent, despite his fervent hopes when Graves recruited him. When they first met, he'd tried to introduce himself. The older man cut him off. "First rule," he said. "Never give your real name. True names have power. You can call me Graves. And from now on, you're Candle. Got it?"

Candle loved it. A code name. He thought he was going to get a gun and a license to kill. Instead, he got a desk and a computer.

Before he joined the Company, Candle received a regular stipend from the CIA as part of its psy-ops division.

In plainer language, he lied. He wrote op-eds for friendly politicians, distributed talking points and cash to talking heads in the media, and engineered cover-ups when necessary, like when a precision-guided Predator drone mistook an elementary school in Iraq for a terrorist hideout.

After he jumped, he did the same thing, but on a much bigger scale. He generated reports to make Archer/Andrews look like a vital piece of the national security machine. He'd been personally responsible for two elevations of the threat level. One of those times had been with a story about female suicide bombers having surgery to get plastic explosive breast implants.

Candle spent a lot of time commenting anonymously on blogs, starting chain e-mails and planting rumors on message boards. It didn't take much effort. He planted the seeds, and they grew like kudzu.

But he thought he should be closer to the action. He'd been excited when Graves pulled him in to work counterintelligence on Barrows. He thought he'd finally get to see some real action.

Now that he had his chance, however, he felt a little nauseous.

Hewitt's special skills unlocked doors and got Candle into the tunnels—the geek part of him was pretty psyched about the secret tunnels. But after that, he was on his own. He got lost twice, even using the detailed turn-by-turn map programmed into his phone.

He was sweating and queasy by the time he found the morgue. He had his gun in one hand, his phone in the other, but he didn't feel particularly dashing. He was pretty sure a secret agent's underwear wasn't supposed to ride up his crack while on a mission.

He peered into the morgue. It was a disaster area. Carefully, he shoved the door open, sweeping first with the pistol, the way he'd been taught at A/A's firearms course. However, he insisted on holding the gun sideways, despite all the times his instructor had yelled at him about that.

It just looked so damned cool.

The lights flickered in the room. Something really bad had happened in here. He could tell. His foot came down on something sticky, and he knew it was blood.

But the bubble of his fantasies—*I'm really doing it! I'm a spy!*—was thick enough to be a force field. Candle literally couldn't imagine anything bad happening to him. In his head, this was all part of the script. This was where he found the way to pry Barrows loose from their group, where he learned a way to control Cade, and he got Graves's approval and Bell would have sex with him.

Then he heard the hissing.

He turned in time to see the Snakehead, battered and half-frozen, a crusted scab over its chest. It looked pissed. And worse, it looked hungry.

Candle pulled the trigger—and just like his firearms instructor warned him, the gun ejected a hot shell casing back into his eye. He recoiled in pain, blinded. He kept pulling the trigger.

He couldn't see a thing between the tears and the pain. He kept firing, bullets spanging all over the metal surfaces of the room, hoping for a random hit.

His slide locked open. The clip was empty. He still couldn't see. Deafened by the gunshots, he couldn't hear the hissing either.

But he was still alive.

Maybe he got lucky.

Then a heavy weight landed on his back, and he felt the skin separate as something sliced through it.

His bubble of fantasy popped. The real world was right in his face, and it was a small square of tile on a cold floor. It finally occurred to him that he was not the secret-agent hero of this movie. He wasn't the plucky sidekick. He wasn't even the damsel in distress, because no one was coming to save him.

TWENTY

Operation OFTEN was the name given by Sidney Gottlieb to the CIA's attempts to "weaponize" black magic. Gottlieb, who was already famous among conspiracy theorists for his part in the CIA's mind-control experiments (see: Operation MK-ULTRA), used untold amounts of taxpayer dollars to hire psychics, astrologers and mentalists in an effort to tap into real magical power for America to use against its enemies. It was even rumored that OFTEN conducted séances to debrief CIA personnel who'd been killed in action. No wonder Gottlieb's nickname was "the Black Sorcerer." A similar operation, code-named CONNECTICUT-HULU, was reported to extend OFTEN's research by using cult rituals and techniques, although no documentation exists to support this charge.

—Cole Daniels, *Black Ops: The Occult-CIA Connection*

GULF OF ADEN

A helicopter rose over the *Virtue*, its spotlight sweeping the deck. It revealed six of the Snakeheads feeding on a single corpse, their slit pupils contracting in the sudden glare. They looked like animals on the highway, feasting on roadkill while caught in the headlights of a car.

Cade didn't drop from the chopper as much as launch himself out into the air. Thirty yards to the deck, then he hit and rolled to his feet, right in the center of the carnage.

The Snakeheads stared at him. He was smiling.

No. Not smiling. Snarling. Showing them his own fangs.

To Cade's surprise, they did not come right for him. They stood, looking as if they considered the idea, then seemed to sniff him out.

Interesting, Cade thought. They sensed his inhumanity. They weren't going to try to eat him; he didn't suit their tastes.

Cade realized they would only fight him if they perceived him as a direct threat.

He could manage that.

"All right," Cade said, still snarling. "Who's first?"

HE PICKED THE BIGGEST ONE, absurdly clothed in a hospital gown still strung around one arm and its neck.

He leaped high above it and kicked.

His heel cracked the Snakehead right at the neck. The kick would have killed one of the creatures on the yacht.

But instead of the familiar snap of bone, Cade felt only a dull thud of impact. The Snakehead fell down, but it wasn't dead. It was barely even hurt. They were like jerky; tough but flexible.

No question about it now. This was an entirely different generation of creature. They were evolving rapidly—too rapidly to be random chance. Someone was refining the virus with each new strain; deliberately producing tougher breeds of the creatures.

Cade just hoped they hadn't gotten any smarter.

It scrabbled back to its feet and slashed at him. He grabbed the Snakehead by the neck and hurled it to the deck. It slashed at his gut with the talons on its feet; Cade moved barely in time to avoid being disemboweled.

The others left them alone, concentrating on the meat. They had no herd or pack instincts, apparently. They just wanted to eat.

The Snakehead suddenly barreled forward and pinned Cade to the deck. Cade held its neck just far enough to avoid those needle-sharp teeth snapping at his face.

The creature kept shifting position, snapping crazily. It didn't want to devour Cade; it only wanted to kill him. Cade had learned he could make them angry. That was a sort of progress, he supposed.

He knew he couldn't keep its jaws away much longer. He was on his back, at a disadvantage. Sooner or later, the Snakehead would get past his guard.

So Cade let it.

He slipped its thrust, driving it face first into the deck behind him. At the same time, he turned his head and bared his fangs.

He bit as hard as he could, tearing free the leathery hide of its neck.

Blood poured over his chin and neck, even dribbling into his ears.

The Snakehead rolled away with a strangled kind of hiss that could only be a shriek of pain.

Cade spat out the snake flesh. It wasn't human anymore; not even close. It made him slightly nauseous.

But Cade noticed the other Snakeheads didn't have any reservations.

Their heads lifted as one from the body, and they narrowed their eyes on the thrashing, bleeding Snakehead.

They ran headlong at it, shoving one another out of the way in their eagerness for the kill. Primal instinct took over. They saw weakness and they pounced on it.

In a second, the creatures were tearing at one another, all trying to find a fresh chunk of the wounded Snakehead. Inevitably, they tore open new wounds, and the fresh blood drove them even crazier. Several more, attracted by the hissing cries of the scrum, joined in the slaughter.

Cade watched from a safe distance as the Snakeheads ate one another.

Now Cade knew how to kill them all.

FIRST, HE MADE a trip to the bridge. He had not piloted a boat in years, but it was easy enough to set the *Virtue* moving forward. He hoped it wouldn't run into anything before he was done.

In the stairwell to the lower decks, Cade found another Snakehead waiting. It sniffed the blood on him and attacked immediately.

Cade was ready. He ducked, grabbed the Snakehead by the leg and slammed it into the metal stairs.

Dazed, it thrashed weakly at him, tried to bite.

Cade's hand darted in between those needle-like teeth, grabbed and yanked.

He came out with the Snakehead's forked tongue and some other things that used to be stuck in its throat. It began choking, scrabbling at its neck in pain.

Now that it was distracted, Cade easily hooked one of its claws and tore it free.

Then he used the claw like a knife to slice open the Snakehead's belly.

It was not too deep—not enough to gut the creature—but it was enough to make the blood run. He punched the Snakehead back to the ground and swabbed it with the bloody tongue. He stomped on its knee, keeping it from gaining its feet.

Cade hooked his hand under the Snakehead's jaw and began running down the steps, dragging it behind. It painted a trail of blood wherever he went.

THE *VIRTUE* WAS a big ship, nearly the length of four football fields. Cade had to settle for making two circuits of the upper decks. He could not go down any deeper; he'd be hopelessly outnumbered and caught.

The idea was to be the fisherman, not the worm.

They came after him halfway through his second trip. Drawn by the blood of one of their own, they began chasing him.

As he reached the main deck again, Cade finally looked back. Dozens—maybe even hundreds—of Snakeheads were following him now, eagerly, jaws snapping, in a frenzy. He heard their claws on the metal like rain. Saw them scrambling over one another. Some peeled off into minor fights and tangles, like little storms breaking out of a massive thundercloud.

The thrill of the hunt had overridden any other caution or instinct they had. All they wanted was the meat.

Cade ran faster and tried not to think about what it meant for the crew if the Snakeheads were still this hungry.

He reached the rear of the ship. Below him, the *Virtue*'s twenty-six-foot propeller churned the sea with enough force to shove the seventy-ton ship through the water.

He didn't let go of the still-living Snakehead until after he'd leaped over the railing.

Unable or unwilling to stop, the mass of creatures surged over the side after him, a green-black wave pouring into the sea below.

His fingers wedged into a seam of the ship's steel plating, Cade watched as they fell. Some even seemed to look at him where he clutched the side of the hull.

The prop caught them in its backwash, drawing them into the metal blades. The Snakeheads were made for the water, but even they couldn't outswim the pull of the giant metal screw. It sucked them down, again and again, cutting them to pieces.

In minutes, there was nothing left but a stew of lizard skin and bone.

Cade watched to make sure nothing else surfaced. Then he began climbing back.

CADE LISTENED CAREFULLY ONCE he reached the top deck.

Not everyone who had been attacked had been killed. He heard the groans of pain, the screams of people asking for help.

The worst part, however, was what he didn't hear: no one was rushing to assist. There were no barked commands from anyone in authority. The Snakeheads had had *hours*. No one was left to come to the rescue.

All that remained was the wounded.

Cade knew they were infected. Given time—almost no time at all, really—these people would become the same things that nearly murdered them. There was no way around it.

There would be no survivors.

He walked toward the closest sounds of pain, knowing that he'd end their suffering, at least.

It was no comfort.

TWENTY-ONE

Then there was the mysterious "Mr. Gray" or "Mr. Grace" who showed up in New Orleans at Guy Banister's offices, which just happened to be the same address given by Lee Harvey Oswald on the flyers of his "Fair Play for Cuba Committee." Banister—who also investigated UFO sightings when he was still employed by the FBI—wasn't known to be a pushover, but witnesses said he did whatever Grace/Gray said, despite the fact that the mysterious stranger was much younger than he was; barely out of college, in fact.

—Cole Daniels, *Black Ops: The Occult-CIA Connection*

CHANTILLY, VIRGINIA

Bell and Zach showed up at the office at nearly the same time. They were a little shy of each other, but not so much that Book noticed.

He had other things on his mind.

"Candle's missing," he told them.

"He's probably just late," Bell said.

"No," Book said flatly. "He's not."

Bell looked to Hewitt and Reynolds. They sat, almost sheepish.

Zach tried to pick up on the subtext. Something wasn't being said out loud.

"How do you know he's not late?"

Book ignored him. Bell didn't reply. Zach got it in a second.

"You know he's not late because you know what he was doing," he said. "And it's something you didn't want me to know."

Bell had the courtesy to look embarrassed, at least.

"He might have followed us to that place we went yesterday."

For a moment, Zach thought she meant his apartment. Then he realized it was worse than that. It was the morgue.

He'd broken protocol, revealed a deeply classified secret lab to an unauthorized private contractor, and allowed some fat bastard who was probably working for the most evil organization he'd ever known to find out where it was.

All things considered, Zach was pretty restrained in his reaction.

"Oh, son of a *bitch*," he said.

IT WAS THE FIRST TIME Zach had seen the morgue and thought it really looked like death. Slicks of blood on the floor and red spatters on the walls. Paper in heaps, tables and medical equipment smashed and scattered.

Book had wanted to come. So had Hewitt and Reynolds. Zach only brought Bell, because he figured that he'd already spilled that milk. And, frankly, he didn't trust the others.

Now it was looking like a big mistake for anyone to be here.

Bell thought the same thing. "We need to get out of here," she said.

Zach walked inside anyway. The fluorescents overhead buzzed and flickered where they weren't broken.

"Zach, did you hear me?"

"Shhh," Zach said. Something was in the room.

Zach looked around. He saw the cold-storage drawer, torn open, and put it together.

"It wasn't dead."

Bell followed his gaze. She got it. "Oh Christ," she said. "We have to get out of here."

She was right. Zach stepped forward to go.

Then he heard the noise again, and knew it was too late. A clicking, hissing sound. He'd never heard anything like it, but he knew where it came from.

The Snakehead reared up behind the overturned autopsy table, showing them its razor-sharp smile.

As it lunged for them, Zach could see bits of flesh lodged in its teeth.

ZACH WOULD HAVE BEEN lunch had he not been training with Cade.

Eleven months earlier on his first assignment, Zach had to admit he'd been basically useless in a fight. Cade had remedied that in his own style.

Zach had been in the Reliquary, doing paperwork at what was now his desk. Without warning, Cade picked him up and threw him down on the floor.

"What the hell are you doing?" Zach had screamed. For a split second, every nightmare he'd ever had of Cade rushed through his head.

Cade simply stood there.

"You need to learn how to fight," he said.

Zach dragged himself to his feet, wincing at the places where he'd hit the stone floor. "Isn't that why I've got you?"

"I won't always be around," Cade said.

"This is not a good time for me."

"You might be killed before we get another chance."

Zach considered this. "I'll clear my schedule."

So Zach had learned, the hard way. Cade would attack, and Zach would defend himself as best he could. He never lasted more than a few seconds. Cade would stop short of the fatal blow.

"That would have been your head," Cade said, his hand like a knife at Zach's neck.

"Son of a bitch," Zach said, panting and sweating. "Haven't you heard of sparring?"

"There's no point. You are either fighting or you're not. No middle ground."

"Yeah, but what if I accidentally hurt you?"

Cade's lip curled.

"Right," Zach said. "Stupid question."

"You can't hurt me," Cade said. "But by all means, you should try. Use whatever you can find. Use your teeth, your hands, your feet, your clothes, anything on the ground. Everything is a weapon. Don't play by any schoolyard rules. Don't be afraid to be desperate. Desperate is better than dead."

So Zach learned. He doubted there was any cool name for the martial art he invented. He knew he must look ridiculous, flailing away, still wearing his coat and tie, eyes and mouth wide open. Maybe someone would call it "The Way of the File Clerk" in a hundred years or so.

But when he began seriously trying to hurt Cade—to kill him—he began to last a little longer.

Not much longer, true. Thirty seconds, instead of three. But Cade said he'd made progress. "You might survive," he'd said.

High praise.

ZACH THOUGHT of that now as he dropped out of the Snakehead's path.

It hit the floor and rolled, then turned toward Bell.

Bell made her first mistake then. She froze up. Disbelief all over her face.

Zach couldn't blame her. It was unbelievable.

Unfortunately, unbelievable was a daily part of Zach's job.

Zach dove over a desk to intercept. His hands automatically grabbed for a weapon. He snagged the scissors out of a pile of office junk spilled from a coffee mug.

With a quick, hard snap, he broke the screw holding the scissors together, giving him two makeshift knives. He put a blade in each hand and stabbed wildly at the Snakehead.

One blade bounced off the folded scales under the creature's neck and fell to the floor. The other Zach brought around and jammed hard into its eye.

The Snakehead let out a high squeal and lashed out, backhanding Zach away.

The blade in its eye stayed stuck where it was.

Without eyelids, it couldn't clear its vision of the fluid and gore dripping from its eye socket. It flailed wildly, still grinning its crocodile grin, shrieking in pain.

Zach came up immediately. Never stop, he heard Cade telling him. Never surrender for a second.

He reached out and snagged the handle of a short, two-drawer file cabinet. He nearly wrenched his arm out of its socket as he heaved it around, swinging it like a club, into the Snakehead.

It staggered, but Zach had given it a target. It turned toward him, knocking the file cabinet easily to the floor. Paper spilled everywhere.

"Hey," Bell screamed. The Snakehead turned as she threw something.

Glass broke. Liquid splashed all over the Snakehead, dripping to the floor. Zach felt its odor sting his nostrils. He needed to get away. Fast.

Zach kicked, pivoting on the ball of his back foot, putting all his weight behind it.

The sole of his shoe connected solidly with the Snakehead's chest, shoving it back. Zach used the space to dive clear.

Bell, on the other hand, did the unthinkable. She got closer. She darted a hand out, holding a lighter to the spilled puddle beneath the Snakehead. She barely needed to touch it. Her hand was caught in the sudden bloom of heat and light.

Embalming fluid is highly flammable.

The Snakehead went up like a torch.

It screeched and squealed, slamming itself into walls and floors and debris before it finally stopped screaming.

It hit the floor, facedown. No movement.

Zach stood there, panting, as the sprinklers above finally kicked in. A fire alarm rattled somewhere. The water did nothing against the chemical fire. It kept burning the Snakehead down to a charred lump.

Bell stood up, cradling her hand. Zach realized they were both soaked.

"I think you got him," he said.

"Yeah," she said, her voice weirdly calm. "Did he get you?"

Zach shook his head. "Are you sure? No broken skin? No infection?"

Zach carefully pulled up his sleeves, then lifted the cuffs of his pants. Not even a scratch.

"Sorry," she said. "I had to be sure. What about Candle? Do you think he might have—"

"I don't know." He turned to look around the morgue again, and immediately slammed his shin into an open drawer, protruding from a desk.

Zach swore and looked down. He was about to kick the desk. He stopped.

The drawer was almost sloshing, filled with sticky, drying blood. Chunks of raw meat, wrapped in roughly cut strips of cloth.

Zach could see the fabric of the cloth. Where it wasn't stained with blood, it was marked with a pattern. He recognized it.

EAT ME, it said.

Zach swallowed bile that had climbed to the back of his throat.

Bell couldn't see from behind him. "What? What is it?"

"I found Candle," he told her. "Most of him."

TWENTY-TWO

The cultist believes he can summon the very hounds of hell to his aid; the intelligence agent can overthrow a government, terminate a politician, or call in an air strike. Either way, the Gates of the Underworld are opened.

—Peter Levenda, *Sinister Forces: A Grimoire of American Political Witchcraft*

USNS *VIRTUE*, GULF OF ADEN

It had been a long night. Cade had been through the ship twice, checking every hiding spot, every blind corner and dead end.

The results were laid out on the deck. Some of them still looked quite human. Others were nothing but scales and teeth.

Cade didn't know if the virus died when its carrier did. He found a fuel hose near the helipad and began splashing it over the bodies.

He looked at the rows. It took him a nanosecond to count: six hundred ninety-seven. God alone knew how many he'd sent over the side to be ground into chum by the prop.

The black smoke rolled into the sky as the fire burned.

He was still watching when Graves arrived.

A Marine chopper dropped Graves off at the helipad but kept its rotors spinning, ready for a quick takeoff.

Graves carried Cade's briefcase, the one Zach had packed for him, in one hand.

"We should go," he said. "I brought your luggage."

He tried to make it sound lighthearted, but Cade was in no mood to act human right now.

"How did they get here?" Cade asked, as much to himself as to Graves.

"Maybe they came up over the sides. From the water. Hell, maybe that Marine was infected, after all. It was my fault, Cade. I'm sorry. But we do have to leave. There's going to be an investigation. The ship will probably have to be scuttled. And we have other places to be. This is a dead end."

Cade said nothing.

Graves snapped his fingers. "You there? Answer me."

Cade looked at him. Something nagged at him again, demanding his attention through the blood and pain. Something about those words, in that cadence. Years peeled away in seconds.

He turned to stand face-to-face with Graves. "You were right," he said. "We've never met before. But we have spoken on the phone."

Even behind the sunglasses, Cade could see Graves's eyes go wide with fear.

It was about time.

G raves could not keep himself from trembling. Long after he'd
commanded his rebellious body to stop, he just kept shaking.

He walked to the door of the cheap motel room, past the office. Nobody saw him. The place was still asleep in the early morning.

He checked the thermometer. It lied. No way it was only sixty degrees. Sweat dribbled down his ribs from his armpits. He felt like he was wrapped in a bag of heavy steam.

He didn't even have to knock when he reached the room. The door opened. Graves gaped.

"You?" he blurted. He couldn't help it. One more shock on top of all the others. The director of counterintelligence himself. CODE NAME: LORD. It was a play on his actual name, which every politician in Washington knew and feared. But he was supposed to be in Europe.

The old man laughed, a wheeze like gas escaping a corpse. "Good to know I can still inspire terror. Come in, son."

Graves was dead. He knew it. He'd failed. He'd clearly punctured some veil of secrecy, because there was no way the old man would be here, not after Dallas, and certainly not if there was any chance Graves could tell anyone about it later.

Graves considered taking off into the night beyond the parking lot, running until he got lost.

"Don't just stand there," the old man said. "You're letting the bugs in."

The urge to run faded. It was useless. They would find him. But more than that, Graves could not do it. He was trained and conditioned to follow orders. From table manners to Boy Scouts to this. There was no breaking free from what he was.

He entered the room.

Lord sat in the room's one chair, a bucket of ice and a bottle of whiskey on the table beside him. Two glasses were already poured, beaded with condensation.

The old man picked up his drink. He nodded, and Graves did the same.

The old man sipped. Graves guzzled despite his best efforts.

"You look better already," the old man said. "Have a seat. We need to talk."

Graves sat on the bed. The whiskey burned, but didn't take much of his anxiety away.

Graves couldn't contain himself any longer. "Sir, the men—all of them, Jesus, all of them, they're all dead, sir."

"Of course they are."

What? Was that part of the plan? Was he expendable? Did they intend for this to happen?

No, it couldn't be. Graves had done everything right.

The old man offered the bottle again. The glass shook in Graves's hand, causing fat drops of liquor to spill on the carpet.

Graves's ears burned with shame. Even after all he'd seen recently, he felt the duty to maintain a stiff upper lip. Chin out, stand up straight, Yale down the spine all the way.

But he gulped the drink anyway. "I'm sorry, sir," he said.

"Sorry for what?"

Graves opened his mouth, then closed it. "For all of this," he said. "For the failure of MORDRED."

AT FIRST, it had been a textbook operation. They'd set it up perfectly. The symbolic King of America, brought down while surveying his people. Their convenient suspect picked up at his rendezvous point by the police.

Graves thought his shooters were safe and clear. Friendly Dallas PD officers escorted them away after the hit, told the press they were "drifters" and let them disappear.

Then things began to go wrong.

While the nation reeled, Air Force One was supposed to be blown out of the sky. Johnson and the grieving widow, taken out in one move. The wreckage would show evidence of a Cuban-made bomb. The Cubans would deny it, of course—because they were innocent—and the Soviets would come to their rescue after the invasion. With a few touches here and there, they were looking at a limited nuclear exchange and troops on the other side of the Iron Curtain within a month.

The Agency would have what it wanted—war with Russia, a war Russia could not possibly win. A great sacrifice, yes, but all for the greater good.

Nothing happened. Air Force One landed safely. LBJ sworn in. An orderly transfer of power.

He went to the warehouse outside Dallas where his fake Cubans were supposed to be waiting.

They were there. In pieces. Something had torn them apart and painted the walls with their remains.

He ran back to his car and drove all night.

He stopped only at pay phones, trying to find the gunmen. They were supposed to be at a series of safe houses, always reachable by phone.

180

No one picked up until Graves was almost to Orange, the sun beginning to breach the sky at the horizon.

Someone answered, but there was no sound. Not even the sound of breathing.

"Mordred," Graves said.

Nothing.

"Mordred. This is Morgan. I need your authentication."

Silence.

"Hello?" In impatience, he'd snapped his fingers, a nervous habit he thought extinguished in training. "Anyone there?"

"I'm coming for you," the voice on the other end said. It wasn't overtly threatening. It didn't even sound angry. But Graves had never heard a voice quite like that. It was perfectly cold, perfectly calm and utterly inhuman.

"Who is this?" Graves asked.

"You'll see," the voice said, and in it, Graves heard dead leaves scraping on a gravestone.

The call ended with a click. Graves had been shaking uncontrollably ever since.

LORD GAVE HIM a kind smile.

"You didn't fail."

"Sir. With all due respect. The terminal phase of the operation. And my men . . ."

Graves gagged, and nearly brought up the whiskey in his stomach. He managed to swallow. His throat burned. "Sorry," he said again.

"It's understandable," Lord said. "You're still trying to comprehend what's happened. I remember the first time I saw him." A shudder, involuntary and quickly suppressed, shook the old man under his suit.

"Him? You know who did this?"

"Oh, yes. I know him."

"Sir, what I saw—what happened to the men—there's no way anything human did that. It looked like some kind of animal."

"Not an animal, no," he said. "A predator, but not an animal."

"I don't understand."

The old man sighed. "Before tonight, you thought you knew secrets. One of the few pressed into service, to carry the burdens of what it takes to keep this country safe. The elite. *Don't* argue with me. Don't look at me with that false humility. Admit it. You loved the idea of power. Of being privy to the real action in the world while everyone else swallowed lies."

Graves nodded.

Lord grinned and moved closer. "Well, boy, let me tell you, you have no fucking idea."

Suddenly Graves was looking into the barrel of a .45, a WWII-vintage Colt Peacemaker.

"Are you sure you want to know the truth?" Lord asked.

Before Graves could say anything, the old man pushed the gun a little closer.

"Think carefully. Do you want to know the real answers? I'm about to bring you inside the knowledge, son. But there is always a choice. Just say the word. I will set you free."

For a moment, Graves considered it. As if it was a real choice. He wasn't sure if he wanted to live in a world where the things he'd seen over the past forty-eight hours could happen. Oddly, he thought of his mother. He hadn't spoken to her since he had taken on his new name and identity. He barely even thought about her anymore, except perhaps at Christmas. But now he wondered, what would she think of what he'd become? Was this what she wanted for him?

For a moment, he thought it might be better to take the bullet.

But that was crazy. He blinked, and the moment was gone.

"I have to know," he said.

Lord nodded and lowered the gun to the table. "Yes, you do. That's our gift and our curse. We have to know the secrets. And we have to carry them, ever after. It's why we chose you, after all."

"What does this have to do with anything? Who killed my men?"

"A vampire," the old man said.

Despite everything, Graves almost laughed. But the old man's face was devoid of humor.

"What do you mean?"

"Every presidential assassination attempt since Lincoln has been carried out in broad daylight. Now you know why."

"Sir, when you say 'vampire'—"

Lord slammed his glass on the table, splashing whiskey and nearly upsetting the bottle. "I mean a goddamned vampire. Clear the wax out of your ears."

Graves apologized, but inside he wondered if the old man was insane, or if he was. If he had not seen the bodies of his agents, if he had not heard that voice on the phone, he would have run for the door.

"There's more to this world than the things you can see," Lord said. "There are hidden chapters to history, and not all of them were written by men. Think about what you saw. Think about the voice you heard. Was that human?"

Graves shook his head. No. That was not human. He was sure of that.

"Just be grateful you didn't meet him in person," Lord said. "You wouldn't be here."

"Who is he?"

"You'll find out. Along with many other things. But first, I want you to answer a very important question."

The old man leaned close.

"Haven't you ever noticed the similarities between spycraft and witchcraft?" Lord asked.

Graves shook his head, confused.

"Think about it. Witches revere true names—they are the way to control demons. While we use false names to get close to people, and then use their demons—alcohol, homosexuality, pederasty—to control them. Witches speak magic words to unlock secrets. We use code words. They talk of crossing over to the 'Other Side,' the place beyond death. We refer to the enemy as the Other Side, and when we find a traitor, we say he's gone over. It's all about who controls reality. That's what we're after. That's what we've always been after."

Graves struggled to keep up. This was all starting to be too much. Sure, he'd heard about some esoteric projects run by the Agency. Things like MK-ULTRA, or CONNECTICUT-HULU, or even the rumors about what they were keeping out at Groom Lake. That stuff sounded like science fiction, and it was real. He'd seen it. But this was past all that, right into fairy tales and nightmares.

"We chose to operate this way. We prefer the shadows. The Order is only one more mask. The most secure form of rule is the one where the subjects don't even know the names of their rulers. That is the purpose of espionage—to hide the true face in the mirror. We lie to the world, but more important, we lie to ourselves. You have no idea. But you'll find out."

Graves felt he'd missed something. "Sir. I don't understand. What does that have to do with a vampire?"

"Never mind that right now," Lord snapped. "What do you want? Why did you join the Agency?"

Graves stammered, caught off guard. "I want—to serve my country, sir. To stand up against communism, and protect—"

"Stop. Stop." The old man's eyes were sharp and mean. "You didn't walk away from everyone you knew for that pabulum. You let us give you a new name and a new life, and you've killed for us in return. And it wasn't for the U.S.A and Chevrolet. Tell me the truth: what do you want?"

"I am telling you the truth, sir, I—"

The old man put his hand on the gun again.

"Do I really need to threaten you with this? I said the *truth*, you mewling little faggot. What. Do. You. *Want*."

Something came loose in Graves. All the tension and fear and anxiety came crumbling down. All that was left was rage.

"Everything," Graves hissed, and it was like gas escaping from under tons of rock and pressure. "I want it all. I want people to do what I tell them to do. I want money—enough to buy anything I see, just because it's there. And I want women. All of them. On their knees, on their backs, I want them all, and I want all of that right now, and I want to slaughter anyone who gets in my way."

The old man leaned close. Graves could smell nicotine and rot on his breath.

"You can have it," he said. "You can have all of it. That's why you are here. That's why we found you. The world is darker than you know. If you are willing to see its true face, you must take that darkness inside you as well. If you want power in this world, you must embrace what other men call evil. And then, you can have everything you ever wanted and more."

Graves thought about it. He knew this was one of those pivotal moments in his life. But he felt like the decision had already been made. Still, he took the bottle off the table and poured. Then he took a drink to steady himself.

Graves tried to gauge how serious the old man was. This was starting to sound uncomfortably close to things he remembered from Sunday school.

"Are you asking me to sell my soul?" Graves asked. He chuckled a little, to try to make it sound like a joke.

The old man beamed, revealing yellow teeth. "You sold your soul a long time ago, my boy. Now you get *paid*."

Lord took Graves's hand in a firm grip as if meeting him for the first time.

"Welcome to the Company," he said. "I think you're going to do very well with us."

TWENTY-THREE

Finally there is the story . . . of Dave Morales, a self-proclaimed CIA assassin who one night, with only close friends present, went into a boozy diatribe against Kennedy for sacrificing his CIA-trained comrades at the Bay of Pigs. Suddenly he stopped . . . and remained silent for moment. Then as if saying it only to himself he added: "Well, we took care of that son of a bitch, didn't we?"

—Jonathan Vankin and John Whalen, *The 80 Greatest Conspiracies of All Time*

Cade saw no reason to wait. Graves had escaped justice for decades.

In the next split second, Graves's throat was in Cade's right hand. He raised the briefcase like a shield, his feet kicking in empty air.

Still, he looked far too calm for a man in a vampire's grip.

Cade paused. Longer than he should have.

Behind them, Cade heard the sounds of weapons being readied. The pilot of the chopper shouted at him over the bird's P.A. system.

"Release the Colonel! Do it now! We will shoot!"

Cade realized exactly how this looked. He saw it from the perspective of the Marines in the copter: a field of smoldering corpses, a man in a known uniform, pointing the finger of blame at someone dressed in rags, covered in grime and blood.

It was an old trick. And a shamefully effective one.

But it wasn't the Marines that made Cade hesitate. He maneuvered Graves between them and himself.

Cade felt something he wasn't accustomed to; something so rare it took a moment to name it.

Uncertainty.

"You can't do this," Graves said, choking out the words.

"Something's wrong," Cade said. He could not harm Graves. It was a fact, simple and inarguable, as solid as bedrock.

The Marines continued to scream at them. Cade paid no attention. He looked at Graves, bewildered. "How—?"

Graves pointed to the inside pocket of his jacket.

Cade lowered Graves so his feet touched the deck again, but kept him as a shield for the Marines.

With his free hand, Cade reached into the pocket and came out with nothing but a single sheet of paper.

It began: "Pursuant to the power granted me by the Constitution of the United States, Article II, Section 2, as President of the United States, I have granted and by these presents do grant a full, free, unconditional and absolute pardon . . ."

Cade recognized the language instantly. It was a presidential pardon for any and all crimes committed. Signed by the previous president on the day before Curtis's inauguration, but without any end date. That made it preemptive, automatically forgiving the recipient for anything done, even after it was issued.

In other words, it was the ultimate get-out-of-jail-free card.

And it had Graves's name on it.

Cade couldn't harm Graves in any way. The pardon was nonnegotiable, just the same as a direct order from the president. Even though that president was no longer in office, Cade was bound by his oath to follow it. Thanks to that paper, Graves was free from any sanction the United States government could deliver. And that included Cade.

Graves smiled, the first genuine expression Cade had ever seen on his face.

"You see," he said, "as far as you're concerned, I'm untouchable."

CADE STOOD there for a moment. He was not used to being taken by surprise, not by anything.

"You're Shadow Company," he said. It was so painfully obvious that he didn't need to say it, but words were all he had right now.

"I think it's adorable that you still call us that," Graves said. "Remind me to get you one of the new business cards."

Without warning, Graves moved faster than a man half his age and shoved the briefcase at Cade.

It bounced into Cade's chest. He caught it by reflex, releasing Graves.

Graves made the most of the chance. He ran away, screaming. "It's him!" Graves shouted, waving his arms. "He's the one who killed them all!"

By then, the Marines were already shooting at him.

They sent a line of bullets across the deck, separating him from Graves. He pivoted and ran the other way. He felt the heat of the rounds as they passed by him. If he were human, they would have torn him to pieces already.

The smoke pouring off the deck in front of him suddenly parted in a thunder of rotors. The helicopter rose just above him. A door gunner had his weapon out and aimed.

Cade was caught in the cross fire. There was no cover anywhere, no place to hide.

Briefcase still in hand, Cade vaulted the railing and went over the side.

The door gunner got off one last burst. One of the rounds tore through him, turning him like a pinwheel in midair, at the arc of his leap.

He fell five stories until he hit the deep black sea, then sank without a trace.

TWENTY-FOUR

The Other Side—

Death, or the land of death. (*Ex.* *"He passed over to the other side."*) Thought to originate from the Greek myth of crossing over the River Styx and into Hades, the realm of the dead.

In espionage, used to refer to the sponsor of enemy agents. (*Ex. "Philby was turned to the other side while at Cambridge."*)

—*Falsworth's Dictionary of Idioms and Phrases,* 1971

WASHINGTON, D.C.

Down in the morgue, the sprinklers finally stopped. Bell slicked her hair out of her face. "Now what?"

Zach pulled out his phone. Down here, it was safer than land-lines, and hooked immediately into the wireless network shared through all the tunnels.

He hit the number listed under CLEANERS.

"Operator" was the only reply.

"Code name: JIMMY CHRISTOPHER," Zach said, struggling to remember the right daily sequence and the right code. "UNDERWORLD. CHARON. STYX. ZOOKEEPER."

"Confirm location."

Zach pressed a button on the phone, activating the homing beacon, then put it back to his ear.

"Got it," the operator said. "Sit tight. We'll have someone there as soon as we can. Good luck."

"Yeah," Zach said. "Thanks." But the line was already dead.

"What was that?" Bell wanted to know.

"Cleaning crew. They'll be here to secure the location and deal with . . ." He looked at the desk drawer as his voice trailed off.

"Not your first time doing this, then."

Zach sighed. "It's not even my first time this month."

"Seriously?"

"It's the federal government. We have procedures for everything. Why do you think I'm inoculated against zombies?"

"There's a vaccine for zombies?"

"Oh sure. HZV, H1Z1, most of the other strains."

"Are you kidding?"

For a second, Zach savored being the guy who knew stuff nobody else did.

"Sorry. Classified."

Bell gave him a dark look that said he wasn't nearly as amusing as he thought.

They both shivered from the cold and the sudden adrenaline crash.

Bell looked around the room. "Do we have to stay here?"

Zach wasn't wild about the idea either. Why not, he figured. They both needed a change of clothes.

Zach led her down one connecting tunnel, then another. Five minutes later, they were in the Reliquary.

Bell looked at all the exhibits with a kind of exhausted wonder. She was losing the capacity for shock and awe: *Oh, so that's what a Chupaca-*

bras really looks like? Huh, who knew? Zach could tell; he'd been there himself.

He found a set of Smithsonian sweats that would fit her and a towel from the stack of things he kept for the nights he slept here.

Bell sat in the growing silence. Zach didn't know what to say. The reality of dying horribly was always there, sort of a steady background music on the soundtrack of his life. But he really hated these moments where it suddenly came to the forefront and dominated the whole scene.

They sat among the dead mysteries in silence.

"You really don't think about quitting?" she asked, with the lopsided smile he'd seen before.

"Oh, I think about it," Zach said. "But I can't."

She shook her head, still with the same funny grin.

"You could," she insisted. "But you choose not to."

"You could quit, too, if you wanted."

The smile vanished. "No," she said. "Not my job. Not at all."

He waited for her to explain, but she left it there.

"You ever want a normal life?" she asked.

"Sometimes," he admitted. "Why do you ask?"

Before she could reply, Zach's phone buzzed. He picked it up.

"Leave it," she said.

"What? Why?"

She pulled him closer. "Oh," he said.

He lifted her shirt and put his lips to her breasts. She leaned back on the table, guiding his head down her belly.

He was kicking his pants off when one of the interior Reliquary doors came crashing open.

Men with wicked-looking guns, wearing full-body riot gear, aimed their weapons.

Zach looked up. Then looked angry. "God *damn* it, Smitty."

The man in the lead flipped up the visor on his helmet, revealing a bearded, grinning face. "You didn't answer your phone," he said, in a Southern drawl, as if that explained everything.

Bell was busy covering herself.

"Who the hell are you?" she said.

"The cleaners I told you about?" Zach said, pulling up his pants. "This is them."

"Ma'am," he said. "Zach, you know we've got protocols for a reason."

"Yeah, yeah, yeah. Don't you have a dead monster to scoop up?"

Zach was pretty sure he heard muffled laughter from under the other riot helmets.

"You weren't in the lab. We didn't know what had happened. Standard operating procedure. Also, I can't help but notice you're here with unauthorized personnel."

"She's with me. Obviously, I'm fine." Zach had regained his pants, if not his dignity.

"Obviously," Smitty said. "But for a minute, it sure looked like you were under attack."

Zach scowled at him. "Go away."

"Sorry, kiddo," Smitty said, still grinning. "I know what it's like when the adrenaline gets going. Shoot, I remember one time, I was out in the field with this operative from the U.S. Marshal's Service—"

"Go away now."

He laughed and signaled his team. The cleaning crew shouldered their weapons and filed out.

Zach looked at Bell, who wavered between anger and laughter. He wasn't sure exactly how to apologize for this.

"What I get for not answering my phone," he said. He picked it up and checked the screen.

Something he hadn't noticed. An e-mail had come through. Delayed by the servers—overburdened government issue, of course, running last year's software. It was from Everett.

"What is it?" Bell asked.

Some instinct told him to read it first. Maybe it was the interruption by the cleaners, or maybe Cade's warning was coming back to him. But he remembered how much classified info he'd let Bell see.

"Just a second," he said. He opened the message and scanned through it.

Everett might have been a little weird, but he wasn't one of those people who bury points in a report just to fill pages. If he found something important, he put it right at the top.

Zach remembered this. Everett had tried to tell him, right before they left.

"The deceased has a steel plate and bolts in the lower right femur, repairing an old fracture," Everett wrote. Serial numbers on the plates were run through the medical manufacturers' databases. The surgical plate was one that was sold in bulk to a Pentagon contractor, later used in field hospitals in Afghanistan. "Specifically, the plate in question was issued to Bagram Air Force Base, where it was used by U.S. Army surgeons to repair the broken leg of an enemy combatant held in custody, Tariq Sharraf," Everett wrote.

Everett might have been a freak, but he was great at his job. Zach realized he had the first real breakthrough in this mess. He had a name.

"Zach, what is it?" Bell said again, impatience growing.

"Give me ten minutes," he said. "I've got an idea."

IT TOOK HIM TWENTY.

Working on the Reliquary's computers, he had access to more information than when he was off-site. Through its encrypted communications lines, he could sift through all the massive paperwork generated by the federal government. It was just a matter of finding the right needle in a haystack made of needles.

Bell sat, stewing, clearly unhappy at being made to play Girl Friday while he worked. But he had to check this for himself.

Tariq Sharraf. Several terrorists or suspected terrorists had that name. Several different spellings popped up on no-fly lists, border-watch lists, INTERPOL, and so on. The one Zach was looking for, however, was also known as Tariq "the Mute" for his ability to resist interrogation. That was where he got the broken leg and the surgical repair job, both courtesy of the U.S. government, while he was held at Bagram Collection Point in Afghanistan.

The prison at Bagram was notorious; some of the things there made Abu Ghraib look like day camp. An interrogator got frustrated with Tariq and hit him with an aluminum baseball bat—not exactly approved interrogation procedure. Because it was a compound fracture of the femur, and because Tariq was considered high-value, he was rushed into surgery and the repair performed. He was given to the CIA in 2003 for further questioning. His paper trail dead-ended there.

Which meant he shouldn't have been turned into a Snakehead and shipped to Somalia.

Zach checked the date of Tariq's release to the CIA again: July 12, 2003.

Couldn't be a coincidence. Just couldn't be.

He flipped open his laptop and brought up Graves's list of assignments and stations again.

There on the screen, just as he'd remembered: *Bagram Collection Point, Combined Joint Task Force—180 (CJTF-180), Afghanistan, 11/11/01 to 08/17/03.*

"Son of a bitch," Zach said.

"What?" Bell said, standing up and crossing to look at the screen with him.

"It's Graves," he said. "Graves is the one moving the prisoners. He's behind the whole thing."

BELL LOOKED GENUINELY DISTRESSED. "That's not possible. How did he get the White House to let him investigate himself?"

"I don't know," Zach said. "If he's Shadow Company, then he's got a connection somewhere pretty high."

"I don't buy it," she said. "You don't have any real proof. Just because he was there at the same time?"

"The guy he was supposed to deliver for the CIA turns into a Snakehead. That cannot be a coincidence."

She shrugged, not looking at him. "You really think so?"

"You *don't*?"

"Close enough, I guess," she said.

Zach wanted to ask her what she meant by that, but Bell kept talking. "What if he had no choice?" she said. "What if he was ordered to do this?"

Zach was amazed. He couldn't figure out why Bell was so anxious to stand up for Graves.

"You think that matters? You think there's any way to say 'Sorry, my bad' for this? More important, you think *Cade* will accept that as an excuse? No way. Cade simply can't let something like this pass."

"Graves isn't a lightweight. He'll fight."

"He doesn't seem that frightening."

"You don't know him. Nobody does. Most of what I know comes from rumors," she said. "But I believe them all. Even the ones that contradict the other ones."

"He's just a man," Zach said.

She gave him a sharp look. "Just because you know Cade doesn't make you an expert on what's scary," she said. "Seriously. You have no idea about some of the things he's supposed to have done."

Zach thought he heard a little fear in her voice when she said that. Fear, and maybe just a trace of admiration. It irritated him, almost like they were arguing over whose dad was stronger.

Only, he was right.

"You've never seen Cade hunt," he said. "He won't stop. He can't stop. Not for anything. No matter what, he'll find a way. Someone has to pay for this. There has to be blood."

Bell thought about that. "You're right," she said.

She grabbed Zach by the hair and slammed his head into the metal desk. Zach's eyes were full of pain and surprise. Bell slammed him into the desk again.

Zach's eyes closed. He fell to the floor, unconscious.

Bell picked him up under the armpits and began dragging him toward the corridor.

TWENTY-FIVE

I Solomon said unto him: "Beelzeboul, what is thy employment?"
And he answered me: "I destroy kings. I ally myself with foreign
tyrants. And my own demons I set on to men, in order that the
latter may believe in them and be lost. . . . And I will destroy
the world."

—F. C. Conybeare, translator, *The Testament of Solomon*, c. A.D. 100

A little less than six miles away, a phone rang in a two-story home
in the suburbs of Fairfax, Virginia.

The man in glasses was at the dining room table with his wife
and kids. She was trying to make it a regular thing—dinner together, as
a family, at least one night a week.

She glared at him when he stood, mobile in hand.

"Sorry, honey," he said, checking the number. "It's the office."

She let out a long-suffering sigh. "Fine. Take it. We're just your
family."

Sarcasm, he thought. If he was lucky, she'd leave it at that. He looked
at his children, a boy and a girl, eight and ten. They were tense, waiting
for the next move.

He really had to take this.

"I won't be long," he said, and got up from the table.

"Eat your dinner," his wife snapped at the kids. They dug into
their food.

The man in glasses felt a stab of genuine regret at causing them pain, and then turned his attention to the phone call.

"What?"

"Complications," Graves said. "The package didn't make it to the carrier."

"That's disappointing."

"Wasn't my idea. The chopper pilot made a detour. Instead of a fully armed aircraft carrier, loaded with young men brimming with testosterone, he put them down on a hospital ship."

"How did the new viral load perform?"

"Hard to say. I'm fairly certain the carrier agent went critical as planned. Cade went in."

The man in glasses felt a headache coming on. This just kept getting better. "How many got away?"

Graves sighed. "None."

"None?"

"You heard me."

"None? Zero? Not one?"

"I can say it again. It won't change."

"Wounded? Any other carriers?"

"He killed them all."

The man in glasses chuckled. "My God. Just when you think that one can't surprise you again . . . Well. Where's Cade now?"

"I dealt with him."

"Permanently?"

Graves paused, which said it all.

"I didn't see the body," he admitted.

The man sucked at a bit of chicken stuck in his teeth. "Well, this is a fairly large pile of shit you're in, isn't it? We were supposed to start the outbreak in the Middle East. You know the progression. We should be at several hot zones by now."

"'No battle plan survives contact with the enemy.' You know that," Graves said. "Cade intercepted our Somali shipment. He was drawn into this much earlier than I anticipated. I had expected our White House contacts to keep him away from us until—"

"You really think the higher-ups will be impressed by those excuses?"

"I don't answer to you," Graves said tightly. "You want to get your hands dirty? Hop on a plane. Otherwise, fuck off and let me do my job."

The man in glasses took a moment. It was still Graves's show. He had to resist the urge to micromanage. "Point taken. But if you didn't kill him, you know you will see Cade again."

"He can't touch me."

"Mmm-hmm. We'll see. What about Barrows?"

Graves laughed. "Barrows is only human. It's under control."

"This is where I would, ordinarily, list all the things that will happen to you if this goes off the rails," the man in glasses said. "But you're a grown-up. I'm sure you can fill in the blanks on your own."

Despite his best efforts, Graves pictured a range of possibilities. "I appreciate your trust, Proctor," he said.

"Of course. Oh, and one more thing: do not call during dinnertime. Ever. Or I'll skullfuck you myself."

The man in glasses flipped the phone shut and looked up. His wife and kids were at the kitchen door, staring. They'd never heard him swear before, not so much as a "hell" or "damn."

"Sorry," he said. "A little disagreement with one of our branch offices."

They kept staring.

He smiled. "Who's up for ice cream?"

TWENTY-SIX

SPRINGWOOD, OHIO—A couple of months ago, you could have called Springwood a "sleepy little town." These days, nobody here is sleeping much at all. The city is in the grip of terror as a serial killer stalks adolescents from the ages of 13 to 19, always murdering the youths in their bedrooms when they are asleep. The killer enters and leaves homes without leaving a single piece of evidence or disturbing the other residents. While police are baffled, the town's teenagers are doing everything they can to remain awake. Illegal amphetamine use is skyrocketing.

—*The Springwood Shopper*, November 9, 1984

GULF OF ADEN

The sky began to turn gray on the horizon. Cade clung to the briefcase, bobbing in the waves. It was just buoyant enough to keep his head above water. The hospital ship was long gone, and the shore was far beyond his sight.

Cade could not have reached it even if he'd known where it was. Vampires are not great swimmers. Cade's muscle and bone were too dense to allow him to float, and though he didn't necessarily need to breathe—he could live off the stored oxygen of his last meal for some time—he would sink like a stone until he hit the point where the water pressure would squeeze his brains out through his ears.

He suspected this was what happened to the vampire who made him, all those years ago. Tossed overboard or otherwise lost at sea, stuck on the ocean floor until somehow, it made its way again to the surface, and Cade's ship.

It looked like Cade was going to test that theory himself.

He couldn't let that happen. He had to get to shore. He had to stop Graves.

Admittedly, he wasn't sure how he was going to work that. Dawn was coming. The wound in his chest refused to close, and the salt water seemed to leach what strength he had left.

He heard a boat in the distance. He paddled around lamely, trying to see where it was coming from.

He marshaled what resources he had left. Perhaps this was one of Graves's men coming to finish him off. Tired as he was, he could try to fight. He could take the boat and hope to outrun the daylight.

In a moment, he realized that wouldn't be necessary.

The boat was a slick, jet-powered racing craft. Cade had seen several of these moored at Eyl. They were fast, but they also had the range necessary to run out to the shipping lanes where the pirates did their work.

Tania stood behind the wheel, hair whipping in the breeze. She looked for all the world like a rich girl out in her daddy's favorite toy. Aside from her utter lack of a tan, she could have fit right in on the Riviera or South Beach.

She drew the boat alongside him. Her mouth quirked into a smile as she looked him over.

"Not your strongest moment, Nathaniel," she said.

Cade opened his mouth to speak and spat seawater. He lifted his chin and tried again. "I've had better days," he admitted.

"Aren't you even going to ask how I found you?" She reached out a hand and pulled him on board.

He collapsed behind the driver's seat and finally was able to open the briefcase. He drank one of the packets of blood dry before he answered.

"I'm willing to call it random chance."

She smiled again. "Really?"

He looked at the briefcase and opened the next packet. "I don't see the need to complicate my life any further right now."

"Smart move," she said, and wheeled the boat around, back toward the shore.

TWENTY-SEVEN

If they can get you asking the wrong questions, they don't have
to worry about answers.

—Thomas Pynchon

LIBERTY, IOWA

Some conspiracy theorists will tell anyone who will listen that the
shadow government—the one behind the scenes, the people really
pulling the strings—built a secret concentration camp under Denver International Airport in Colorado. They'll point to the project's
budget overruns, its massive complex of underground concrete tunnels,
its razor-wire fence, and tell you its real purpose is to hold enemies of the
New World Order—without trial, indefinitely, turning ordinary U.S.
citizens into the same kind of detainees held at Guantánamo.

They're wrong, of course.

It's not under Denver Airport. It's actually under the Liberty Mall,
outside Liberty, Iowa.

LIBERTY MALL was one of the largest shopping centers on the North
American continent, the local chamber of commerce was proud to say.

The members even had a plaque made and a special ceremony to celebrate the grand opening. They knew that without the mall, there wasn't much going on in the greater Liberty area. Farming had been a losing proposition since the early '80s for most of the residents, and attempts to rebrand the town as a new kind of high-tech Mecca—"The Silicon Prairie," as one of the expensive consultants they'd hired called it—only drew a few companies that withered and died when they ran out of venture capital.

But the Mall—it was always *the* Mall, capital M—drew over ten million visitors a year to gawk at its three million square feet of retail space. Everyone in the area depended on the Mall, in one way or another.

This probably explained why the locals minimized or ignored some of the Mall's unusual aspects. For starters, not many people knew the Mall was actually owned by a defense contractor, PKD Ltd. Or that its construction actually used three times as much concrete as specified on the blueprints filed with the city.

There were other things, too. While standard rent-a-cops patrolled the upper floors and common areas of the Mall, the basement level was always guarded by private security wearing uniforms without any insignia or identifying badges. Some area kids complained of brutal treatment when they were caught trespassing after hours. These incidents were hushed up, as were a number of disappearances of Mall employees who worked late. And there was the razor-wire fence on the outskirts of the mall's farthest borders, which angled inward, as if to keep someone from climbing over the fence from inside.

The most visible anomaly, however, the one nobody in town would ever mention out loud, were the delivery doors built into the foundation of the Mall that were never used for deliveries. They were enormous, made of steel and concrete, like something designed to withstand a nuclear blast. They never opened, at least not when anyone was around to see it. If anyone in town had any idea where those doors led, they would have been glad.

GRAVES ENTERED THE MALL just as the last of the shoppers were leaving. The movie theater would stay open for a few more hours, and so would the Hooters, but the rest of the place was locked down tight.

He made his way to an elevator in the food court, marked by a somewhat disturbing mural on the adjacent wall. It was supposed to depict the brotherhood of mankind as well as the local Native American creation myths, but nobody who saw it ever had any warm and happy feelings. Instead, it seemed like a giant black bird was looming over a group of helpless children, ready to carry them off to feed some squirming nest of its young.

Graves put his thumb against a keycard reader below the button panel, like the ones used in hotels for penthouse access. If anybody else touched it, that's all it was. But behind the plastic face, a special DNA-encoded scanner sent a signal to an internal computer. The elevator began its descent, leaving the surface far behind.

Half a mile into the earth, the doors opened again and Graves walked out into the place where the Shadow Company birthed its nightmares: the Black Site.

He was home.

THERE WERE SIX LEVELS below the Mall, the largest being Level Five, which contained the cells. There were over a thousand in all, based on the supermax model of federal correctional facilities. Each cell was fitted with a sink, toilet, timer-controlled shower and poured concrete bed.

The Site was nowhere near full capacity. The staff was basically a skeleton crew now. Most of the lab personnel were gone, and it didn't take many people to handle the prisoners. Only ninety-four Shadow Company operatives, including Bell and Book, were there at the moment.

Graves would have liked to fill each cell, but he was out of time. It wasn't as easy as some civilians thought, making someone vanish from the real world. This was where the disappeared sank down, out of sight and out of mind, each one meticulously scrubbed from all records above-ground, until they existed only in the memories of the few people who'd loved them.

Along with terrorists and enemy combatants plucked from the battle-fields in Iraq and Afghanistan, Graves collected dissidents of all stripes from within the U.S. He didn't hold any political prejudices. His cells held militia members filled with hate and rage for the New World Order, firebombers who used animal rights as an outlet for pyromaniac fetishes, college students who wore the wrong T-shirt to a campaign rally, hitch-hikers who wandered too close to classified airfields, and people who were unlucky enough to catch a glimpse of the Shadow Company in action.

He had 532 prisoners now. That would have to be enough.

Correction: 533 prisoners.

ZACH'S WORLD SLOWLY filtered back in around the edges. He could feel the concrete floor under his cheek, the cold metal of a drain touch-ing his forehead.

His eyes snapped fully open. There was no light.

He tried to sit up, and his head sloshed like a water balloon. He got a hand out in time to keep from planting his face back on the floor.

He closed his eyes as pain radiated from the swollen lump at the crown of his head. Bell. Bell had hit him. He was concussed. He didn't know how badly, but it wasn't good.

He closed his eyes and felt the world spinning. He opened them. Didn't help. There was no light.

Lost time. Maybe passed out again. He was against a wall now. He got his feet under him, pushed himself up to a standing position. His head still hurt, but the spinning had stopped.

The air was cold and sterile. Something used-up and dead about it.

The overhead light clicked on, and Zach blinked until he could see.

The cell was a standard four-by-eight block, with a steel toilet and a cot built into the wall. There was a door with two slots; one for trays of food, and another for someone in the corridor to check inside.

It took Zach a moment to realize the viewing slot was open and he was being watched.

He cursed, jumped and nearly fell down as his head started spinning again.

He heard Graves laugh.

"'A rag and a bone and a hank of hair, but the fool he called her his lady fair . . .'" Graves recited in a kind of singsong. "No need to be embarrassed, Barrows. Bell is a professional. You barely qualify for the amateur rankings."

Zach was too hurt and too tired for banter. "Cade is going to kill you," he said flatly.

"He tried. Didn't take," Graves said. "You're all alone down here. No one is coming to save you."

"I've heard something like that before. You know what happened? Cade found me. He'll find you, too."

"You know, I almost hope he does," Graves said, and set off down the corridor, leaving Zach alone.

TWENTY-EIGHT

Memorandum for: Mr. Tolson (FILE ONLY)
From: John Edgar Hoover, Director
Subject: The so-called "Cross-Country Killings"

I notice another report in the sensational press of bodies found alongside the road. I assume that some of the descriptions are hyperbole, given the source. (What else can one expect of a paper that boasts "crime scene photos—IN FULL COLOR," and headlines such as "Strangled in Silk!") However, some of the details lead me to believe this is part of the vendetta of Mr. Cade. For starters, the three men found—in various bits and pieces—were all contractors known to be on the payroll of our sometime friends and constant nuisances at the CIA. For another, all were seen in New Orleans and Dallas in recent months. I shouldn't have to tell you what this implies. Nor should I have to tell you what this might mean if it should find purchase in the minds of someone outside the tabloid press.

And yet, I find myself telling you. Get a leash on this, Clyde. I don't want to see another word in the press.

—United States Department of Justice Memorandum, 5:53 P.M.,
  December 12, 1963 (classified)

CAIRO, EGYPT

C ade walked into the bar, located in the lobby of a hotel that catered entirely to tourists. The designers wanted a spot where
guests would be comfortable. The menu offered burgers, fries
and Miller Lite. There were movie posters and old license plates on the
walls. The air-conditioning was kept to a frosty sixty-eight degrees, and
the TV screens showed nothing but football and old sitcoms. The end result could have been airlifted directly out of a suburban mall and plunked
down in Egypt.

Cade stood out. He'd needed clothes to seek out his contact, and he
let Tania do the shopping. As a result, he was dressed in an Armani suit.
It wasn't his usual off-the-rack poly-wool blend, but he had to admit it
fit very well.

The man Cade was looking for, in contrast, seemed to be right at
home. He sat at the bar, drinking a beer and eating a plate of buffalo
wings that glowed neon-red with hot sauce.

He belched and wiped his hands on a napkin as Cade sat down on
the next stool.

Cade knew he could not contact the White House—Prador was compromised. He'd tried calling Zach, but there was no answer. He threw
his own phone into the ocean. If anyone tracked its GPS chip, it was on
the seabed, where Cade was supposed to be.

Without Zach, he had no direct way of reaching the president. And
he was stranded half a world away from the U.S.

It was his own fault. He'd only been reacting since this started. Graves
had planned, thought tactically and improvised. Cade had come into the
game late, but that was no excuse for playing like such an amateur. Now
he was forced to rely on his own networks and resources.

In this corner of the world, this man was his only option.

He certainly didn't look like the World's Greatest Secret Agent. And in truth, those days were long past.

His once hard jawline was gone, replaced by a double chin. His hair was combed over a bald spot that refused to hide. And his days of filling an Armani tux were gone; now his belly slopped over the waist of his Dockers stain-resistant pants.

Years ago, he had worked the back alleys of global politics, making sure the Cold War stayed perfectly frigid. He discovered plots that never made the news: secret space missions, vanishing islands, strange weapons and deadly assassins with steel teeth. With that much time in the dark, he soon found the same nightmares Cade was sworn to fight. They compared notes, traded information and even saved each other from time to time.

As he got older, he was moved to the farthest outposts of the American empire. His set of skills was considered obsolete, and the files of his missions were forgotten or shredded. As far as the current heads of the world's intelligence services were concerned, he was just another bureaucrat in a sweltering third-world country. That suited him just fine. A spy doesn't live long if he draws attention to himself.

Cade could never be certain where his loyalties actually were—or if he even had any. But he was unquestionably the very best at his job, once upon a time.

And more important, he owed Cade a favor.

"Cade," he said. "How's Griff doing?"

"Dead. I need something."

"You're even more sociable than I remembered."

"I'm pressed for time."

He took a swig of his beer and motioned the bartender for another. "The world ending, forces of evil on the march, doomsday clock running down to zero? That sort of thing?"

"Something like that. What am I calling you these days?"

"Flint," he said, and grinned. "I'd offer to buy you a drink, but I don't think they carry your brand."

Cade regarded him carefully. "You're not being very discreet."

"Nobody cares anymore, Cade. Or hadn't you noticed?" The bartender, a young man with a patchy beard and a surly look, brought over another beer, bright yellow in a frosted glass. "Take Nawaz here. He knows I'm just another fat American bastard sitting in a country where I don't belong. Isn't that right, Nawaz?"

The bartender curled his lip at Flint, then walked to the other side of the bar.

"See? He doesn't care. Back when he started, Nawaz spent every day eavesdropping on conversations, hoping to have something to report back to the Mukhabarat."

Nawaz barely flinched at the mention of the Egyptian Secret Service.

"Now he daydreams about all the ways he'd like to violate the waitresses and wishes they would show the soccer matches on the screens here. Not going to happen, Nawaz. It ain't football if you don't wear a helmet. And to top it all off, he can't even make a decent martini."

Nawaz kept his back to them.

"You see what I'm talking about? It's easy to keep secrets when nobody gives a damn."

"You know why I'm here."

"I have an inkling," he said. "You threw quite a party on that boat."

"It was unavoidable. It's not like Innsmouth. It's contagious this time."

Flint's eyes sharpened.

"How contagious?"

"It spreads in the bites and the blood. Transformation begins immediately."

Flint thought about the implications. For an instant, Cade saw the cold warrior emerge from his doughy features again. In that moment, he imagined he could see Flint struggle with the urge to rise from his bar stool and ride into action.

But the moment passed. Flint took another drink and turned to watch the game on the nearest screen.

"So what do you want from me? I told you about the bodies in Uganda. I kept you in the loop. But that's all I know."

"I don't need any more information," Cade said. "I know who's behind it. A man called Graves—"

Flint turned at the name. "Graves?"

"You know him?"

"Same church. Different denomination."

"He's on his way to the source of the contagion now, a black site. I don't know where."

"I don't mess with the Company. Not anymore."

"I need an exact location and transport. That's all."

"That's all? You know what will happen to me if they find out I not only gave you the address, I drove you to the front door?"

Flint pretended to consider it, but Cade knew he'd already decided. He simply had to make it look good for anyone watching.

"Fine," he said. "But you do something for me."

"What?"

Flint checked his watch. "In a few minutes, a hit squad, tipped off by Nawaz, will enter the bar and spray everyone down with automatic weapons. In turn, they are supposed to be killed by Egyptian security forces. Islamic militants will be blamed. But it's all a cover for the real target: me."

"You said no one cared anymore."

"Sometimes they get nostalgic. Take care of them and I'll arrange your ride."

"You're sure about this?"

"Damn well better be. I told Nawaz to make the call an hour ago."

Cade looked at the bartender, who smirked.

"He's coming along nicely, don't you think?" Flint said.

"You must be very proud," Cade said. He noticed the three men enter the bar, wearing what they thought were the outfits of typical college students. They had to wear jackets over their weapons, short, stubby machine pistols that bulged under their arms.

They were sweating. Nervous. Trying to work up the courage to open fire on a room of unarmed civilians.

Cade's fangs emerged. He pulled them back with effort. Too many witnesses. This had to be handled quietly.

"Back in a moment," Cade said.

Faster than the eye could follow, he was across the room, standing behind the men.

Instantly his whole face changed, turning into a happy, gassy balloon inflated by a five-beer drunk.

He clapped his arms around all three men, hanging on them and laughing, as if hugging old friends.

The two on the outside froze. They were the followers, and they didn't know what to do. The first hit man was their leader, and Cade had pinned him between the other two, unable to move.

Cade used their moment of hesitation to grip their necks, right at the base of the skull. He popped their vertebrae cleanly in two, severing their spinal cords from their brain stems. Their lives went as quietly as a lamp unplugged from the wall.

The first hit man turned his face to Cade, struggling against the press of the bodies. He didn't know what was happening, but he opened his mouth to shout something as he struggled to get to his gun.

Cade still had to hold the other two men up, as if they were all drunk and stumbling together. He had several options. But as it turned out, he didn't need to use any of them.

Tania appeared in front of them, squealing with sorority-girl glee, and rushed to join the embrace. Along the way, she drove her hand into the hit man's sternum, sending shards of bone into his heart and lungs.

His face grew purple and his eyes grew panicked. He tried to get something out of his mouth, but he was too busy drowning internally on his own blood.

Tania and Cade, meanwhile, spun all three of the bodies out toward the hallway again, walking arm-in-arm like old friends.

"I had him," Cade said.

Tania shrugged. "Sure you did, dear."

If anyone looked, Nawaz was there, by their side, to make it appear as if customers were being escorted by the hotel staff.

Cade left Tania with the corpses in the meat locker. He didn't want to watch her feed. He returned to Flint.

Flint had a freshly poured beer in front of him.

"You haven't lost your touch," Flint said.

"You either."

"You have a suspicious mind, Cade," Flint said, lighting a cigarette. "Just so I can prepare for the fallout. How bad is this going to be?"

"Do you remember 1963?"

Flint didn't say anything. Just gulped what remained of his beer, then closed his eyes tight, as if trying not to see whatever memories Cade had evoked.

The building was largely deserted when Cade entered. Most of the employees had gone home. But not the man who was—for a few more days, anyway—their leader.

Cade walked into the office without knocking. The attorney general did not seem to notice him. He was holding one of his brother's suit jackets, as he often did these days. He stared into space, looking at nothing.

Cade waited. The AG noticed him a moment later, jumping slightly in his seat.

He covered it well. "Cade," he said. "Thank you for coming. How goes it?"

"It's over."

The AG appeared to shift gears in his mind. He forgot, like most people did, that Cade's personality didn't allow for many social graces.

"What do you mean, over? I thought—"

"I've tracked each man as far as possible. It ends with anonymous notes from unknown superiors. Money left in dead drops. A cutout system. I cannot go any further."

"What about the last men—they wouldn't talk?"

"They talked. They had nothing to say."

The AG took a cigar from a desk drawer—another habit of his brother's that he'd picked up since Dallas. He chewed it for a moment, then lit it. "You believed them?"

"It doesn't matter what I believe," Cade said. "I can't find the men who gave the order to murder your brother. I've failed."

The AG shook his head. "No, you haven't. You went as far as you could from the bottom up. If anyone failed, it was me. I never should have used them."

Cade usually never questioned his orders, or the people who gave them. But he wanted to know. "Used who?"

Pain filled the man's face. "There are levels of government even you don't know about, Cade. There are men in our intelligence services who will do—well, they will do things—"

"The jobs I wouldn't," Cade finished for him.

"Yes," he said. "Sometimes, we need someone willing to cross the lines you won't."

"Those lines were drawn for me."

"All the more reason to have someone with a little more flexibility on the team."

"And you believe these men were behind the killing of your brother?"

The AG gave him a sad grin. "I can't prove it."

Cade didn't move, but the AG felt the whole room shift along with Cade's attitude. His anger was a thing that seemed to join them in the office.

"Give me their names."

The AG looked at Cade calmly. "No," he said. "I can't prove anything. And I don't want to dig this up again. The body's practically still warm."

Cade understood. The AG and his brother had things to hide.

"They shouldn't get away with this," Cade said.

The AG rose from his chair.

"They won't. I just need to play this a bit smarter next time. Put the lessons I've learned here to use, when I get back."

Cade was puzzled. The AG's resignation to run for the Senate was well known. "Back?"

"To the White House, Cade," the AG said. "You got as far as you could, working from the bottom. I fully intend to finish the job—from the top down."

There it was. The AG planned to run for president someday. And whatever dealings led to the assassination—whatever secret plots that Cade was not privy to—he didn't want those spilling out. Not just for his brother. But for his own chances as well.

Cade felt something almost like disappointment.

The attorney general stubbed out his cigar and put on his jacket. Then he folded his brother's over his arm and carried it with him to the exit.

"See you in the Oval Office, Cade. I'm sure you'll still be around."

Cade didn't say anything. He had no gift to see the future. But he was certain he would never see the man again.

TWENTY-NINE

We've long theorized that the purpose of occult ritual is to reprogram the human brain. It's been demonstrated that new thoughts and new ideas actually create new neural pathways in the brain. The chanting, sleep-deprivation, music, visual and other stimuli of the occult ritual—especially as it's repeated, over and over—create a similar effect, until the brain conforms to the purpose of the ritual. In one sentence: the rituals reinforce certain thoughts until the brain is capable of thinking only those thoughts.

—Dr. William Kavanaugh, Sanction V research group

After he left Zach, Graves walked a few dozen yards and turned to the doors of the main lab. This was the heart of the Site, dead-center in the middle of Level Five, with prisoners located in spokes of cells radiating outward. Everything in Level Six below was maintenance or utilities.

There were good, logistical reasons to keep the main laboratory so close to the cells. During the initial development phase, the Company's scientists and technicians went through test subjects at the rate of six or seven a day, and it was easier to cart them a short distance from their cells.

But there were other, less rational reasons. Designs for the Black Site came from both government blueprints and old translations of even older texts. There were ley lines to be considered, the position of the stars and the rituals of sacrifice.

Graves knew better than to question these touches. After a while, he began to think of them as another section of the building codes, like occult OSHA regulations.

He pressed his thumb to another encrypted lock, and heavy bolts thudded back. The steel-plated doors moved steadily, powered by self-contained hydraulics. Even in the midst of a total power outage, the doors would still operate. Graves hadn't been in charge of the witchier sections of the Site's design, but he planned for every other possible contingency.

He walked inside the long bays and lab tables of what he had come to think of as the Hatchery. A year ago, even six months, the place would have been crawling with mad scientists, disgraced biochemists, rogue theorists of every discipline. The Company had a small battalion of men and women willing to test the boundaries of science and sanity, who found the ethical constraints of academic and corporate R&D too confining. They needed a place to work, unlimited budgets and human test subjects. The Company was glad to supply all of these in exchange for everything they could produce.

Today, however, the Hatchery more or less ran itself. The process was fully automated, and only one man, a technician, was necessary to watch it work.

He had his feet on his desk, reading a white paper filled with molecular equations. He didn't bother to get up.

"Colonel," he said.

"Everything going smoothly?" Graves asked. "Anything I should know about?"

"Production is right on track. Quiet as babies on NyQuil."

"You delivered the supplement to the last meal?"

The technician nodded, but now he looked a little nervous. "I hope the cells hold," he said. "They're going to be hungry."

"You let me worry about that," Graves said to the technician. Then he turned and fired a shot from his pistol, blowing the man's face through the back of his head.

For a second, the technician's lifeless body teetered in his desk chair. Then gravity won and he fell over backward, legs comically up in the air for a moment before he hit the floor.

Graves didn't think of this as a cruel betrayal. He barely thought about it at all. As far as he was concerned, everyone in here was going to die, sooner or later.

In this case, sooner was better.

THE TRAY SAT ON the floor of Zach's cell. Someone had shoved it through the lower slot. Nutraloaf: dried potatoes, flour, maybe some cheese or milk mixed in, all baked to a hardened brick. Standard prison food.

Zach had seen it before, but never tasted it. He didn't think today was going to be the day that changed.

He heard a hissing noise from the next cell. He started, then realized the noise was human. Someone was trying to get his attention.

Zach scooted over to the slot and listened.

"Don't eat it," a voice warned from the next cell. The tones were cultured, almost British.

"Wasn't planning on it," Zach said.

"They have put something in the food. I heard them talking about it. The guards."

"They told you about it?"

A slight chuckle. "Not intentionally. I am on a hunger strike. They were preparing food to force down my nose through a tube, when one told the other they still needed to get the supplement. I knew what that meant. They left hours ago."

"Maybe they're busy," Zach said, hoping that an assault by a pissed-off vampire was the cause of the delay. "What's in the food?"

"The blood of demons. I've seen them. Serpents. The guards take men away and turn them into snakes."

"Yeah. I caught the live act."

The prisoner's voice lost some of its certainty for the first time. "What?"

"Never mind. Is it just you and me here?"

"You're the first person I've heard since they moved me here. The others are all on a different cell block. This corridor is reserved for the disciplinary problems. The ones who don't obey."

"That's just you and me?"

"Most people don't live long enough to disobey."

"Super. What's your name?"

"It doesn't really matter now, does it?"

"Why would you say that?"

"We are both going to die. Unless we are already dead, and this is Hell."

Zach sighed. "That's the spirit."

THIRTY

1925—Red Hook, New York—Authorities investigate a series of
child disappearances and murders. The crimes stop suddenly
after an old lodge building is demolished.

—BRIEFING BOOK: CODE NAME: NIGHTMARE PET

56,000 Feet Above the Atlantic Ocean

The jet engines were a constant, comforting thrum as the aircraft
cruised at a fraction over Mach 2.

Cade had not quite believed it until he'd seen it, but decided
it made perfect sense. Who else but the top agent of the Space Age would
have access to this craft, sitting in a private hangar, waiting for a chance
to fly again?

The Concorde he and Tania now rode in was supposed to be decom-
missioned like the others of its kind, a casualty of the world economy
and higher fuel prices. But Flint couldn't let it go. It represented something grander than a fast airplane to him. It was a piece of a time when
a ninety-minute commute from New York to Paris was supposed to be
a regular occurrence.

Flint took the plane so many times he was finally able to convince his agency to buy one out of confiscated funds. It came in handy when he had to haul large weapons across the world. And it fit his lifestyle: champagne on every flight, nineteen-year-old stewardesses in microskirts serving New York steak grilled medium rare, the end of the world waiting on arrival. When Flint was put out to pasture, he managed to keep the jet and all the memories it contained from his glory days.

But for once, Cade didn't mind the human tendency toward nostalgia. Not when it was going to get him to the Black Site an hour after sundown, local time.

Tania wasn't complaining either. Cade recalled that the Concorde would have been the height of cool when she was human. She seemed to be enjoying it. She held a flute of champagne, even though she couldn't drink it.

"Can we keep this, Nathaniel?" she said. "It's better than the cattle car Zach provided."

Cade looked at her.

"Oops," she said, not at all convincingly. "I might have spilled a secret. What a terrible spy I am."

"Zach recruited you to backstop me."

"Surprised?"

"Not by him. By you. You're not bound like I am."

"I'm working as an independent operator. Your boy Zachary decided it might be a good idea to have another vampire on the job, just in case. Turned out he was right, wasn't he?"

"Do you really think this is the way we can be together? You are still a killer. I have my duty. Eventually—"

"Not everything is about you," she sniffed. "I thought it might be interesting to see the world from your position for a while. I get bored easily." She tossed the champagne to the floor. "Speaking of which. We have nearly five hours left."

Cade's lip curled slightly. "I think there's a movie."

"*The Towering Inferno*," she said. "Saw it. In the theater. There is, however, a bed in the back."

"I saw. I believe he used it to relieve tension between missions."

She stood and, surprisingly, took his hand. It was an uncharacteristically tender gesture. He grasped her fingers, feeling the cool, bloodless skin.

He let her lead him back down the aisle.

"This won't end well," he warned her.

"Nothing ever does," she said.

THE CONCORDE LANDED at Offutt Air Force Base, where Flint still had a few contacts from the old days in the Strategic Air Command. The plane was quickly hidden, and an old Sikorsky MH-53J was made available to ferry them back the hundred and fifty miles they'd overshot Liberty.

It was already well past sunset. Cade was growing anxious, although no human would have seen it.

Tania, standing by him in the open bay of the helicopter, felt like slapping him.

He showed far too much worry about his humans. It really left no question about where his loyalty would be, if—no, *when*—it came down to her or them.

She wondered if this would work, or if she should just cut her losses now.

She was not doing this just to be close to him. Maybe it started that way, although she had trouble admitting that. But there were other ways to be near Cade, and despite what he said, he wanted to be with her. They would have found each other. Tania did not need Zach's assistance. She didn't have to be a recruit. She certainly didn't have to help Cade on his pointless missions.

Now, however, she had to know: Why did he do this? What drove him? It wasn't just the oath. She was sure of it. What was inside him that was so hollow inside her?

Tania believed she might glimpse his secret if she only stayed close enough. She could learn the source of his strength. Once she knew that, she could decide whether or not to stay with him, willingly, as an equal— or whether to use it to kill him before he could kill her.

Every relationship has its trade-offs, she thought again.

She looked at Cade, practically on point, leaning into the wind, ready to fight.

It stirred something strong and unusual. She couldn't name what he evoked in her, not anymore. When it gripped her, she could almost remember what it was to feel warm.

THIRTY-ONE

I know this will cause you some embarrassment, and for that I must apologize, but I cannot remain any longer. Ghastly things are afoot and I fear I shall be caught up in the wrath of your president's bloodhound, if not by the other hounds on my trail. Perhaps, for my sins, I'm to be denied any peace or the golden evening of my years. But you and I know that it is always for the greater good.

Yours,
Kim

—Intercepted letter from Kim Philby to CIA head of
counterintelligence, 1963, the year of Philby's
defection to the Soviet Union (classified)

LIBERTY, IOWA

The management company that ran Liberty Mall had a problem: as the recession dragged on, people were choosing to spend their money on things like mortgage payments and heat rather than high-end TemperFoam pillows. That left a lot of inventory on the shelves, which was even more useless to the sellers than it was to the buyers. They had to make room for the shiny new stuff coming for the holiday season, and their storerooms were still clogged with leftovers from the spring lines. People visited the Mall, but they weren't buying anything. The place was turning into a museum, or worse, a city park. People even brought their own lunches.

The managers held a meeting with representatives of all the stores, including execs from the national chains that anchored the Mall. They offered an idea that would increase foot traffic and clear out the surplus: a one-day sale, involving every store and restaurant, the biggest sale in America for the biggest mall in America. (Sure, sure, Liberty wasn't exactly the biggest mall, but that was just a detail.)

The retailers were skeptical. The whole thing smelled a little desperate, like the reek of the items laid out on blankets at a swap meet. And the discounts being suggested—fifty percent in most cases—those were brutal. Even kids in the third world had to be paid something to make this stuff.

Liberty's managers held firm. They needed a big event before Thanksgiving, or they were looking at reducing the Mall's hours. The food courts, the concession stands, the movie theater, the kiddie rides—the places that depended on visitor numbers—were all running in the red, or close to it.

The retailers balked again, and the managers brought out the secret weapon. They'd been covertly surveying in-store sales, by monitoring the high-speed fiber-optic lines in and out of the Mall. They'd found a disheartening twenty-nine percent of credit-card purchases were being declined at the registers. People weren't just running out of cash; they were out of credit, too. If the stores didn't do something drastic, they'd be looking at a ghost mall, and nobody wanted that.

Faced with the hard truth (after the predictable sputtering about privacy and corporate secrets), the retailers caved. One day only. An event, never to be repeated, that would break all sales records. They could sell that to their shareholders. The doors would open early, at midnight on November 1. People would be encouraged to camp out in the parking lot. There would be prizes, TV coverage, T-shirts.

It would all kick off the night of Halloween: a one-time-only "Great Monster Sale."

It worked better than even the Mall's managers hoped. Shoppers lined up outside the Mall's main entrance days in advance. Some fights had even broken out. News copters flew overhead like flies above a corpse, shooting endless footage of the crowds, waiting on the potential riot.

For the most part, however, people were cheerful. Tourists came from as far away as Japan. The parking lot was full of tents and RVs and cars. Three of the surviving members of Night Ranger played their hits and assorted oldies from an outdoor stage.

Kids ran around in Halloween costumes. Mall employees handed out candy while their parents drank cider and ate doughnuts. There was a kind of state-fair feeling in the air.

CADE AND TANIA walked among the throngs of people gathered at Liberty Mall. In his Armani suit, Cade stood out more than she did. Several people complimented her on her "really cool" and "sexy" vampire costume.

"See?" she said to Cade. "*I* look like a real vampire."

"Yeah, like that chick in *Underworld*," one girl, maybe fifteen, said to her. "You know, maybe a little bigger than her, but . . ."

Cade held Tania's hand tightly, to keep her from punching it through the girl's skull.

"Enough," he said. "We need a way in."

He broke through the lines of people along one side of the Mall.

"Hey," someone protested. "End of the line is back there, pal." Others around him joined in, secure in the strength of numbers and the rules.

Cade gave them a hard look, and suddenly, no one was interested in proper etiquette. They all turned back to the apple-bobbing stall.

"Livestock," Tania said. "Would you mind if I stopped for a quick—"

"Yes." Cade pointed. "Look over there."

She focused her vision on a ramp near the back of the Mall. Its doors were not large—no bigger than the rear of a semi truck—but they were heavy.

In front of them stood two mall cops. At least, they wore the uniforms of mall cops. But everything else about them—their stance, their heavy muscles, shaved heads, and most of all, the pistols on their belts—advertised who they really were.

Archer/Andrews.

No one from the Mall's celebration was anywhere near them. It was as if the civilians had been trained not to see them, like a dog given beatings every time it even came near the dinner table.

If Graves had his men in front of the doors, it had to be the way inside.

TANIA MADE THE FIRST APPROACH. Her leather jacket was zipped down almost to her navel, offering the guards a distracting view.

Neither of them fell for it. They put their hands on their guns and warned her away from a safe distance. "Back away now," they said, low and mean. "You won't get a second warning, honey."

"Oh for crap's sake," Tania said. "I told you this was stupid."

Neither man knew whom she was talking to.

Cade reached from behind and snapped their necks, so fast it appeared nearly simultaneous.

They were deep enough in the shadows that no one had noticed at the main celebration. Cade checked both men for keys and found none.

He examined the door. There was a palm reader built into the side of

the wall. He put one of the guard's hands on it, then the other, and repeated the process with the other body.

Deactivated.

Cade noticed the metal view-slot. It was eye level and welded into the
shutter of the door. It could be pulled back to look outside, or to fire a
weapon.

He put his ear to the thick metal and listened. He could hear them.
Two sentries, still at their post. Talking fast. The words were indistinct.
But they were clearly nervous.

Tania was still messing with her jacket. "You think I should open
it more?"

He looked at the corpses again. "I know how we're getting inside."

He sized them up by height and picked up the one who was closer.

He stripped the corpse of its fatigues, and then exchanged his suit
with the cadaver's.

"That's never going to work," Tania said.

Cade didn't reply.

Once he was dressed, he leaned down and gripped the corpse by the
hair. He slid his thumbnail around the dead mercenary's face, starting
at the hairline, carefully tracing a line to the ears, the jawline and down
the chin, all the way around again.

Thin red drops trickled out from the skin, but not much. Corpses
don't bleed; they leak. Cade was able to resist the sweet stink of the fresh
human blood.

He reached in with his fingers, under the cut he'd made in the forehead. He pulled hard and tore the dead man's face clean off.

He set the flap of skin aside. The lips and nose looked deflated without muscle and bone under them.

Cade steeled himself for the next step. He wasn't immune to pain.

And this was going to hurt.

He put his thumbnail to his own skin, right where the forehead met the hairline, and pressed down. Hard.

Even Tania was a little disturbed at what he did next.

"Ah. Yeah, okay," she conceded. "That might do it."

CADE POUNDED ON THE DOOR. A voice buzzed through the intercom. "What?"

He pounded again and gave an unintelligible bellow of pain.

The view slot slid open. The barrel of a pistol pointed out first. Then a pair of eyes looked at Cade.

"Kemper? What the hell, man?"

Cade had his hand to his nose. That never looked quite right, despite his vampire body's vessels and nerves worming their way into the dead skin, colonizing it and making it their own. The mottled bruising, the pallor—all that worked in Cade's favor. He looked—or rather, Kemper looked—like he'd just been on the losing end of a fight.

Eventually, the skinned face would mold and conform to Cade's features and he would look like himself again. But that would take at least an hour. Until then, he was Kemper, at least from the chin to his hair.

Cade nodded and coughed and hacked, almost bent over. He had no real idea how Kemper had moved when alive. Pretending to be injured would mask that deficit long enough to get him past the door.

He hoped.

"Jesus, man, hold tight, we're gonna come get you," the voice on the speaker said.

Cade nodded again and slumped down a little farther. Before the speaker cut off, he heard an argument begin:

"We can't open this door. Are you crazy?"

"Fuck that, man, I'm not leaving him—"

Cade wondered who'd prevail. He got his answer within seconds. With a heavy thud, the door's bolts slid free and the door swung open.

One of the guards put out a hand to Cade and helped him up.

"You fucking idiot," his companion said while pressing a button to close the door again.

"Shut up," the first guard snapped back. "You're okay, Kemper, you're going to be—Jesus Christ!"

Cade straightened up. The guards could see his face now. By their reactions, he assumed it wasn't pretty.

His fist darted out twice, knocking them both cold.

He didn't bother killing them, but it was no real mercy.

He hit the button again and Tania came inside, licking blood off her teeth.

He knew she would take the two guards next, and didn't really care. No one was getting out of here alive, with one exception:

Zach.

AFTER A WHILE, Zach heard the other prisoner talking again.

"What?"

"I said this can't be Hell."

"Why not?"

"Because I did my duty. I should be in Heaven."

"Your duty?"

"I helped kill Americans. Many of them. And other infidels, of course."

The mild tone and the cultured inflection of the man's words somehow made them that much worse.

"You did what?"

"I see no reason to lie. I had a background in finance. I facilitated the flow of arms, arranged credit, disbursed cash to the families of the warriors. I directed money to people who used it to buy bombs. To kill Americans. I've seen the videos. The bombs really are quite effective. Metal ball bearings are packed into bricks of C-4 or dynamite, and wired to a single trigger. The ball bearings shoot outward, tearing open flesh, crushing bone—"

"Yeah. I've seen it," Zach said. "So you're just another death-to-America asshole. Color me impressed. Takes a real man to pay a poor Palestinian kid to splatter himself."

"I asked to become a martyr. I was refused. My talents were better suited to moving the money."

"How lucky for you. And what do you get out of this? You really believe you're going to God's Champagne Lounge with free lap-dances for eternity?"

There was no answer. Zach thought the prisoner had given up talking, then: "Do you have children?"

"Why? You want to threaten them, too?"

The prisoner spoke again, his voice far away.

"Imagine seeing your only daughter running toward you from your front door. She just learned to walk a month ago, and now she's running. You've been out all day, looking for work. You were a banker before. Now you're lucky to get paid for moving concrete rubble around.

"You know she's supposed to stay inside. So does her mother. It's not safe. Your neighborhood was once filled with children playing in the streets. But now, people huddle in their homes as the militias fight for each city block. You know you should scold her and tell her to run back the way she came.

"But you can't stay mad at her. She only just got her front teeth, and she's smiling at you. This is what makes your whole day worthwhile. This is the air you breathe and the ground beneath your feet. She has her arms out for you to lift her.

"And then the bullets hit her. You can see the first one. It nearly severs her head from her body. You can't help remembering how fragile her neck was in your hands after she was born, how carefully you had to cradle her. It took so long for her to be able to raise her head on her own.

"And in an instant, all that care and effort are gone. Shredded. Turned into nothing but bone and meat.

"Your only daughter. And you are still standing there, your arms out for her. Because even though you just saw it, you're still hoping she will somehow reach you. That you will somehow be able to shield her. To protect her.

"But you've already failed.

"That's when the Americans come and tackle you to the ground. And after you have been bound and gagged, after you have been jailed and kicked and beaten, a man will come to you. And he will tell you about bad intel and an unfriendly quarter and stray bullets. He will tell you it was unfortunate. He will tell you she was collateral damage, the inevitable cost of war. He will tell you all of that, and he will tell you they are sorry. But he will never tell you why he is in your country in the first place. And he will never be sorry enough."

The prisoner went quiet again.

"You think killing people will get you your daughter back?" Zach asked.

"No," the prisoner said. "But perhaps, if I kill enough of you, I will get to see her again."

"Maybe," Zach said. "And maybe you belong in Hell."

They didn't talk after that.

THIRTY-TWO

1928—Dunwich, Massachusetts—An unknown creature destroyed several homes and killed or injured more than a dozen people before being killed itself by a group of scholars from neighboring Miskatonic University. Possibly related to the Innsmouth incident.

—BRIEFING BOOK: CODE NAME: NIGHTMARE PET

They must have been digging for months, Cade thought.

The door led down a long vehicle ramp. At the bottom, it opened into the entry hall of the Black Site, where vehicles sat in a motor pool. There were cars, Humvees and even an armored personnel carrier. Archer/Andrews could overthrow a city with the ordnance stored in the garage.

At the center of the wide, open space was an elevator shaft and platform large enough for the vehicles. It ran on rails that went straight down into the Site. Smaller, passenger elevators lined another central wall. At both ends, doors led to stairwells.

Even a secret prison had to respect fire safety, it seemed.

Inside, the Site seemed more like a hospital than a jail. The floors were painted with the same slick gray coating used in garages all over America. The walls were spotless arctic white under the glare of the fluorescent panels above.

A human being might be fooled into thinking it was sterile. But not Cade. He could smell the truth under the disinfectant in the air: sweat thick with adrenaline and fear; the sweeter odor of ketosis as starving bodies began to eat themselves; the acrid burn of tear gas and pepper spray; the roast-pork scent of high voltage applied to human flesh; underlying it all, the base notes of shit and piss and puke and blood.

His mouth would have watered at the slaughterhouse odors, if not for the stink of waste.

Cade knew about torture. He was not so much of a hypocrite as to claim moral superiority over those who did it. But he was always amused at the attempts to minimize it. Cade was a horror; he knew it. He supposed the same involuntary recoil humans felt when they saw him caused them to flinch from what they did to one another.

The smell of shit, for example. He knew it came from the deliberate efforts to make the prisoners here lose control of their bowels. Even Cade, who hadn't shat or pissed for over a century, knew that it was utter humiliation. It reduced a man to an infantile state, with the full adult knowledge of how low he had fallen into waste and filth and foulness. It took the most basic notions of self-control and literally turned them into shit.

And this was considered one of the more humane methods of interrogation.

Cade wondered why they didn't just kill the prisoners. For some reason, that was going too far. He supposed that was ironic. Honestly, he wasn't really sure what the term meant anymore.

A COLOR-CODED MAP BY the elevators marked different routes through the facility.

The main shaft drove straight down, through six levels radiating outward. Level Five appeared to be the cells; it was the largest. The staircases looped around the whole facility, touching all ends of all levels. Looking at the map too long might induce a migraine in a human, Cade thought. The Site looked like a kinked DNA helix bulging with mutations.

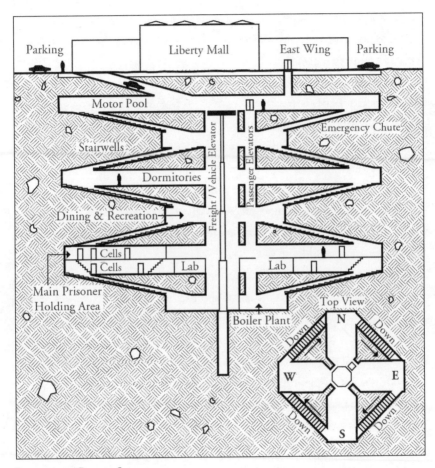

LAYOUT OF BLACK SITE

He'd have to find Graves and get Zach's location from him.

He turned to Tania and explained what he needed from her while he was looking for Zach. She was less than thrilled at the division of labor.

"It's a prison," she whined. "All that caged stock, dizzy with panic and fear. You can't ask me to pass that up."

"You've had plenty to eat."

"Is that a crack about my weight?"

Give me strength, Cade thought silently. Out loud, he said, "I would take it as a personal favor."

She thought it over. "I do like the idea of you being in my debt. I even know what I want."

"This isn't a negotiation."

"You don't tell Zach you know about my deal."

"Why not?"

"Not your concern. Take it or leave it."

Cade nodded and turned to go on his own errand.

"Promise you'll save at least a couple for me," she said to his back.

He didn't respond.

"No fun at all," she said, but he heard her walk in the opposite direction. Cade had to hope she'd do as she was told.

IT WAS, SURPRISINGLY, no trouble at all to find Graves. He was one level down, sitting calmly at a desk in an office. He shuffled paper as if he were preparing a tax return.

"Where is he?" Cade said.

If Graves was surprised at Cade's sudden appearance six thousand miles from where he'd left him in the ocean, he did an admirable job covering it.

Graves looked at Cade's face, still distorted and rubbery, wearing the other man's skin. "Have you had some work done?"

Cade leaned down to stare directly into Graves's mirror-shaded eyes. "I have no more patience for you. Your life now depends on the answer to my question. Where is Zach Barrows?"

Graves leaned back in his chair and smiled. "Nah. You're just not convincing me. Try it with a little more growl in your voice."

Cade very badly wanted to snap Graves like a broom handle over his knee. He wanted it so badly he felt the oath impose itself on him, felt the beginning of the pain. As long as Graves had his pardon, Cade could do nothing.

Enough of this, Cade decided. He'd find Zach himself.

But Graves spoke before he could go.

"Hold on, Cade. We have some things to talk about."

"Unless it's Zach's location, I don't want to hear anything from you."

"Really," Graves said. "How about I tell you why all this is happening?"

Cade cocked his head. He was listening.

Graves leaned forward, eager.

"Think about America," he said. "Do you really believe it's possible for a nation to just stumble into the greatest power in the history of the world? We didn't get where we are by God's grace or by clean living. There's always a price. Someone's got to pay the bills. You know the kind of currency I mean. For this kind of prosperity? There's only one payment that will do: blood. And even with all the little wars we've kicked up, the tiny atrocities, the kids picking up land mines, America is still way, way, behind on the dues. We haven't had major casualties since Vietnam—hell, World War II, if you think about it. There's not enough suffering going on. We *owe*. And I believe you know who is coming to collect."

Cade's lip curled. "Disappointing," he said.

"What?" Graves was insulted.

"You think I've never heard anyone predict the end of the world before?"

"I'm not wearing a sign and ringing a bell, Cade. It's already happened. No matter what you do, you're already too late: the world has ended."

"Then why are we still here?"

Graves smiled. "You think the new world will be empty? We'll need workers. The new management will require worshippers as well. Human beings, most of us, we won't fit properly. But some of them can be adapted. Remodeled. Made to serve."

"The Snakeheads."

Graves nodded. "Exactly. Deep down, everyone knows this is the way it's going to be. Hell, they're even anxious for it. Why else do you think they're all stuffing themselves with zombie movies and apocalypse books? They're getting ready. They know what's coming, and they want to get it over with."

"But not you. You really believe your masters will protect you from the Hell you're trying to unleash? They didn't stop me from killing Bin Laden."

"He was a tool, nothing more. My masters have plans for me. There are places reserved. When the smoke clears, we will emerge, better and stronger. And we will be rewarded. The new world will require enforcers, governors, supervisors—"

"Traitors," Cade said. "Predictable. Selling out your own kind for the Other Side. You're just another pawn. Another servant."

Graves didn't look offended. "Everyone has to serve someone. There are advantages to being on the winning side. You'd find out, if you joined us."

Cade's mouth twitched again. Really, Graves was cracking him up. "I can't do that."

"Don't be so sure. How could you be loyal to the United States if it didn't exist?"

For an instant, the vampire side of Cade rose to the idea. Freedom. To run wild, to kill whomever and whenever he wanted, even to slake his never-ending thirst.

Cade shook it off almost as quickly as it hit him. He was more than his baser instincts. Graves had made the same mistake as many others in assuming Cade was a prisoner of his duty. An oath only works if both sides agree to it. Cade had made his choice over a hundred and forty years ago. He would not break his word now.

"I've had stronger temptations from more terrible demons," Cade said.

He turned to the office door.

"That's it? You're just leaving?"

No reply.

"I asked you a question." Graves was shouting now. "You can't just walk away from me."

Cade had no interest in trying to explain it to Graves. He couldn't do anything here, but neither could Graves stop him.

He had work to do, and it wasn't here.

SOMETHING ABOUT CADE'S total disregard for him stuck in Graves's craw. He'd admit it to himself, if no one else. He'd been frightened of Cade, haunted by the mere idea of him, for so long. And here he was, human-sized and unable to lift a finger against Graves. It was a chance that would never come again.

He reached behind his belt and pulled out the Gigli saw.

The Gigli was a loop of tempered steel wires with finger rings at each end. It was invented to cut through skulls for brain surgery. But the CIA knew a good tool when it found one. It could saw through a wooden two-by-four or even iron bars. It could be hidden inside lapels, heel compartments, even shoelaces.

It was listed in the official catalog of clandestine weapons as an escape device. Even in its own documents, the Agency liked to hide the truth.

Back in the Cold War, the Technical Services Division used to hand the things out like they came at the bottom of a box of Cracker Jack.

Graves got his first one not long after he'd joined the CIA, before he was sent to Vietnam. He'd lost count of the number he'd used since then. The one in his hand came from a reputable surgical-supply firm.

He put his fingers through the rings and stepped behind Cade.

Used properly, the Gigli would behead a man in under thirty seconds.

What the hell, Graves decided. Let's see how long it takes for a vampire.

CADE REALIZED HE'D UNDERESTIMATED Graves when the steel wire flashed past his eyes. Even with his reflexes, he was taken by surprise. Graves did not move like an old man. Cade barely got his hand up in time.

The looped wires bit into the flesh of Cade's palm and sliced through to the bone. Graves didn't hesitate. He put his knee in Cade's back and pulled with all his might.

Graves didn't have the strength of an old man, either. In a remote corner of his brain, Cade wondered what, exactly, had been done to Graves in order to give him this vitality.

Then Graves began to saw, and Cade felt the steel grinding his bones. That put the question more or less out of his head.

Cade was handicapped by the pardon covering Graves like a shield. He could not kill Graves, or even hurt him. But neither could he allow Graves to keep him from his mission.

Graves kneed him in the back again, and again. Cade pushed against the wire. It wouldn't break. His hand was pinned against his own throat.

Cade felt his fangs emerge. He was starting to lose himself to his rage. But no. He was not about to forget who he was. He was still in charge of himself.

He snapped backward, rolling in the same direction that Graves pulled him.

Graves couldn't hang on. He fell over.

Cade was on his feet, standing over Graves, on the floor. Graves realized he no longer had the saw in his hands. He looked around for it, and then looked up.

It was buried deep in Cade's palm, the flesh trying to close around the wound already.

Graves was panting like a dog. His unnatural burst of strength had deserted him. Now he just looked like an old man who'd slipped in the kitchen.

He grinned at Cade. "Can't blame a guy for trying," he said.

Cade stared directly at Graves as he grabbed one ring of the saw and pulled. The saw came free of his hand with a slick pop.

He dropped it on Graves's chest. And left.

Graves bellowed after him as the vampire moved down the corridor. "You're an idiot. What do you think you're going to do down there?"

"My job" was all Cade said.

GRAVES WATCHED THE VAMPIRE GO. He shook his head. Stubborn. No reasoning with some creatures.

Graves took out his radio. "Baker team, this is Graves. Report."

"Vaughn here, sir. We're holding," the answer came back. The squad leader sounded nervous. "We're hearing some strange noises down in the cells—"

"That's not your concern now," Graves said. "I want you to move your men to Level Two, Sector B. Intruder moving west, on foot. Find him and kill him."

"You said it was crucial to guard this corridor, sir. If anything were to get past us—"

"I'm giving you new orders. Understood?"

A slight hesitation. "Clear, sir."

"Good," Graves said. "One more thing. Your target will be alone, and apparently unarmed. Do not let that fool you."

"Just one man." Vaughn managed to make it sound like he was clarifying the order, not questioning Graves again.

Not exactly a man, Graves thought. But this wasn't the time to get into it.

"Don't give him a chance, Vaughn. You get one shot, then you're lunch."

He clicked off the radio before Vaughn could respond and turned to his keyboard.

He entered a series of commands, followed by codes and passwords. The software behind the Site's engineering and environmental protocols kept asking him to confirm the orders, like a bartender checking on a drunk who keeps asking for another round. *Are you sure you want to do this? Y/N?*

Graves was sure. Proctor and the higher-ups in the Company might balk, but he was tired of waiting for the Apocalypse. Maybe they weren't prepared to light the fires, but he'd always believed in taking initiative. It's why he'd come as far as he had.

And if anyone questioned him—if there was anyone left to question him, in the aftermath—well, then, he could disavow all knowledge.

But he didn't think he was going to fail. Cade couldn't stop him. No one could stop him. Armageddon was about to begin in the heartland of America.

He entered the final command: *Open all cells.*

Are you sure you want to do this? Y/N?

Yes. He was sure.

He hit ENTER, and with the tap of a key, set everything he'd been hiding in the Black Site free.

It was time to open the reptile house to the general public.

THIRTY-THREE

1955—Marineland, Florida—Locals report encounters with a reptilian, amphibious "Gill-Man," supposedly captured from the Amazon. Several deaths are attributed to the creature, who vanishes into the ocean.

—BRIEFING BOOK: CODE NAME: NIGHTMARE PET

LEVEL SIX

Tania took the elevator shaft down to the final level of the Site. She levered the doors open by hand and slid down the cables. The elevator car blocked her descent at Level Five. She crawled down the side of it, headfirst, and then down the wall to the bottom level of the Site.

The rudimentary map of the Site told her that utilities and pipelines would be down here. This is where she'd find the task that Cade set out for her.

She thought it was a waste of her talents, but she supposed this is what it meant to compromise in a relationship.

Moving silently down the corridors, she found the generator room in a matter of minutes. There was only one sentry.

She smiled. Cade may have ordered her away from the prisoners, but that didn't mean she couldn't enjoy herself.

SEAN EARLY WASN'T a bad guy, as Archer/Andrews employees went. He wasn't bounced out of the military for rape or murder or anything like that. He hadn't participated in the prisoner beatings at Bagram. He'd never gotten his jollies beating guys with batons or shoving light sticks up their butts. But when the investigators had come around, asking questions, Early kept his mouth shut. He was no snitch. He was granted an honorable discharge as part of the general effort to minimize the P.R. damage to the War on Terror.

Archer/Andrews, however, could use a guy who knew how to keep a secret. After a series of rotations at ever-more-secret prisons, Early was finally given a job at the Black Site under Liberty.

It didn't seem like that big a deal, honestly. Most of his time was spent monitoring the Site's power plant. He sat in a chair, watching the big 200-kilowatt generators spin away the hours.

The Site ran on a pipeline of compressed natural gas that could pump a thousand gallons per minute through twenty-eight miles of pipes. It fed the big generators and provided heat and fuel to the rest of the complex. The whole power plant was automated. Early wasn't required to fix or maintain anything. He was just there to watch it.

There were worse assignments, of course. He supposed the stink of fuel, the constant thrum of the engines and the endless boredom were better than having your ass shot off.

Still, he thought there would be more excitement in being part of a top-secret military installation.

Then he saw the redhead.

She sauntered up to him like he was in a bar. His jaw dropped. He'd been down in the Site for nine months. The last woman he'd seen had been a tech who wore heavy sweaters and a lab coat all the time.

This woman was wrapped in an outfit that looked like it had been applied by a paintbrush.

It threw him so completely that he almost didn't get his weapon free of the holster.

He pointed it at her. He knew, no matter how many porn movies he'd seen, that this couldn't be right. At best, she was a prisoner from Level Five who'd gotten free. At worst, there was a breach, and he was in a world of shit.

She looked at him over the barrel of his gun and frowned. "Oh come on," she said. She didn't sound scared. Just annoyed. "Am I completely losing my touch, or are they feeding you guys something?"

"Don't move," he said. "Don't even think it."

He reached for the radio attached at his shoulder, ready to call for backup.

Then his gun was gone and he was pinned to the wall. Her hand was a steel clamp at his throat.

She smiled. He saw her fangs.

"You really took the fun out of this," she said, as his vision began to go gray around the edges. She still sounded upset.

Early's last thought was that finally, something interesting happened, something right out of a spy movie, and it was over in a moment. First hot chick he'd seen in a year, and she was a monster.

TANIA FINISHED HER MEAL before she looked over the power plant.

She sought out the main generator. It only took her a moment to figure out the fuel line and trace it back to the main pipeline.

She found a toolbox with everything she needed. It was nothing more than a matter of removing some nuts and bolts and finding a feeder line into the fire-suppression system.

Tania had been raised with seven brothers when she was human. Even before she became a supernatural killing machine, she'd never bought into the notion that women were supposed to be useless with anything mechanical.

THIRTY-FOUR

There are more than a hundred of these deep underground military bases (also known as DUMBs) in the United States alone, according to the believers. Some of the more famous include the base at Dulce, New Mexico, the base under Area 51, aka Groom Lake, Nevada, and beneath Mount Shasta in California. No government map will show them, of course, but dedicated researchers have spent hours painstakingly tracing the routes and locations onto their own hand-drawn atlases and exchanging their work over the Internet and at conspiracy conferences. If this is a secret plan to rule the world, a lot of people seem to know about it.

—Cole Daniels, *Black Ops: The Occult-CIA Connection*

LEVEL TWO

Cade worked his way methodically through the Site, room by room. It was time-consuming and frustrating, but to find Zach, he had no choice.

That Zach might already be dead didn't slow him down in the least. Zach's life was his responsibility until one or the other of them was dead. Until he found Zach's body, he moved forward. Simple as that.

He kept checking the rooms, one after another.

Sirens blasted at him. Enormous steel shutters slammed down across the corridors. This wasn't just in his wing. He felt the change in the air pressure in the Site. All throughout the complex, exits were being sealed.

Cade held himself very still and listened even more closely. He heard the thrum of the air forced through the ductwork. He heard the vibrations still moving through concrete and rebar like the aftershocks of a quake. And finally, he heard the oiled slide of a thousand doors being opened.

This could not possibly be good news for Zach, or anyone else locked in here.

If he were human, he might waste a moment in denial. But he knew what had happened instantly. Graves had released his prisoners. Cade was almost certain none of them were human any longer.

Cade found a door at the end of the corridor. It was like a hatch on a submarine—a sally port, designed like airlocks, with two doors on a connecting space. They were common in prisons. One door can only be opened when the other door is closed and locked, so only one or two people can go through at any time. Even if a guard were forced by a prisoner to open one door, the tight spaces would prevent more than one prisoner from going through the passage.

Down the other way, thick metal shutters, from floor to ceiling, created seamless new walls, blocking the stairwells.

Still, Graves would have left a way to the surface. He wouldn't leave the Snakeheads to starve down here. For a man like him, that would be like refusing to fire a loaded gun.

He would have left a path for the creatures, Cade knew, because he'd already prepared a meal for them. He and Tania had walked through them on their way into the Site: tens of thousands of happy shoppers, waiting outside the Mall.

He felt a familiar surge of anger welling up inside.

Fortunately, a group of heavily armed men showed up at that moment, giving him the perfect targets to take it out on.

THE SQUAD OF ARCHIES dropped into firing formation as if they'd practiced the move all their lives.

Cade stood completely still, hands at his sides.

They were sealed head-to-toe in a combination of biohazard protection and body armor. Faces were hidden behind tinted-glass visors and sealed behind gas filters. Stubby antenna poked up from their helmets for the radios that clicked behind their masks. They looked as if evolution had taken a different, insectile path, and equipped gleaming beetles with heavy artillery.

Red dots of multiple laser-sights danced over Cade's chest and face.

"I'll make you an offer," Cade said.

Cade heard one soldier in the back snicker, even through his gear.

"Every man who puts his weapon down will not spend the last minutes of his life in agonizing pain."

A moment.

"Last chance," Cade said.

Almost as one, they opened fire.

LIEUTENANT DAVID VAUGHN never thought much about firefights or explosions. The sound of the bullets barely made him flinch, even on his first tour of duty. He didn't know why, but somehow it didn't register with him the same way as with other people.

Maybe that's why he was fast-tracked through Special Forces training and assigned to Delta. His temperature just ran cooler than most guys'. He could focus on the mission, even with shrapnel and slugs tearing inches past his face.

About the only thing that got his pulse above sixty was when he would go back to the States on leave and spend a few hours carving up a teenage girl with a knife. He'd spend days roaming the streets of small cities in the Northwest in his unregistered truck, looking for hookers, homeless and runaways. He'd leave the bodies in a river or near a rest stop or on the side of the highway.

He kept the sides of his life separate and clean. He'd always had a knack for organization, and the military had nurtured those habits in him. Vaughn never left any trace evidence; he wasn't one of those pathetic psychos who could only get it up while masturbating over his kills. Vaughn would never be caught because he never stuck to any pattern. His leave would end, and he would return to combat. Nobody really missed the girls he selected anyway. He varied his itinerary around the Northwest, making sure to put at least six months between cities.

Vaughn liked Portland especially. Nice place. They still trusted people there. Vaughn thought about maybe buying a house in the city when he retired. Near a school. A good neighborhood, with lots of kids.

Someplace with a basement.

When his third tour was almost up, an A/A recruiter came to see him. His CO knew the guy from way back and gave him Vaughn's name. They offered him five times his Army salary to kill the same people. His superiors could have stop-lossed him, or hindered him in some other way, but they were happy to see him go. Despite what you see in the movies, most officers aren't stupid. They smelled something wrong on Vaughn. He knew it and they knew it. Maybe it was the spring in his step when he came back from leave. Maybe he just gave them the creeps.

So he took the job. The pay was better, the gear actually worked and he didn't have to buy his own body armor anymore.

He wasn't thrilled when he was assigned to the prison. For a guy who found combat uninteresting, working security was almost dull enough to put him in a coma. He was in charge of one of the emergency response teams. The ERTs were supposed to put down riots, fights or unruly prisoners. That was in theory, anyway. Most of the detainees at the Black Site were broken by the time they arrived, and if they weren't, it didn't take much more than a few days. A guy sitting in his cell sobbing quietly to himself wasn't much of a threat to a trained Delta commando.

Still, he got a bump in pay, and he was able to keep pursuing his hobby.

Lately, however, his job had been getting interesting. Vaughn wasn't sure he liked the change.

The prisoners had been fighting the guards with surprising strength and desperation, like animals cornered by something bigger and meaner. A week earlier, he'd had to break a prisoner's collarbone just to get him back inside the cell. Even previously cooperative (or comatose, which was pretty much the same thing) detainees had turned into vicious spitters, biters and fighters. And the uncooperative prisoners now required three or four ERT members to wrestle them down.

They didn't seem to be fighting the guards, at least not directly. They just wanted out. It didn't seem to matter that the double-locked doors beyond their cells could not be opened from inside. Or that they were a mile underground, or that some of them didn't even speak English. They were like dogs at the racetrack, seemingly conditioned to run as soon as the doors opened, making a direct line for anywhere but here.

Vaughn wasn't stupid. Delta didn't do stupid. He could see the pattern developing. On some atavistic level, the prisoners knew they were running out of time. It made them desperate, and desperation was dangerous.

He was happy, at first, when Graves gave the ERT their orders: post outside Level Five and shoot whoever tries to get out. Straightforward. He could deal with that.

But not for long.

The screams coming from inside Level Five were god-awful. He'd heard human beings make all kinds of noise while in pain. He could identify the age, race and gender of a victim by the type of sound that came out of them, like a wine taster picking up hints of the grape's home soil on his tongue.

But he'd never heard anything like that before. He had no idea what was happening in there.

That implied some freaky shit. He double-posted sentries at the doors—just in case.

It was a relief when Vaughn got the call from Graves, ordering him to fall back and intercept the hostile moving toward Level Five.

His men hit their marks and formed up on his position.

One man wearing a stolen uniform. No weapons.

The hostile just stood there, and despite what Graves had told him, Vaughn couldn't believe they were supposed to take this guy seriously.

Maybe that was why Vaughn gave him the chance to speak.

In response, the dumb bastard threatened them.

"Last chance," he said.

Vaughn almost laughed, and tightened his finger on the trigger. He began to squeeze.

He didn't have time to wonder why he felt so nervous now, even more than outside the cell blocks.

He only realized, at the last moment, that the tickle under his arm was a single bead of cold sweat.

Vaughn suddenly understood. He was scared.

By then he was already shooting.

HE HAD TO GIVE the mercenaries credit: they were more than merely competent. They had covered every possible angle of fire.

They were using AA-12 combat shotguns—possibly the deadliest gun ever made, capable of delivering 300 rounds of 12-gauge ammunition per minute.

His reflexes accelerated so that seconds stretched like taffy.

The metal-jacketed slugs looked like snowflakes, drifting in the air, to Cade. He had all the time in the world.

He chose the least crowded section of air and leaped for the ceiling, his fingers clawing into the smooth concrete.

Pain—and surprise—nearly made him lose his grip. Despite his speed, one bullet from the swarm caught him in the leg—and tore right through the meat of his calf.

Regular ammo couldn't do that. Fully fed, as he was, Cade was close to bulletproof. A Magnum load at close range would raise a bruise, but not much more.

Cade hit the ground behind the mercs. He was moving much slower now. The mercenaries ceased fire, realizing their target had vanished right in front of them.

The man closest to Cade began to turn around. Cade grabbed his helmet with one hand, his vest with the other, and yanked. The mercenary's neck snapped; his head nearly twisted off.

Cade grabbed the weapon from the man's nerveless fingers before the body fell. He snapped open the ammo drum and examined the shells.

Depleted uranium rounds. Loaded with the same material used in tank-piercing weaponry, these weren't supposed to exist in this size. The Shadow Company had made sure its men could hurt things like Cade.

Cade allowed himself a small smile.

This just got interesting.

Another merc turned when he heard the body of Cade's first victim hit the ground. He didn't waste time in shock or disbelief. He aimed and began firing.

Cade dropped the drum and the gun. His leg flared with pain, and he only barely managed to avoid being hit again.

He'd already been hobbled. If the mercs got another chance to pin him down, he'd be shredded.

So he dived into the center of the squad.

The mercenary stopped firing as Cade moved among his squad. Before he could shout a warning, two more soldiers went down with crushed windpipes.

Three down. Nine left.

Shouting. Random shots. The squad leader screaming orders at the men.

The confusion didn't last.

They turned inward, breaking into smaller three-man groups, back to back, guns out.

Cade at the center of the ring, the bull's-eye.

Cade really was impressed. These men were well trained and well equipped.

But it wouldn't save them.

Cade hit the ceiling again. Even limping, he moved too fast for them. They shot at the empty space where he had been.

Cade smelled fresh blood as a DU round tore through the armor of one of the men. Friendly fire.

Eight left.

Cade dropped from above. The mercs had as little hope of touching him as they did avoiding him.

Fact about Kevlar helmets: they will prevent a bullet from going through your skull, but they cannot stop the laws of physics. The shock wave from impact can still jelly a man's brains, killing him instantly.

Three of the mercs discovered this as Cade's fist connected with their heads at the velocity of a tank shell.

Three bodies hit the floor.

Five left.

Cade didn't bother going up again. He just ran, right into the remaining mercs. His fingers, pointed like a knife, went clean through a mask and helmet, into the man's face, then his skull, mashing it to pulp.

Four left.

Now panic set in. One of the mercs lost it. He began shooting at everything, emptying his drum on full automatic. He tore up a lot of concrete in the walls and ceiling. Then he took a grenade off his belt and threw it, a wild pitch in Cade's direction.

Cade ducked it easily. The man behind him didn't.

There was a searing blast of heat behind Cade's back. His shirt caught on fire and his skin felt crisped.

He didn't slow down, but kicked, catching the grenade-tosser in the jaw. The man's spine broke neatly at the C3 vertebra, ending autonomic functions like breathing and heartbeat.

Cade checked behind him. The man hit by his comrade's grenade was still burning.

White phosphorus. It burned on contact with oxygen and clung to skin and clothing. Impossible to extinguish with water. Technically outlawed by international conventions for use as a weapon. It was supposed to be used as a smoke bomb or a marker.

The burning man stopped thrashing as he was cooked down to the bone.

Two left.

One ran.

Cade caught up with him in a leap, landing heavily on the man's legs. He heard the crunch of bones and tendons as they splintered and tore. He was crippled. Cade left him there.

One more.

It was the squad leader. He reached for a dead man's switch on his front vest. Cade had intended to take him alive to question him, but the runner had already broken. He'd be easier. So the squad leader was no longer needed.

Before the leader could reach the suicide button, Cade crushed his fingers, then hurled him as far down the corridor as he could.

Which was about the length of a football field.

Lieutenant David Vaughn was traveling at about thirty miles per hour when Cade heard the impact of the body against the wall. It was like a car crash, minus the car. The mercenary's body slid down the wall and rested in a puddle on the floor.

Cade didn't bother to look. Moving at human speed now, he walked to the sole survivor, lying among the corpses.

He had a little fight left. Cade removed the pistol from the Archie's hand, fracturing a finger on the way.

Cade held the back of the mercenary's head and tore open the biohazard suit like a candy wrapper. The Archie's face was gritted teeth and sweat.

"I have questions," Cade said. "Believe me when I tell you that you'll want to answer them."

A sound—half laugh, half sob—emerged from the soldier.

"Do what you want. It doesn't matter," he said. "I'm dead. You're dead. We're all dead, everyone in here."

"Why would you say that?"

"There are things down there. Worse than you."

Cade leaned in close and showed his teeth. "There's nothing worse than me."

The soldier grinned so hard Cade could see his back teeth. There was a crunch from the soldier's mouth. A scent of bitter almonds.

The soldier went limp. A cyanide capsule in a false tooth.

Cade dropped the body.

These men were very well equipped, indeed.

He peeled away the scorched shirt, then scavenged a new one from the corpse. From the others, he collected the items he thought he'd need and loaded them all into a backpack.

He kept walking, deeper into the Site.

THIRTY-FIVE

Some of my colleagues question why Cade doesn't drink human blood when it would make him stronger. I think the more interesting question is, Why is Cade so strong when he refuses to drink human blood? We already know from our studies of Cade and his kind that vampires gain power as they age— whatever processes are at work in them only grow more efficient at survival over time. But we also know that these biological engines are designed to run on human blood, and that animal blood is a lower-grade substitute. Yet, at over a hundred and twelve years since his transformation, Cade shows no signs of disease or degradation. (Indeed, he has already killed vampires stronger than he is.)

—Dr. William Kavanaugh, Sanction V research group

LEVEL FIVE

The Snakeheads worked their way through the guards on Level Five quickly. There were only a few of them, and their calls for the ERT were not answered. They were overwhelmed as the Snakeheads came streaming from their cells.

That wasn't much meat for so many to be fed. Their frenzy ebbed as the facts of their situation began to sink into their brains. Like reptiles, they could feel the vibrations running through the floors of the Site. Like fish, some of their new organs were more sensitive to smell and taste. With their tongues, they could scent bodies filled with warm blood. Instead of turning on one another in a frenzy, the Snakeheads did something new for them, as old instincts woke up in response to their new situation. They began to hunt.

THE DOORS SLID open so easily Zach thought his eyes might be playing tricks on him.

He stood up. He heard a siren squawk and go silent, and then watched as the lights flickered.

He wondered if this was a trap, then felt stupid. Any trap that started with letting him out of a prison cell was very badly designed.

Still. Something was wrong here.

He stepped outside the door. He heard a hissing again.

But this was not the prisoner in the next cell. This came from down the corridor, around a bend.

It was not just one hiss, either. It was the sibilant noise of many snakes rising in chorus. Not all at once, but all together, hissing, as if talking to one another.

Zach noticed all the doors on the cell block were open.

The hissing got louder.

It didn't take him long to understand. Snakeheads.

All the doors were open.

The hissing got even louder. It was the sound of dozens—maybe hundreds of them—stepping across the threshold of their cells, just as Zach had.

They were all free.

It was only then he noticed the other prisoner in his cell, one door down the hall, one across.

He sat in a restraint chair, a jailhouse appliance that looked like something from a medieval torture chamber. Zach had seen this before, too.

The prisoner was strapped in, unable to move.

"Please. Let me out."

Zach looked at him, then back over his shoulder. The hissing was getting closer. He could have sworn he heard the clicking of claws as well.

"I know what is happening," the prisoner said. "They're coming. Aren't they?"

Zach looked down the hall. He heard gunfire and a short, strangled scream.

"Please," the prisoner said, panic creeping into his voice. "Do not leave me in here. You can't leave me to face those things alone."

Zach hesitated.

"I swear I will not harm you."

A human being or a monster. It was really no choice at all.

I am ten different kinds of stupid, Zach thought, even as he ducked inside the cell. He began unbuckling the restraints.

As soon as his right hand was free, the prisoner clouted Zach in the head, knocking him backward and to the floor. He bounced off the wall on the way down, and his vision blurred again.

He lurched upward just as the prisoner got his feet free. He staggered out the door, getting a kick to the side on the way.

Zach's head still ached from Bell's blow. Now he was dizzy and sick. He hit the floor hard.

The prisoner hopped out of the cell, moving quickly and surely. In one hand was a shard of metal, a jailhouse shiv, sharpened along one edge.

Zach put his hand up, and the prisoner stabbed at him.

"Idiot," the prisoner hissed, holding the shard like a knife in front of him. He giggled. Zach had heard the phrase "laughing like a maniac" before. But he'd never actually heard the sound until that moment; a horrible, high-pitched noise like a bird strangling on a worm.

"Don't do this," Zach said, struggling to keep his voice calm. "You don't have to do this. We can still get out of here."

There was a weird gleam in the prisoner's eye. "What do you think is happening here? God is coming. He will judge. It's finally time."

"You're wrong," Zach said. "You don't know how wrong. It's not God. Not even close. Come on, man. Don't be stupid your whole life. You can at least choose a better way to die."

The prisoner snarled and slashed at him again with the knife. He tensed to leap, to cover the distance between them.

Zach saw it then. Behind the prisoner, light played over a group of round, wet objects, just beyond his shoulder. It looked like a stream running over pebbles.

It took Zach a moment to realize the pebbles were eyes. Lidless eyes with diamond-slitted pupils. Snakeheads. Moving quietly, stalking prey.

Some still had prison uniforms. Others had the A/A corporate fatigues, torn in places, sagging like old paper bags on their changed bodies.

The Snakehead at the lead tensed and prepared to strike.

For a split second, Zach considered warning the prisoner. He could see the low comedy that would ensue, something out of an old movie or cartoon—"Look behind you." "Oh, no, I'm not falling for that one." And so on.

But as the Snakehead levered open its jaws, Zach stayed quiet.

The prisoner must have seen something in Zach's eyes, however. He turned just as the jaws snapped shut.

Zach heard the scream, cut short by the sound of crunching bone. He didn't see any more, because by then, he was running for his life.

LEVEL FOUR

Sims and Miller were on their way back from the dining hall, locked in their usual struggle. The rest of their squad listened, cheering them on, tallying points.

Like all the A/A employees assigned to the Site, they lived totally belowground for the duration of their tours. It wasn't too bad, but it could get boring. They had to find their own ways to fill the time. Miller liked to bullshit.

Miller didn't mean to be a dick, Sims told himself. He was just a little delusional. He told amazing, fantastic, awesome stories—with Miller himself as the hero of each one. The moral of every one of Miller's stories was how Miller was the most incredible human being in existence. Somehow there was not an incident in his life that didn't end with him winning a fight, banging some gorgeous chick and meeting some celebrity.

For a long time, Sims listened, half irritated and half entertained, like the others. But it just got under his skin. So he started calling Miller on his shit.

That led to a ritual even more entertaining for the rest of the Archies: watching Miller try to plug every hole Sims found in his lies, and watching Sims's frustration mount as he did.

Sims tried to ignore it. He really did. But sometimes, it was just too much.

Like right now.

"So I'm banging this chick, who was, I remind you, Miss Nevada USA, right there in the casino—"

"Oh come on," Sims said. "You mean to tell me, she vanishes for hours while the Miss America pageant is going on and nobody notices?"

"Miss USA pageant," Miller reminded him. "Much sluttier than the Miss America pageant. Everyone knows that."

The other guys all nodded, as if saying, sure, everyone knows that.

Sims rolled his eyes. This one looked like it was going to land in familiar territory. Sims would bet anything this adventure ended in another three-way.

"So yeah, I've got her ankles locked behind my neck, she's screaming 'Harder, harder!' at the top of her lungs, and I don't even know where she got the vinyl suit. Of course, this is when her roommate opens the door—"

Called it, Sims thought.

Then sirens wailed to life, at a decibel level designed to induce ear-splitting pain. Even Miller had to shut up. Then they cut out with a squawk, leaving them all slightly stunned.

"What the hell?" one of them said.

Some kind of major equipment failure. Something was fucked up, that was for sure.

They milled about near one of the sally ports, unsure if this meant they should return to their stations or their posts.

Then the shutters came down. It was like the air turned to steel over their heads. They all had to jump for it. Sims and Miller just missed being crushed.

That was when they really should have known they were dead. The shutters were designed to come down, to seal off the tunnels, only if there was a breach. It was a fail-safe, hardwired deep into the security systems of the Site.

They weren't worried about just the prisoners getting out. Any of them could have handled that. But there were pens that held much worse things. The shutters were only supposed to come down if those got out.

It was one of those things in the manual nobody could ever bring himself to really believe. Nobody ever thought any of them would get out. It was, really, too horrible to consider.

On an animal level, they knew it. But in places in their minds, they still had to be convinced. They had to hear the rest.

Down in the dark, at the other ends of the tunnels, they heard something else, faint but unmistakable. The sounds of metal moving against metal, the clanging noise of a hundred doors to a hundred cells opening at once.

Sims finally put his hand on his holster and popped open the snap. The others had already done the same.

The lights flickered. The shadows seemed to get deeper.

Sims's heart pounded. They were all staring the same way, all waiting to draw.

He heard a noise coming from the dark, like the last stubborn kernels of popcorn in the microwave. A kind of clicking on the concrete floor.

It got louder, and faster.

They all had their guns out now, aimed down the hall. It wouldn't help. They knew it. But they had to do something.

Sims thought of something that almost made him laugh out loud. He wondered, if he asked, would Miller be able to finish his story?

The first one came skittering around the corner, low and fast. Miller froze where he stood, and it took him down to the floor.

The rest of the Snakeheads came around a second later. Only three of them, but it might as well have been dozens. Something had gone very wrong. Where was the Emergency Response Team? What had happened to the locks?

Even as he thought this, Sims and the others were shooting. They had to do something, even if they knew it wouldn't work. The Snakeheads were impossibly fast. They leaped up the walls and angled down at the men. Sims watched one whisk a claw past Choi, and then saw Choi's carotid artery spurt open a second later.

Before he knew it, Sims realized he was on the floor. He wondered when his legs had gone numb.

The creatures stood over him for a moment. He looked up into their blank eyes and wondered what they were waiting for. He was bleeding out.

Whatever it was, he wasn't going to waste the opportunity.

Somehow he still had his gun. He put it under his chin and pulled the trigger.

Piranhas, when starving, have been known to reduce an entire cow to a skeleton in under a minute. The Snakeheads did the same thing to Sims · in just under five, but there were only three of them.

Then they moved on to the bodies of the others.

LEVEL FIVE

Jefferson Davis Obadiah Marsh huddled quietly in his cell. He wasn't scared—not exactly, not anymore.

Marsh had been at the Site longer than any other surviving prisoner. Six years ago, he'd been in the Chipley lockup down in Florida. Drunk and disorderly again. Marsh's adult life played like a highlight reel from *COPS*: meth bust, shirtless in the back of a squad car, kicking at the glass barefoot; bar fight, tazered and convulsing on the ground; meth bust, fleeing through a trailer park with a dozen sweaty cops behind him; DWI, meth bust, resisting arrest; a high-speed car chase in an unlicensed Chevy that might have actually made prime time if it hadn't ended suddenly because Marsh had tried to outrun the police with the gas gauge already on "E."

He hadn't been disadvantaged as a kid; his parents came from money, and they'd done whatever they could to help out. But after the fourth arrest, they wrote him off as a throwback to the old New England Marshes, like his great-grandfather, the one who was never mentioned, even though it was his wealth that established the Marshes throughout the South.

Back in Florida, he was sleeping off a hangover and a beating he'd received from the other prisoners when he was wakened by a guard's nightstick. The casual cruelty was something Marsh accepted. People tended to dislike him on sight. Something about his face—weak chin, gaping underbite, flat nose and bulging eyes—made it look as if he was always gawking at everything.

He struggled up on the cot and sat there, staring. "These people are here for you," the guard said and left. Marsh was alone with two men in dark suits. They hustled him out and into a waiting Humvee. Nobody even signed any papers. Marsh went along with it as they drove across state lines. He didn't have much choice. They treated him like some kind of super-criminal, keeping him handcuffed at all times, except to piss and eat, never letting him have a minute alone.

Then they injected him with something and when he woke up, he was in another cell.

He spent the next few years in the same routine. His blood was drawn every day. Occasionally, the doctors who came did spinal taps—he fucking hated those, they felt like a nail gun in his back—and occasionally shot him up with other drugs. Some made him high. Most made him sick.

It wasn't all bad. He had his own TV with all the pay channels. They didn't even mind if he watched porn. And they'd give him fried chicken and pizza on Friday nights. He got comfortable in his limited world. His stringy crystal-meth muscle bloated to fat, so he looked like a man-sized toad on the day the sirens blared and the cells opened.

Marsh had no idea what to do. He sat there for the longest time. He called for the guards, but they weren't around.

Then he saw the Snakeheads, moving down the corridor next to the cells, drawn by his voice.

He wasn't completely stupid. He lurched back into the cell and tried to slam the door after him. But it was locked into the open position. He tried to hide under his sink, but he was still grossly exposed.

The Snakeheads—two of them—came ticking into the cell on their clawed feet. They stared at him with their reptile eyes, white teeth stained with blood. He noticed some wore prison jumpsuits, in tatters. Others were dressed in what remained of jeans and T-shirts, lab coats or guard uniforms.

He trembled and pissed himself.

The Snakehead in the lead, one with the bare remains of a prison coverall, seemed drawn by this. It leaned forward, extending its serpentine neck, examining Marsh closely. Its tongue darted out and tasted Marsh's sweat.

Marsh nearly lost it right there. But then the Snakehead pulled away. It moved backward, and the others did the same.

Marsh was about ready to believe he'd escaped when, almost as a parting gesture, the Snakehead reached out one claw and sliced a furrow deep into Marsh's cheek.

He screamed and hid his face, tried to worm his bulk further into the corner of the cell, ready for more pain.

Nothing happened. When he finally opened his eyes, he was alone again. And despite the burning gash on his face, he felt pretty good.

It was almost as if they'd recognized him, he realized. As if they'd marked him as one of their own.

LEVEL FIVE

Zach was a dead man.

He'd seen Cade take on these things and he knew what they were capable of. They would run him down in less than a hundred yards. They would rip him apart like a crocodile snatching a gazelle from the bank of a watering hole. They'd open a hole in his chest and tear out his organs. They were faster and stronger. He was going to die.

He ran anyway.

He heard their claws on the floor, not too far back. He wasn't sure where he was going—the place was laid out like a maze, but he kept turning corners, trying to keep the distance between them.

It wasn't until he saw the steel door that he realized he'd just turned down a dead end.

He still wasn't going to give up. Just like the idiots in the horror movies, he tried to open the door. When he found it was locked (of course), he pounded on it. Nothing.

Now he was really dead.

Maybe it was just as idiotic as pounding on the door, but he wanted to see the end coming.

He turned to face the Snakeheads.

Only there were no Snakeheads.

Somewhere along the way—Zach had been too busy running to notice when—the Snakeheads had stopped following him. He couldn't even hear them now.

Zach waited, doubled over, trying to catch his breath.

The corridors behind him were eerily silent. As if the creatures had simply given up on him.

Zach had no way of knowing that he'd stumbled on the one thing the Snakeheads truly feared: the door behind him. All of them remembered, on a dim Pavlovian level, being taken behind that door. They knew horrible things had been done to them there. They knew that not everyone taken behind the door would come out. Even as twisted as their brains now were by the change, they knew that the door meant pain and death.

They weren't going to get close to it again. Not ever.

Zach didn't know this, but he wasn't about to waste the chance he'd been given.

He waited as long as he thought possible, and then carefully made his way back to the main corridor.

He started looking for a way out.

LEVEL FOUR

Darnell Pendle was off-shift, dozing in front of a TV screen in the rec room, when the alarms sounded, only to be stopped in mid-screech. Huh. That was weird. He went back to sleep.

A little while later—he wasn't sure how long it was—Pendle sat up. He thought he heard something. It almost sounded like someone whispering, "Hush." Now he knew something was off. Nobody in the dorms was ever quiet, especially when he was trying to sleep.

"Anyone there?" Pendle called.

He heard it again. Hush, hush.

He knew what made that noise.

Pendle went for his gun.

Something lashed out at him, whip-fast. He felt a quick, sharp pain at his wrists.

He looked down and realized he didn't have the gun. He couldn't hold it because he had no hands.

At the ends of his wrists, there was nothing but exposed white bone and empty air.

There should be blood, he thought numbly, and then it came jetting out of him.

He heard himself screaming, although there was no real pain, not yet. Or if there was, his brain simply hadn't caught up with it yet.

He looked up, and the Snakehead's claws were coming down again. This time, he saw the long, knife-like edges—

It tore across his face, and his right eye no longer worked.

He knew someone had to hear him screaming by now.

His one good eye saw the blood all over him. The Snakehead ducked in with his teeth, right at Pendle's chest.

He was no longer screaming, he realized. Maybe it was because he couldn't feel much of anything. Or more likely, it was because he couldn't seem to get any breath into his lungs.

He looked up again and saw the Snakehead over him. The white teeth, peeled back in what looked like a grin.

He raised the stub of his arm, but the Snakehead nuzzled it aside, almost gently, and then opened wide again.

Pendle felt cold all over, but he still wanted to ask how this happened. How did the thing get out of its cage?

The Snakehead didn't have any answers, of course. It just kept grinning, tearing away great strips of skin with each jerk of its head.

LEVEL FOUR

Marsh walked the corridors with a crooked smile. He listened to the occasional sound of gunfire, the occasional scream. He nodded his head, agreeing with some unspoken question.

A soldier ran screaming down the hall, blood all over him. Marsh didn't even look twice.

The bleeding on his face had stopped. It seemed stupid to wait inside the cell any longer. And he didn't feel like he was in the slightest danger. He couldn't explain it. But he didn't stop to think much about it, either.

Suddenly, Marsh was pulled into a room off the main corridor. A small group of soldiers blockaded themselves inside.

They shouted things at him he didn't bother to understand.

After a while of shouting, they left him alone, his back against the wall, as they looked out into the hallway, standing guard against whatever was out there.

Marsh decided he could wait here awhile. He wasn't sure what he was waiting for, but he knew it was coming. Whatever it was, he was looking forward to it.

He had never felt so happy in all his life.

LEVEL FOUR

Dobbs walked into the toilet. He wasn't the typical Archer/Andrews recruit. He was out of shape, with an undistinguished service record. But he was the guy who could get you anything. Someone had dropped him in supply and logistics at the start of his army career, and an obscene kind of genius flowered there. He supplied soldiers the world over with illegal drugs, porn, hookers and guns.

Then he discovered the real money was in livestock.

It began with a fluke. An Afghan warlord wanted to celebrate a victory with some Special Forces guys. Only problem: they were in a desolate section of the mountains where all the local livestock had been bombed, along with the people. Dobbs found himself transporting a dozen live goats, in crates, in a top-secret military aircraft.

He was pissed. He'd been ordered to do the job, so he didn't make any money. He even had to clean the plane afterward, because the regular crews didn't have security clearance for it. Everything about the mission was classified, even the goat shit.

Dobbs had one of those lightning flashes of business genius. He could transport more than just goats. Those crates with air holes could fit something far more valuable.

The U.S., Europe and Saudi Arabia all wanted children. For all kinds of different uses. And the one big surplus in any war zone or disaster area was kids. Wandering around, stunned and stupid, ready to follow anyone with a uniform and a candy bar.

So for a year before he was recruited by Archer/Andrews, Dobbs ran a successful child-smuggling ring. That's how he joined the Company.

Like any good middleman, Dobbs didn't think about what happened to his cargo once he got it from Point A to Point B. With the magic of the U.S. Army's international transport system, he could have those orphans, sleeping quietly in a ketamine-induced coma, anyplace in the world in seventy-two hours or less.

You had to allow for some breakage in-flight. Not enough air in the container, overdose of sedatives, whatever. But the profit margins were amazing; even better than drugs.

Dobbs lowered his bulk onto the toilet.

The lights went out.

Bastards, Dobbs thought. "Hey," he said. "*Hey!* I'm in here!"

No reply. He heard the sirens wail, then die almost immediately. Must be a power outage. The P.A. would have an announcement, but there were no speakers in the latrines.

"Asshole!" Dobbs yelled, just in case.

He heard the restroom door slam. A scratching noise, tentative at first. Like a dog or cat trying to open the stalls.

No, Dobbs thought. His throat closed. He began sweating wildly. There were no pets at the Site. There was only one thing that could be scratching.

The scratching continued. It went down the line of stalls, opening each door in turn.

For some reason, Dobbs thought of one of his shipments.

The missing fingernails, the broken knuckles. The skin gone blue and cyanotic at the edges. He'd seen this hand when he pried open a crate on

275

one of his first deliveries. He'd misjudged the amount of air, and he'd lost six of ten of his cargo.

The kid on top had tried to scratch his way out of the crate, but the lid was nailed shut.

Dobbs remembered it so clearly, because he'd had to give back half his fee; he barely made anything on that deal.

The scratching stopped when it reached his stall and the door wouldn't open. Dobbs looked down and saw the clawlike feet on the floor. The stall began to rattle and shake, and then the Snakehead was looking back at him, staring up from the floor as it slithered under the obstacle to reach him.

Ten minutes later, it left. What remained of Dobbs was stuck, head-first, in the toilet, limbs splayed at disjointed angles.

He looked as if he had been flushed and spat out again, as if he was too foul even for the sewer pipe below.

MARSH KEPT SITTING THERE, waiting in the blockaded room with the other people. He'd listened, and he'd learned their names. He might have been happy to stay there forever, but something kept interrupting his peaceful daze.

The one called Copeland was cracking his gum again. Marsh hated that.

Marsh could even smell it. Copeland had a big wad of some sugary brand Marsh hadn't seen since he stole candy as a kid. Marsh listened to the sound, like a cow mashing up its cud—and then, snap, pop goes the tiny bubble.

It wouldn't be so bad, Marsh thought, if only there were some pattern to it. But it came at random moments. Snap. Snap. Snap. Then a long pause. Nothing but chewing. Then, just when he was used to the relative silence—another snap.

He decided to kill Copeland. That would end the noise.

The more the idea buzzed through his head, the more Marsh liked it. He still wasn't exactly sure where the notion came from, but it made him feel warm. It made him feel better.

Because something was going on in his body. Something was making his heart beat faster, and making him angry. Way angrier than he'd ever been on meth, and he'd once punched through a wall of glass bricks while on meth. But at the same time, the anger made him happy. Filled him with all kinds of other images and feelings—

Snap. Snap. Snap.

Enough.

He stood up and immediately stumbled. One of the men, a guy with a blond crew cut, noticed.

"Take it easy, man," he said. He helped Marsh sit back down. "You don't look good."

Marsh was a little premature. He kept breathing deeply. He looked at his skin and began picking, and saw the green-black scales under the sores. He felt the teeth behind his teeth, pushing forward.

No, Marsh was not good. But he could be worse.

Much, much worse.

They had their backs to him again. Marsh stood up once more. This time, he stayed on his feet. This time, he began walking.

He started with Copeland.

Snap.

LEVEL FOUR

The Snakeheads regrouped. They were running out of prey on the lower levels. Something told them they could find more as they rose up.

Like cattle in a chute, they began to stream through the only pathway left in the maze of corridors, stopping when they hit steel walls and turning in the new direction.

Some of their victims, not quite dead, rose up and followed them as soon as the change hit them. It transformed their bodies and healed them, but left them famished.

Clusters of Snakeheads still got stuck in the sally ports as they overloaded the hatches and tried to squeeze through. Biting fights broke out that left some of them wounded and an easy meal for the rest.

But the creatures still made their way to the surface, drawn by the scent of prey, rich with fat, heavy and slow on its feet, noisy and complacent. They twisted upward, more like one long serpent than individual creatures, slithering from a hole in the earth.

LIBERTY MALL, GROUND LEVEL

Twenty-six hundred feet above the Site, people were still arriving. They got into the spirit. Estimates put the crowd at a hundred thousand or more. They all waited, more or less patiently, standing room only, waiting to be funneled inside.

10:49 p.m. A little more than one hour to go, and all the doors would open. Then the fun would really begin.

THIRTY-SIX

A 1975 Trilateral Commission report concluded that the United States was plagued by an "excess of democracy," when "what is needed is a greater degree of moderation in democracy," to improve "governability." Trilat co-founder Brzezinski recommended a study on "Control Over Man's Development and Behavior" to devise "new means of social control," especially in "advanced societies." In the coming New World Order, the natives apparently have yet to be civilized.

—John Whalen and Jonathan Vankin, *The 80 Greatest Conspiracies of All Time*

OSCEOLA MUNICIPAL AIRPORT, IOWA

The pilot was right on time. Graves met him in the hangar at the small, private airport outside Liberty. He carried only a duffel bag.

After takeoff, Graves sat comfortably in the leather chair of the Gulfstream and watched the Mall recede in the distance. By first light, this would be Ground Zero. People would not believe it, even when they saw the proof on TV, even when it was right in front of their eyes. From the center of the country, the new dominant species on the planet would spread outward.

Graves figured six months, a year at the most, before humanity was reduced to a few thousand people, not including those selected for the special shelters—like him.

The speaker above his seat clicked on. "We'll be at Dulles before you know it, sir," the pilot told him.

Graves pressed his own intercom button. "Thank you. Let me know when you've got an exact landing time."

"Yes sir," the pilot said, and clicked off.

Graves was no movie villain, no mad scientist who sticks around to see if his experiment works. He'd done everything he could. He'd fulfilled his duty to the Company. And Cade? Well, if Cade made it out in one piece, he could witness the new world. The Company could try to fit him into its plans then.

He had one last job to do; a reward, or a punishment, depending on the loyalty of his aides.

Just before he'd left the Site, he'd called Book and Bell from their quarters to his office. He figured they would be waiting there by now. He took out his sat-phone and dialed his own line.

It rang three times before Bell picked up. She always was the curious one.

"Put me on speaker," he ordered. He could picture them both, standing more or less at attention in front of the desk, more or less baffled.

"Where are you?" Bell asked. "The cells have been opened, and the fail-safes are down. It's a nightmare down on Level Five, and I don't think it's going to stay contained."

"It's not," Graves said. "Within a few hours, everyone at the Site will either be infected or dead."

Silence. He quite liked imagining the shock on their faces.

"You're gone, aren't you?" Bell again. Her voice was flat.

"Approaching cruising altitude," Graves agreed. "But I trust you to monitor the situation."

Book finally spoke up. "You've fucking killed us, haven't you, old man?"

"I wouldn't repay your service like that," Graves said. "Look on the desk."

By now, they would have seen the vials and the jet injector guns he'd left for them.

"This is the new, final strain of the virus," he explained. "You'll retain most of your intellect, probably most of your memories as well. You'll be the Alphas of the new people. Stronger than the basic-model Snakehead. Faster, too. And much smarter. Within a few hours, there will be thousands of those creatures, basically mindless, operating only on instinct. They will be looking for leadership. This is your chance to forge your own nation."

"Are you out of your mind?" Bell screeched.

Book didn't say anything.

"I'm offering you this duty and this reward," he said. "I hope you choose to accept it."

Bell began to scream other things at him, but he shut off the phone.

Graves was done. He'd completed his mission. It had taken him almost fifty years and dozens of false starts and aborted plans, but he'd done it.

Tomorrow, he would turn on the TV, and he would be living in the new world.

He pressed the intercom button again. "Tell me, is there any booze on this thing? I feel like celebrating."

THIRTY-SEVEN

1951—Antarctica—An expedition is sent to the Arctic to retrace the steps of the Pabodie explorers, with the hope of finding some trace of the discoveries left behind. After a brief radio report of finding what appeared to be an alien craft, the expedition lost all contact during a massive storm. No survivors were found.

—BRIEFING BOOK: CODE NAME: NIGHTMARE PET

LEVEL THREE

Bell burst through the stairwell door, putting as much distance between herself and Book as she could. She knew he was bug-nuts enough to look at being a six-foot lizard as a bright spot on his résumé.

She hadn't signed on for that. And even though Graves had locked the Site down, there were still ways out. She knew the place as well as he did. Maybe better.

She would never use the hypo he'd given her. She had her sidearm, and she'd put that in her mouth first. All she had to do was make it to the surface.

The elevators wouldn't be anything but coffins now. The stairwells would be full of Snakeheads. There were only one alternate route. She just had to get there alive.

She heard a tack-tack-tack on the floor behind her. She glanced back, and realized she wasn't merely running now.

She was running from something.

A lone Snakehead was bounding after her, using arms and legs, on all fours.

Bell grabbed her gun, but the tack-tack-tack stopped. Oh shit, she thought, in the split second before the Snakehead landed on her. It had leaped through the air and taken her down.

The A/A fatigues had incorporated body armor, which protected her a bit. But it wouldn't keep the Snakehead from chewing through her neck.

She managed to flip over and get her hand up, but her gun was somewhere far away, and the creature was lunging in for the kill.

Something grabbed it by the snout. Something yanked hard, pulling its jaws back toward the ceiling, until the creature's head touched its back. Bones snapped through the scales at its throat.

The Snakehead was tossed aside, out of her field of vision.

Bell only really got scared then.

Cade stood above her. She looked into his eyes. And if he was frightening before, now he was terrifying. Because now he was angry, and he let her see it.

LEVEL FIVE

Hewitt and Reynolds were the only ones inside the Black Site who were not trapped. They could fold themselves into shadows and emerge outside at any time they wanted.

But to them, the sounds of pain and torment, the rending and tearing of human flesh, were like grand opera delivered via cocaine injection. Everywhere they went, there was more to see, more to hear, more to sense.

The Shadowmen hung on the walls and watched as the Snakeheads ran down former friends, coworkers and prisoners alike. Some died fast, while others began the insanely painful process of turning.

The Snakeheads had little interest in the Shadowmen. In fact, they seemed to actively avoid the darkness, as if they knew something even more unnatural lurked there.

It didn't reduce the Shadowmen's fascination one bit. They were like kids in a toy store, promising, "Just five more minutes, just five more minutes."

The Shadowmen found an empty corridor. The cells had already been picked clean by the Snakeheads. Only bodies and the echoes of screams remained.

Then they saw Barrows cautiously working his way down the cell block, looking for an exit.

Behind the darkness that hid their faces, both Hewitt and Reynolds broke out into huge smiles.

They'd never liked that little prick.

Their talents were not as obvious as Cade's. Their abilities were not made for direct confrontations.

But there were other punishments, other tortures than the merely physical.

And they finally had Zach where they wanted him: alone.

LEVEL TWO

Book picked up the vial Graves left for him with only a moment's hesitation.

Bell ran out of the office as fast as she could.

She knew him better than he thought.

Book sat in an office chair in front of Graves's desk. He was only playing at making a decision, he knew. He sat there not because he had anything to consider, but because he was scared.

For the first time in years, he could admit that to himself. He was frightened.

He wasn't a sociopath, despite all he'd done. Book was capable of feeling things. There were times, undercover or in a fight, when he felt fear. You'd have to be an idiot not to. It never stayed with him, never kept him up nights.

But what was in the vial frightened him.

He saw, for the first time, how small and petty he was compared to the predator waiting in that vial to be born. His rage, his viciousness, his power to harm—these were the things he'd used to make his way in the world, and to convince himself he was truly strong enough, bad enough, to make the world step out of his way. In the end, it was nothing more than the mewling cry of an infant who was not held enough, who was not given the toys he wanted or the attention he demanded.

But he looked into the vial and saw real strength. The creature inside was indifferent to the suffering it caused because that would imply it cared about its victims. Its power was untainted. It was stronger, and it fed off the weak. It had no need to prove itself. There was no wish for peace at its source, no secret wound to be healed. It simply killed, and did so because it was made to kill. It was pure.

Looking at it, seeing himself, Book had nothing to offer. He was a matchstick before the sun. He was nothing compared to the thing contained in the vial.

Nothing.

Book was scared because he had never wanted anything so much. He was about to become perfect.

As the needle punched into his skin, Book almost wept, he was so grateful.

LEVEL THREE

"Where's Graves?" Cade demanded.

"Gone. I don't know where," Bell said.

"Where is Zach?"

"I don't know."

"Very well," he said, and reached for her throat.

"Wait, wait, wait," she blurted. "I delivered Zach to Graves and Graves took him to a cell. I swear to God that's all I know."

Cade kneeled down and got very close. He didn't lay a hand on her. He didn't have to.

"Then can you give me a single good reason to let you live?" Cade asked.

Bell mustered every bit of control she had. Her pulse hammered behind her ears, she felt sick, but when she spoke she managed to make her tone level and even.

"I can give you two," she said. "I'm your only way out of here. The Snakeheads are heading for the surface. They'll cluster around the main exit. But I know another way. You'll never find it without me."

"Why shouldn't I kill you once we get there?" It wasn't spoken like a threat. Cade sounded genuinely curious.

"Because the only elevator still working is DNA-encoded. If I'm not on it, you won't get anywhere."

"I could tear off your hand. Or some other body part."

Bell shuddered, but held her ground. "Biological scanners. Won't accept cold meat. You're stuck with me."

Cade shook his head. "I can find a way out."

"I told you there was another reason."

"What is it?"

"I can show you how the Snakeheads were made," she said, a smile of triumph escaping despite her fear. "If you don't know that, you'll never stop Graves from starting this all over again."

LEVEL FIVE

Zach crept along in the murky gray cast by the emergency lights along the floor.

So far, nothing had jumped out to eat him. But the night was still young.

The shadows seemed to deepen and swirl around him. The emergency lights fluttered, spat and finally gave up entirely.

There was no light at all now.

Zach tried to take a step, tripped over the threshold of a cell, and found himself sprawled inside on the tile.

So much for the other senses compensating for blindness, he thought.

Then again, maybe not. He felt, rather than saw, something move.

Zach didn't hear anything. But he couldn't escape the feeling that he wasn't alone.

His eyes had to be playing tricks on him now.

There was no light.

So how was it getting darker?

THE DARKNESS MOVED over Zach like cold fingers, prodding and stroking his skin with a malicious familiarity, a kind of casual violation, as if to let him know his boundaries, his body, his person meant nothing at all.

Then the whispering started.

He couldn't quite make out the words. Couldn't quite place the voice, either, because it was doubled, in stereo, and too low to hear properly. But he could hear—and feel—the tone. The hate that was in every mumbled word. The curdling note of contempt.

Zach didn't allow himself to be scared. He got angry instead.

"You're trying to haunt me? Seriously?"

The whispering paused, then started again.

Zach laughed. "I work with the scariest bastard you'll ever meet. You're going to have to do better than that."

His voice echoed in the dark.

The silence deepened.

He heard footsteps. Leather soles on the concrete.

Zach wondered if he'd just made a huge mistake.

A figure appeared from the shadows, forming as if out of solid darkness.

"Hey, kid," it said. "Been a while."

Zach suddenly placed the voice. He knew who was speaking to him. "Griff?"

At the sound of his name, former Special Agent William H. Griffin stepped out of the shadows.

He still wore the suit he died in, and the wound that killed him: a massive hole in his chest, his viscera spilling out through the broken remains of his rib cage. His skin was gray and mottled purple, decay setting in around the edges.

He smiled at Zach, revealing teeth painted like fingernails with crusts of blood.

"So," he said, in the same deep voice that had introduced Zach to this world. "How are you liking the job so far?"

THIRTY-EIGHT

January 24, 1946—The Central Intelligence Agency is unofficially founded by President Harry S Truman, who hands a ceremonial black cloak and wooden dagger to Sidney Souers, the agency's first director.

—Cole Daniels, *Black Ops: The Occult-CIA Connection*

Cade and Bell found the access shaft, Bell's secret way around the Site, nestled next to the concrete wall of the giant elevator platform. He gestured for her to lead and he followed.

They moved down into the Site. Bell's head was just below the ceiling. Cade had to duck. The shaft corkscrewed around, following the odd layout of the Site in a kind of descending staircase pattern. But it was so twisted even Cade would have had trouble navigating it without a guide.

Occasional hatches—Cade assumed for maintenance workers—gave them a glimpse of what was happening in the rest of the Site.

Many of the Site's personnel were nothing more than piles of bones now. Bell stopped looking after a while.

At Level Four, through the hatch and on the other side of a sally port, they saw a crowd of Snakeheads moving toward the surface. Through the port's windows, the creatures' heads bobbed as they streamed through the narrow space. There were hundreds of them.

Once, they found another Snakehead, wandering on its own, but it seemed lost in the shaft and confused without the herd.

One-on-one, Cade killed it easily.

Bell still had her gun. She kept it holstered. Maybe Cade forgot it— unlikely—or just didn't think of her as a threat—more likely. Either way, she didn't want to give him any reason to question his decision to keep her alive.

She was sweating, not entirely from exertion, by the time they emerged at the lab, the chamber at the heart of the Black Site.

LEVEL FIVE

Bell thumbed the scanner to unlock the door. It opened, revealing the interior of the lab.

Cade looked inside. For a moment, he was still as a statue.

Bell wondered what he was waiting for.

When he turned to her, she got the impression of great effort, as if he was pulling against gravity.

She realized he was struggling not to kill her.

"You knew about this?"

She couldn't lie. She nodded, afraid to move any more than that.

Cade tore his gaze from her and stepped to enter the room.

"Are you letting me go?" She could hear the hope in her own voice, creeping in around the disbelief.

"Stay here," he said.

She glanced, involuntarily, down the corridor, measuring the distance back to the access shaft.

Cade gave her a look that would keep her from sleeping soundly ever again. "You think I won't find you?" he asked.

He slammed the door shut behind him.

CADE WALKED AMONG the surgical equipment and lab tables. He walked slowly. He struggled not to make a mockery of this by his mere presence.

He still had his pack of tools, but they were useless here.

There, buried deep in the ground, in the middle of America, he saw how Graves had managed to build his monsters.

It even made sense on an obscene level, one Cade understood almost instinctively. Graves needed people as raw material. He needed people who could be disappeared, whose absence would not cause the world to pause, even for a second.

Most of his prisoners were malcontents, nobodies, homeless, insane, wanderers or criminals. But even among the unwanted and forgotten, there were one or two who had people who cared what had happened to them. Even some of the ones who went missing from the battlefields and the POW camps were names in systems and on registries, so they could not vanish without someone marking their absence.

But there was a rich supply of children who barely even had names, living in bone-grinding poverty all over the world. In a war zone, or after a disaster, dozens of them could vanish at once without so much as a ripple in the surface of the greater world.

Cade already knew Graves had used children in his first attempts to create the Snakeheads. When no more bodies showed up, he simply assumed that Graves had stopped using them. Not out of morality, but because they were of no more use.

He realized how horribly wrong he'd been.

The children lay on hospital beds in two neat rows. Respirators pumped their lungs. IVs dripped chemicals into their sticklike arms. Most of their eyes were closed, or stared unseeing at the ceiling.

They were almost corpses already, shriveled like raisins around their bloated, distended bellies.

That was the only sign of life in the room, in each child's swollen abdomen. Their skins stretched tight as drums and translucent, revealing the writhing masses inside them.

They looked like the same eggs he'd seen on the shore at Innsmouth in 1928. Tiny, amphibious creatures turning and twisting. But they thrashed without hope of escape. Cade saw the needles and hoses plugged directly into the children's bodies, sucking out the eggs and slurping them into a central collection tank. Inside, they were strained and shredded, sucked through more filters and tubes, until they were distilled into serum at a final dispensing point.

Even as the eggs were drawn from them, Cade could see the other embryos beneath the skin, dividing, filling up the space, waiting to be harvested.

The virus, or whatever it truly was, lived in that serum, ready to fill syringes, bottles, or maybe the tanks of crop dusters.

Graves had turned these children into incubators. He had made them nothing more than warm nests to spawn horror.

There was nothing here for Cade to fight. All he had to do was end life. All he had to was kill.

For him, this was the easy part.

He went to each bed and shut down the life-support machines. There was no last gasp, no sudden clawing reach for air. There was nothing left in these bodies except death, and they slid into it quietly.

The machines made more noise. They bucked and protested and finally churned to a stop as their supply was cut off.

He knew he didn't have much time. But this was something that required some kind of mourning, even from a thing like him.

Cade held his cross until his hand burned like fire.

It reminded him that he was not human. And at that moment, at least, he was grateful.

THIRTY-NINE

Evidence has linked the CIA to the spread of crack and heroin; the start of wars in Asia, Latin America and Africa; the murders of JFK, RFK and MLK; even dosing innocent civilians with everything from LSD to smallpox. Given all that, is it really such a stretch to believe the agency might be in league with the actual forces of darkness?

—Cole Daniels, *Black Ops: The Occult-CIA Connection*

LEVEL FIVE

"You're not Griff," Zach insisted. He could hear the childishness in his voice, but he clung to the truth of what he was saying.

"How would you know?" Griff asked.

"Because Griff would never let himself be used as a puppet by whatever fist is up your ass."

The Not-Griff scowled. "You've got a big mouth, kid. I never liked that about you."

"You can't hurt me. That's why you're screwing with my head."

"You look ready to piss your pants. I'd say it's working."

Zach hesitated. "Doesn't matter. Whatever you are, you're not Griff."

"Part of you knows I'm telling the truth, Zachary. The part that's honest. I know things about you that you'd never admit to anyone else.

Look at Cade. The closest thing you've got to a friend. And you betray him every day."

Not true, Zach thought. That's not true.

"Do you even know what's true anymore, Zach?"

"I know Griff isn't anywhere your side can reach him. I'm sure about that."

Not-Griff shrugged, and some bit of organic matter fell from under his arm.

"Maybe. Maybe not," he conceded. "Part of Griff is gone. But he left behind plenty. I'm the part that gets left behind when everything good goes away. And trust me, kid: he left a lot of hate for you. He always thought you were worthless and weak."

Zach's legs trembled, but he stood his ground.

"I don't believe you."

The shadows gathered tightly around Zach again. He could barely see Griff now.

"That's why your father split, Zach."

"I dealt with all this in therapy. Try again."

"Really?" Griff asked. "That's not how I hear it."

He stepped back completely into the shadows. His voice kept droning on, however.

"Your mother knew. Look at how she tried to protect you. Tried to shelter you from the truth of the world. Where you could never compete on your own. And you failed her, too."

Not fair, Zach thought. "No. I was there for her."

"She died alone."

"I only left the room for a moment. I had a call. We were in the middle of a campaign."

"Do you want to see it? Since you missed it before."

Griff's voice had changed. It became higher, softer and raspier. Zach knew it instantly. He closed his eyes.

And then he was there. Both the younger version of him, getting up and walking away from the hospital bed, phone already to his ear. Zach remembered the boredom and irritation he felt back then. The need to take a shower, to get back to his apartment and to get some work done. The election was in two weeks, and the voice-mail was piling up.

His mother reached after him, her eyes suddenly open. It was the end. The doctors said she'd felt no pain.

They'd lied.

Without his hand there, she'd had nothing to hold on to. She could hear him talking in the hallway on his phone, too loud, disturbing other patients despite all the signs that warned against using cell phones in the hospital.

The one time she really needed him. Her hand fell. Her body spasmed, and the life went out of her as she fell into the dark. All alone. Her last word was his name. He wasn't there to hear it. He left her alone.

Zach screamed so hard he tore something in his throat, screamed until his lungs ached, and still it did not release a drop of the despair he felt filling him, drowning his soul.

EVENTUALLY, ZACH STOPPED SCREAMING.

From the shadows, Zach's mother stepped forward. She still wore her hospital gown, the IV trailing behind her, hollowed out by the chemicals and the pain.

"You're glad I'm dead," she said. "You wanted it to happen. You were happy to be finished with the inconvenience."

Zach was sobbing, fat tears flowing down his cheeks.

"No, Mom. Please don't say that."

"You failed me. That's all you've ever done. Failed in every way. You never loved me."

"Mom. Please. I love you. I'd do anything for you."

"It's too late. I'm dead."

"No. Please. I'll do anything."

"There's only one thing you can do, Zach. You have to die. Can you do that for me? Are you ready to die?"

FORTY

Part of this resilience we can attribute to the fact that Cade was more durable as a human than most of us in the modern era can understand. He was born in a time without vaccines, antibiotics or even decent sanitation and hygiene. He survived malnutrition and poverty in his childhood to become a sailor at a time when the physical demands of life on the seas were unbelievably grueling. After all that, he lived through an attack from what had to be a King Vampire.

—Dr. William Kavanaugh, Sanction V research group

LEVEL FIVE

When Cade exited the lab, he found Bell backed up against the wall by Tania.

"She says she can get us out of here," Tania said, not looking at him. "I'm pretty sure she's better as a snack."

Bell trembled, her chin up in the air as she tried to push herself even further back into the wall.

"Don't kill her," Cade found himself saying.

Bell and Tania both looked at him with some surprise.

"Not yet," Cade added.

Tania stepped back, frowning.

"It's done?" Cade asked her.

She gave him a withering look.

"I only wanted to know."

Cade was about to say something else when he heard the scream. So did Tania. Even Bell heard it faintly, though it was at the far end of the Site, muted by tons of concrete and steel.

Zach.

Cade had never heard anything so terrible from him. Not ever.

He looked at Bell, who was horrified, but not by any fear of the unknown.

She had the look of someone who knew exactly what was happening to the person doing that screaming, and exactly how bad it was.

"Tell me," Cade growled at her.

"Hewitt and Reynolds," she said. "Oh God, they must still be here."

"Who?"

"The Shadowmen. They have Zach. They must be . . ." She swallowed over a catch in her throat. "They're *playing* with him."

FORTY-ONE

SHADOW PEOPLE: A creature or entity that shares many of the characteristics of a ghost, but also seems to have a palpable physical presence, these strange beings appear to be shadows without bodies to cast them. Witnesses report seeing a variety of types, including a man wearing an old-fashioned hat, others wearing cloaks or trench coats, and some with both. These shadows are nearly always malevolent. Rumors of a similar shadow creature preying on criminals in the 1930s and 1940s are probably urban legends, or an attempt to "domesticate" a truly frightening—and still unexplained—phenomenon.

—Cole Daniels, *Monsterpaedia*

LEVEL FIVE

Cade walked down the corridor. He couldn't see a thing.

That in itself was unusual. His eyes were sensitive to the slightest amounts of light or heat. But it was as if the darkness lay over everything in the cells like a great blanket, smothering any possible detail.

He listened, instead.

He was unarmed.

He'd given his pack to Tania and told her to take Bell and go into the access shaft. If he and Zach didn't show up at the elevator, she would know what to do.

He'd considered taking one of the guns with him, but Bell only shook her head.

"You can't shoot them. They're barely even there."

He didn't have time to ask what that meant.

He kept listening, moving down the corridor, his mind forming a picture from the sounds in the darkness.

There. Through the metal of a cell door locked open. The sound of a heartbeat. Zach's heartbeat.

Faint. And getting fainter.

Cade stepped over the threshold.

A single, half-dead fluorescent tube flickered in the ceiling overhead. The murky light washed everything blue-gray in a small patch at the center of the cell.

Zach huddled on the floor, nearly catatonic. His body temperature had dropped. Cade's senses barely registered Zach's breathing. From the rustle of Zach's clothes on the floor, Cade could hear him twitching— but slowly. Even his involuntary muscle movements were failing.

Cade had to get him out of here.

Again, he hesitated.

Someone else was in there with him. Even if he couldn't see him. Or scent him.

The entire place seemed soaked in dread. All the terrors of the night were coiled in the corners, waiting to spring. It would have been quite frightening if Cade hadn't been one of those terrors himself.

They wanted him inside. Zach was bait.

Cade knew it. He stepped over the threshold anyway.

He saw something, out of the corner of his eye. He moved, barely in time. He saw a daggerlike shadow retreat back into the dark.

Immediately, behind him, another stabbing attack. A blade—a

wooden blade—appeared from nowhere in the dark. It sliced at him. He turned and caught it in his arm, rather than his back.

It was pulled from his flesh with a wet kiss of a noise, and vanished again.

He whirled and sent a kick back at his attacker, but nothing was there. If it weren't for the cut, there'd be no evidence of any attacker at all.

Interesting.

There was still enough fresh blood in his system for the wound to close.

Behind him. The slightest scraping noise, a shoe touching the pavement, broke him from his thoughts.

He jumped this time, not waiting for it. A blade made of shadow sliced through the air where his head had been.

If he hadn't moved, decapitation.

The follow-up attack came from behind, as he expected. This time he was ready for it, and avoided another cut from another razor-edged shadow.

What had Graves made here? They were not as fast as he was—not in thought or reflex, anyway. But they vanished without a trace. He spun around in a complete circle, trying desperately to see something. Anything.

He cranked his reflexes to their limit again. Everything in the room slowed. The darkness thickened, and this time, he could see the silhouette of a dagger, the edge looming like a battleship in the sea. Standing behind it was an outline, a man in a dark trench coat and old-fashioned fedora.

It was just a shadow. Only darkness, given form.

The shadow of the dagger raised over Zach's head.

Cade had no time for other options. He threw himself into the shadow's path.

It skidded along his ribs. If he had not leaned the right way, redirecting the force of the thrust, it would have pierced his heart.

They could have used flamethrowers and burned him. It would have been more effective. But all things in the dark hated and feared the light. It was instinctive. Fire was man's first and oldest weapon against the Other Side. That told Cade something about what they were. They didn't use the same equipment as the A/A soldiers, either because they didn't have it or because they feared it like he did.

Of course, they didn't need DU rounds or white phosphorus. They could just keep picking at him until they got lucky and got his heart. They could end him with a dollar's worth of surveying stakes from Home Depot.

He hunched over Zach, trying to guard his chest and protect Zach at the same time.

He heard something.

Laughter. From the dark, from everywhere at once.

They were laughing at him. They took a moment to enjoy his helplessness. They loved being stronger. You could hear it in the echoes off the walls.

That's how he knew for certain the Shadowmen were still partially human, whatever else they were.

That gave him something to work with.

He'd fought an invisible man once. This was different. That was no contest: he still breathed, still left footprints and still bled when Cade got to him. These Shadowmen didn't just drop out of sight; they dropped completely out of the world.

As unbelievable as it was, they were somehow crossing back and forth between this world and the Other Side. They jumped over the border at will.

Cade marshaled everything he knew about the Other Side, trying to find a strategy.

He'd seen ghosts, and they were random and unstoppable and unfathomable. They belonged fully to the Other Side, and they only pushed through with great effort. He could outlast ghosts.

These two, however, didn't appear to be slowing down.

But nothing human could survive on the Other Side. The things over there were starved for life. Anything real, anything alive—even as little as a drop of blood—was like a light, drawing a billion buzzing insects. They would swarm for even a small taste of the living. And they would take any chance they could to breach the vital world again.

They must be protected somehow, Cade realized. As invisible over there as they were over here.

The strain must have been enormous. The Other Side didn't let go of live meat that easily.

He could use that.

For that moment when they stepped into reality, they were vulnerable. The question was, how would he know when they were about to step through?

They count on being untouchable, Cade thought. Let's test that theory.

Cade quit moving. Stood at the center of the dark space in the room, perfectly still, guarding Zach. He waited.

He didn't see the Shadowmen emerge from the dark behind him. He seemed like a perfect target.

Cade felt it. Somewhere, in the quiet place where his soul used to be, he felt the first step of darkness entering this world. Like a silk nightdress hitting the floor. The Other Side opened behind him, and the Shadowmen coalesced and stepped through.

They were still human, and humans were predictable. Give them a defenseless target and they can't help themselves.

They came at him from both sides, so there would be no escape.

They thought they had him. They stepped in for the kill, wanting to make it intimate, wanting to see it up close—

And Cade lashed out, plunging his hands into their shadows, and grabbed. He grabbed hard.

He connected with something warm amid all the dark and cold. Bodies, struggling under his hands. In his right, he had a man by the neck. In his left, he had the other man by the arm. Warm and unmistakably human.

They immediately retreated back into the shadows, but Cade would not let go. He felt true cold, for the first time since he had changed. The blackness bubbled around his hands, colder than liquid nitrogen, slicker than oil, but he managed to keep his grip.

He got them just as they were about to emerge into the real world, trapped between this reality and the Other Side.

They were stuck.

Cade stood between the two Shadowmen as they struggled, one man in his right hand, the other in his left.

They tried to get back into the dark, where they would be safe. But Cade had managed to get hold of their core—the part that was still human. That was still fragile. They squirmed and panicked. Cade smirked and tightened his grasp. He felt the bones snap under his left hand. First the radius, then the ulna.

The cold soaked him to the bone, but he didn't let go.

The men thrashed and pulled. On his right hand, Cade's fingers kept slipping—he didn't have as good a hold. He felt skin shredding. At the same time, his left hand began to slide off the arm of the other one. The bones were being crushed to powder; it was like trying to hold a greasy sock.

The Other Side had let him in, he figured, because he already belonged to it. His vampire side was connected with the darkness there. It was almost like coming home.

Getting out again was another matter altogether.

The cold crept up his arm, into his shoulder, his chest. Stealing whatever heat was left from the blood he still had inside.

The Shadowmen kept pulling.

Cade pulled with everything he had, dragging them almost back into the real world.

He could see them, panic in their faces, behind the thinnest veil of darkness.

He almost had them out. But it wasn't enough. He was about to lose his grip.

So he let them go.

But not before scratching them both with his thumbnails, deep enough to open skin and capillaries. Deep enough to spill blood.

Instinctively, both of the Shadowmen retreated, back to the Other Side. Mistake.

Fresh blood. Like ringing a dinner bell on the Other Side.

Screaming began from the darkness.

Both of them tried to escape. Their outlines reappeared, but it was as if they were drowning in quicksand.

The Shadowmen began to condense, to sputter out, like a bad TV picture.

The first one almost made it back. The shadow opened once more, and a man's face appeared, his eyes wide with terror. He seemed to be up to his ears in a pool of ink. He was still screaming, but no sound escaped his lips.

The darkness reached up and covered over him, almost gently. Then it dribbled away, running off into itself, as if a plug had been pulled. Cade could have sworn he heard a burp as it vanished completely.

The other Shadowman made it all the way.

The darkness spat, and a man hit the floor. The shadows behind him closed up and whispered away.

He could have been a thousand years old. Skin like parchment. Bones jutting from strings of dried-out muscle. The dark stuck to him, here and there. Filled his mouth, clung to his teeth.

He looked at Cade once. Cade saw nothing in his eyes. The man's mind was broken. The trip back had been too much.

He coughed, giggled once, then curled into a fetal position and quietly died.

Cade picked up Zach. His pulse was stronger already. Whatever nightmares were tormenting him, they died with the Shadowmen.

FORTY-TWO

That's probably the other, more important reason for Cade's unusual strength and endurance. Since the vampiric transformation is accomplished by lateral genetic transmission (through retroviral bodies in the saliva or other fluids), it's probable that the traits of the carrier can be transmitted to the infected, as well. In other words, Cade most likely inherited a set of vampire genes from a much purer, much stronger source than most of his kind. Honed by centuries of constant struggle, these genes turned Cade into as close a copy of that King Vampire as they could manage.

—Dr. William Kavanaugh, Sanction V research group

Zach was unconscious, exhaustion and his head wound combining to put him down. Cade looked him over, opened his eyes to examine his pupils. He was concussed. Cade had to get him awake. He sat Zach against the wall.

"Zach," he said. "Zach, wake up."

His breathing was steady, but he didn't open his eyes. Cade slapped him lightly on the face.

"Zach. You have to wake up."

Nothing. Cade smacked him again.

"*Zach*," he bellowed, as loud as he could. Zach's hair actually ruffled. Zach opened one eye. It glared at Cade.

"If you woke me just to say I told you so, I'm gonna be seriously pissed," he said.

Cade's lip curled. "I need you on your feet. I can't carry you and fight at the same time."

Zach struggled up against the wall. Cade didn't help him. He knew he had to get him to medical help, and soon. But he also knew Zach had to walk, and the sooner he found out if that was possible, the better.

Zach wobbled, but stayed upright.

"Let me tell you something," he said. "Any girl who works for the Shadow Company offers to show you a good time, you tell her—"

He vomited.

Cade noticed Zach was shuddering all over. He wondered what he'd seen in that room. He stank of fear and regret in a way Cade had never sensed before.

"Are you all right?" he asked.

"Super," Zach said, lifting his shoulders as if pulled by a crane. "Don't suppose you have any gum?"

Cade started walking for the access shaft.

Zach followed. "No? That's fine. Touched by your concern, though."

LEVEL TWO

On the other side of the Site, Marsh stood in a long line of Snakeheads, filing toward the surface. Their twisting path had taken them all the way up to Level Two.

Marsh was far at the back of the line. He wanted to follow the trail of scent to whatever was waiting at the end. Even though the blood of his first victims was still wet on his snout, he was hungry. He hoped there would be something left when he got there.

The line came to a complete stop. The Snakeheads jostled and crowded one another, but none of them moved. Marsh knew what that meant: there was something in the way.

Marsh was curious. He moved forward. He seemed to have retained more of his own mind than the others. Maybe they recognized this, because they made room for him, let him pass ahead.

The stairwell above them was blocked. The other Snakeheads scratched furiously at a steel plate that covered the opening to the landing. Marsh began pushing, and the rest of them followed his lead.

Strong as they were, it was no use. The plate didn't budge.

They had no way of knowing the plate was a steel shutter from the fail-safe system. Or that an Archer/Andrews Armored Personnel Carrier, along with desks, office equipment and the wall—much of it broken slabs of concrete now—lay on top of it, sealing the passage shut.

Cade had seen no reason to leave the stairs open. After finishing with the strike team, he'd used the freight elevator to bring the APC down. Then he put one of the merc's tactical batons against the gas pedal. It tore through the interior of the Site, finally ramming into a steel shutter and knocking it loose from its housing before crashing into the stairwell.

The APC alone weighed 12.3 tons. It would take hours and heavy equipment to open this pathway again. That was time Cade had already ensured the Snakeheads wouldn't get.

Their frustration became a yowling, thrashing rage as they hurled their bodies against the metal over and over.

Marsh felt like he'd let them down somehow.

Then he heard something. Like the other Snakeheads, he'd lost his ability to speak English, but these words resonated with him. They seemed to drill right into his brain.

A figure appeared below them at the door.

"You want out. You want food," he said. "I can show you the way."

He turned, and they followed without hesitation. Marsh and the others knew, on some basic level, there was no questioning this. It was simply the natural order of things.

FORTY-THREE

THE BLOOP is a cute and harmless name for what might be the largest sea creature on the planet. In 1997, an ultra-low-frequency and extremely powerful underwater sound was detected by the U.S. National Oceanic and Atmospheric Administration (NOAA). The sound was *several hundred times louder* than the call of a blue whale, the largest known creature in existence, and human sources—such as underwater detonations or submarine propulsion—were ruled out. Some have suggested that the location of the sound—50° S 100° W, off the Pacific coast of South America—is near the fabled underwater city of R'lyeh, the home of the massive underwater creature Cthulu in the stories of H. P. Lovecraft. Of course, Cthulu and R'lyeh are completely fictional. The true source of the sound remains unknown.

—Cole Daniels, *Monsterpaedia*

LEVEL ONE

Bell and Tania waited at the top of the access shaft. Tania eyed Bell as if she contemplated snapping her head back like a Pez dispenser and sucking her dry.

"What is this?" Tania asked.

"Emergency escape route. Graves had it made, off the blueprints. I oversaw construction."

"You are just full of surprises." She gave Bell a completely neutral look. Somehow that was worse than Cade's active hate. Bell mattered less than zero to Tania, except as food, and, currently, as a key.

She checked a watch. Bell noticed it was Hermès.

"How long are we supposed to wait?" Bell asked.

"Don't worry," she said. "I plan on giving myself plenty of time to get out."

"Before what?" Bell couldn't help asking.

"Before this entire place goes up in flames," Tania said. She seemed almost eager to tell Bell what she'd done. Unlike Cade, Tania was chatty.

When a fire broke out, the Site's fire-suppression system sprayed inert gases through ceiling-mounted nozzles, smothering the flames by removing oxygen.

Tania had rerouted the Site's natural gas line into the system. Now when a fire broke out, the nozzles would spray pure methane into the air all over the Site.

Everything inside would be cremated almost instantly.

"I'm not sticking around for that," Tania said. "Sacrifice is Cade's problem, not mine."

"You're just going to leave him here? I thought you were—I don't know, what do vampires call it?"

Tania gave her a cold smile. "We don't call it anything. We don't fool ourselves like you."

Then Tania laughed. At her, Bell realized.

"What?"

"I said 'like you.' I know what you did to Zach. I don't have to explain a thing about survival to you, do I?"

Bell didn't say anything.

"I can't tell you how long it's been since I've had a good girl talk," Tania said. "I might even give you a head start when we get to the surface."

"I'm touched," Bell said.

"My pleasure."

Bell thought about what it meant that she was being judged by a creature whose only purpose was to kill.

She thought about a lot of things in the next few minutes.

TANIA HAD MARKED the way to the top levels by painting arrows in the phosphorescent goo from a broken glow stick.

Cade stayed a few steps ahead of Zach. He tried to keep him talking. He never imagined that would ever be a problem.

"So. Tania?"

"Yeah, you figured that out, did you?"

"She asked me not to tell you."

"I thought you'd freak out if you knew. How did you think she'd been showing up on your assignments lately?"

"I assumed she was stalking me."

"Get over yourself," Zach said. He was panting. Cade didn't let him stop.

"Then what does she get out of it?"

"Mainly the chance to stalk you," Zach admitted. "Although I think she's also interested in our pension plan."

"Do you really think you can manage her? Make her an employee? There's no one who can administer the Oath to her. Even if there were, she'd never agree to it."

"Maybe she'll come over to our side."

"You didn't learn anything from your experience with Bell, did you?"

Silence. Then: "Thanks, Cade. That's a big help."

CADE EMERGED into a narrow passage, less than five feet across, made for one person at a time. Tania and Bell were there.

It was Zach who couldn't meet Bell's eyes, as if embarrassed.

The elevator was right where Bell said it would be. Its door was as narrow as the tight passage. They moved fast.

Bell put her hand on a biometric scanner. It beeped, and the elevator doors opened.

Cade reached for the fire alarm on the wall. He prepared to yank the handle down. In minutes, the air would be saturated with methane.

The Snakeheads would all burn.

Someone grabbed Cade from behind and slammed him into the wall. Cade, drained from his fight with the Shadowmen, didn't even hear it coming. He lashed out wildly, throwing the attacker off him and back down the tunnel.

Bell looked back from the elevator and screamed.

Book stood there, but he was no longer human in every way it counted.

He was naked before them, covered with plated armor, a row of spikes running from the crest on his head down his back.

He'd been fully transformed. Snakehead 4.0. More like a dragon than any reptile living today.

Book's staring yellow eyes retained a cruel intelligence, and Cade was not at all surprised when he opened his mouth, revealing a human-shaped tongue, and spoke.

"Did you think you were the only one who knew about this exit?" Book asked.

His voice was the only thing that remained unchanged. He didn't even hiss on the *s* in "this."

Cade hit him. Book's head bounced back as if attached with bungee cord.

Book smiled.

Cade noticed the others behind Book for the first time.

Snakeheads, lined up behind him. Watching him, crowding forward, eager to help.

They'd found a leader.

"You can't stop us," Book said.

His arm snapped out, whip-quick, and he slapped Cade. Cade felt bones break. He went skidding into the floor, stopped only by Tania's body behind him.

He shook himself and regained his feet.

Book just stood there. He waved Cade on. Inviting him to try again.

"See? You can't even slow us down."

FORTY-FOUR

Of course, it's entirely possible the reason Cade is so formidable might simply be due to individual temperament: Cade is unusually stubborn and willful, dedicated and tough; what some people call—and I mean this with all due respect—a total bastard.

—Dr. William Kavanaugh, Sanction V research group

What's the matter, Cade? Nothing to say now that you're in a fair fight?"

Cade looked up at Tania. She nodded. She understood.

Whatever improvements Book had undergone, the vampires still thought faster than he did.

She swung the pack of weapons off her shoulder, into Cade's hands, and turned for the elevator.

Zach realized what was happening, a moment behind.

"Cade, no," he said. "I order you to—"

Cade shoved him hard enough to send him flying into the elevator.

Bell and Tania were already inside. The doors closed.

In one smooth motion, Cade reached into the pack and pulled out the last thing he'd taken from the mercenaries.

Book found himself staring down the barrel of the AA-12 automatic shotgun.

"I have no interest in a fair fight," Cade said.

THE ELEVATOR STARTED its slow ascent to the Mall.

Zach got his wind back. "Get us back down there," he ordered Bell.

"Not a chance," Tania said. "You touch that button and I'll tear your arm off."

"Shut up," Zach said.

"It doesn't matter," Bell said. "We have to reach the top first. It's an elevator. We can't turn it around."

"Cade's doing his job," Tania said. Bell realized she was speaking to Zach. "He's probably been dreaming about dying for his country for a hundred and forty years. Let him."

Zach looked like he wanted to slap her, if that wasn't suicidal.

He pointed at Bell. "Once we reach the top. You are sending me back down there."

Tania snorted. "What possible good do you think that will do?"

"He's not dying alone. That's good enough for me."

"Idiot," Tania said.

"Shut up," Zach said again.

They rode the rest of the way in silence, except for an instrumental version of "Baby One More Time," piped through the Mall's sound system.

FIVE MINUTES TO MIDNIGHT. The crowds were pressed up against the glass of the Mall entrances now. At the east wing of the Mall, some people were pounding their palms, hitting the glass in rhythm, chanting, "Open up! Open up!"

A contingent of mall cops went out to calm them down and keep them from shattering the big panes of the windows.

Almost time. Four more minutes, and then they would stampede inside. Like cattle on the hoof.

BOOK'S FACE was no longer human enough to register surprise as he looked down the 12-gauge barrel.

Then it was simply gone, along with the rest of his head, as Cade pulled the trigger and fired at point-blank range.

Book didn't fall right away. He stood there, leaking blood all over the floor—more than it seemed possible for him to contain.

The Snakeheads behind him waited a moment, suddenly lost without their leader.

Cade took the moment. He shattered the fire-alarm glass with his right hand. Sirens and lights began blaring. Nozzles popped from the ceiling. Methane sprayed invisibly into the air. It was lighter than oxygen. It would take a while before it reached the floor of the passage.

The Snakeheads surged toward him. Whether they wanted out, or wanted revenge, or both, they were coming for them.

Cade pointed the shotgun again.

The Snakeheads stopped cold. They couldn't rush him more than one or two at a time. The advantage of their numbers was removed by the narrow chute. While no longer intelligent, they recognized that something capable of removing their leader's head was not good.

Cade had enough ammunition, he thought. All he had to do was keep them at bay until the air reached the saturation point. Then the muzzle flash alone would ignite everything around him in a fireball.

THE ELEVATOR FINALLY reached the ground level of the Mall.

Tania stepped out immediately.

"Hey," Zach said. "Where are you going?"

Tania smirked. "Don't push your luck, Zachary. Tell Cade goodbye for me."

She walked quickly away. She could see the crowds outside, pressing against the glass of the Mall's giant outer windows.

"Hey!" someone yelled from the crowd. "They got in early! No fair!"

"Morons," she muttered to herself.

Zach paid no attention at all. He turned back to Bell. "Let's go," he said.

She got back in the elevator, pressed the scanner again, and they went down.

THE SNAKEHEADS GOT their courage back. One at a time, they came at him, running as fast as possible in the confined space.

One at a time, Cade pulled the trigger and blasted them into pieces.

They fell, and the next Snakeheads scrambled over them.

Cade fired again. They kept walking right into the blasts, gaining an inch for the next one in line.

The only problem was, Cade was going to run out of shells before they ran out of bodies.

Just a few more minutes, Cade thought. That's all it will take.

THE SONG ON the way down was "I Will Always Love You." Bell started giggling uncontrollably.

Zach even managed a smile.

"Yeah," he said. "I know. Some job, huh?"

She felt tears at the corners of her eyes. She was on the verge of losing it completely, she knew.

"You're going to die," she said.

"Everyone dies," Zach said. "Just let me out and close the door as fast as you can."

"Why would you—?"

He shrugged. "Beats hell out of me," he said. "Maybe the world needs you in it."

The elevator chimed. The door opened.

CADE WAS ALMOST out of shells.

The Snakeheads had backed him to the elevator. The pile of bodies now almost blocked the narrow passage. They still came at him, only slower.

Cade picked off another Snakehead, barely three feet from him.

He heard a string quartet murdering Whitney Houston.

He didn't have to look behind him.

"You Christ-forsaken moron," he spat.

"Don't blaspheme," Zach said. He coughed and gagged on the sulfurous odor. The air was almost filled with methane now. "Get your ass on the elevator."

"No," Cade said. "They'll get up the shaft. And someone has to be here to make sure the gas ignites."

"I could order—"

The rest of Zach's words were lost in the blast of Cade's shotgun shattering the chests of two Snakeheads, one behind the other.

"You know it won't work," Cade said. "This is protecting the nation. Above all else."

Zach muttered some curse lost beneath the hiss and shrieking of the creatures, the spray of the gas and the hollow boom of the gun.

He reached into the pack, still by Cade's feet. He came up with a white phosphorus grenade.

"All right, then. Butch and Sundance time," he said.

Neither Cade nor Zach realized that the door to the elevator was still open. Bell stood there.

She had her gun in hand, finger on the trigger, as she stepped into the passage.

AT THE EAST ENTRANCE, the regular mall cops had finally calmed the crowd. People still grumbled about the early birds, but when the security guards looked inside, they saw no one there.

Anyway, it was midnight. They unlocked the doors and let the throngs of people rush inside.

"BUTCH CASSIDY DIDN'T DIE," Cade said to Zach. "And neither will you. Get out of here."

At that moment, his shotgun clicked empty.

Zach felt a tap on the shoulder. He turned. Bell had her gun up and aimed at his head.

"Get down," she screamed.

She fired a round the instant he ducked. It caught a Snakehead in the eye, sending him to the floor.

"What are you doing?" Zach started to ask.

She cracked him across the skull with the pistol. His eyes rolled up into his head. "Son of a—"

He was down. Bell shoved him into the elevator.

Cade used the shotgun like a club; the Snakeheads had gotten bold. They were close to escaping. They could feel it.

Bell put her gun right against the temple of the first creature in line. She pulled the trigger. A crater appeared in its head.

Cade used the Snakehead's body to shove the others back.

It was all the time Bell needed.

She shouldered her way by Cade, close enough to kiss his cheek. As her mouth passed his ear, she whispered a name. She told him what she'd learned, the small fact that she'd always saved, just in case. It was useless to her now. But Cade would be able to do something with it.

Then she shot Cade point-blank in the chest.

It didn't kill him; she only had standard ammunition, and he was still close to bulletproof.

But combined with the broken ribs Book had inflicted, it was enough to knock him off balance. She pushed with her whole body, and he fell into the elevator with Zach.

Her hand hit the scanner and she ducked out again.

Cade's icy calm was lost in an expression of pure bewilderment.

He mouthed the word "Why?"

The doors closed.

THE SNAKEHEADS OVERWHELMED her only a few moments later. Her gun was empty, and she had no spare clips. And she couldn't make enough head shots to stop them from getting to her.

She tried to remain calm even as they grabbed her. She thought about what she wanted to say to Cade in response to his last question.

In truth, she hadn't done it for him. Or even for Zach. She'd done it to prove something to herself.

"The world needs people like you in it," she would have said. "Because it has too many people like me in it."

Just as the Snakeheads slammed her to the floor, as they lowered their heads to feed, an appetizer before the main course they knew was waiting up above, Bell opened her hand.

The grenade she'd taken from Zach fell and rolled to touch the clawed toe of one of the Snakeheads.

The pin was still around Bell's finger.

Everything went white and hot, like the birth of a new star.

BELL, AND EVERY LIVING thing within a hundred yards of her, was vaporized.

The explosion ignited the air. The flames surged through the confined spaces of the Site, washing against walls and flowing down tunnels like a wave. The temperatures inside topped out at 2,500 degrees Fahrenheit—roughly the melting point of steel.

It was like sticking a blowtorch in an anthill.

Marsh felt something like the sun on his back. It was pleasant at first. Then it hurt. It hurt a lot. He wanted to run, but there was nowhere to go, and it just kept getting *hotter*—

Marsh and the rest of the Snakeheads were burned down into charcoal.

CADE FELT THE WAVE of fire chase them up the elevator shaft.

The elevator was too slow and too close. He and Zach would have to escape, or burn.

He grabbed Zach and slammed the emergency exit in the roof open. He slung Zach over his shoulder and skittered up the wall of the shaft like a roach.

The fire and superheated air hit the elevator car like a bomb. It ground to a halt, the hydraulics bursting and shattering as the fluid went from room temperature to boiling in under a second. The car broke free and skidded down the shaft, collapsing to slag at the bottom.

Cade was hit with only a fraction of the backdraft, but it nearly took him off the wall. He almost lost Zach. With his free hand, he wedged his feet against the walls and levered the ground-floor doors open with one hand.

He fell forward and spilled Zach onto the ground.

The elevator doors closed behind him, allowing only a small puff of smoke to escape.

People rushed by, buzzing happily as they headed for the stores, paying no attention to him at all.

He picked Zach up again. The latest blow to the head, his exhaustion and the concussion had all combined to send him deeply unconscious. Cade needed to get him medical attention—and fast.

There was no trace of Tania anywhere.

THE "MONSTER SALE" at Liberty Mall was considered a massive success.

Shoppers went home with armloads of merchandise, and the retailers cleared out their stale inventory. It was discussed at marketing conferences as a textbook example of shifting perceptions during an economic slump.

Only two things marred the otherwise-perfect event. One elevator, by the ugly mural in the east section of the Mall, was out of order, forcing a long detour for those in wheelchairs or assisted-mobility scooters.

And many of the shoppers reported a peculiar smell. Some said it was like burning BBQ, while others blamed the Porta-Johns outside.

It dissipated after a few days, and no one thought much about it again.

FORTY-FIVE

1957—"Pod People" Incident—The California town of Mira Loma is nearly entirely wiped out by a cryptobotanical fungal outbreak that creates plant-based duplicates of human beings. The fungus, which appears to be some kind of sentient, mass intelligence distributed through its network of spores, was destroyed when the town's lone survivor alerted proper authorities. However, a number of spores were known to have been transported outside the city limits via truck, and have never been accounted for.

—BRIEFING BOOK: CODE NAME: NIGHTMARE PET

Zach checked out of Offutt's base hospital the next morning. He and Cade were on a military transport an hour after that. It had only taken a couple phone calls for Zach to reinstate Cade's RED RUM clearance.

He didn't speak for the longest time on the flight back to D.C., staring out the window instead.

But at one point, he turned to Cade. "Why do you think she did it?"

Bell. Cade had seen no reason to hide the truth about her from Zach.

"I don't know," Cade said. "Perhaps she thought it would make up for some of the things she did."

"Do you think so?"

"No," Cade said. There were crimes that were beyond forgiveness; something he knew all too well.

Zach winced. "Once again, you're a huge comfort."

They sat in silence. Then Zach spoke without looking at him. "Thank you for going into that room after me."

"Part of the job," Cade said.

Zach shook his head. "I was in there. I wouldn't have blamed you if you left me. That's not just one of those things people say, you understand? That's how bad it was, Cade."

Cade nodded.

"You've saved my life dozens of times. This was different. There was a moment—" Zach paused. "This was worse. That's all I can tell you. So: thank you."

For a moment, Cade could see, it all came back on Zach—the blackness, the fear, everything he'd learned about himself in that room, everything he'd lost.

This would have to be handled delicately. Cade knew there was only one thing to say.

"Ain't no thang, homeslice. Who's got your back?"

Zach looked at him for a second like he was insane, and then his face split into a smile. He couldn't laugh. Not yet. But he smiled, and something of the old Zach was back.

"Homeslice?"

"I'm trying to update my slang."

"Please don't."

"Whatever you say, dawg."

EPILOGUE

WASHINGTON, D.C.

Zach blew past the secretary guarding the door of the Oval. She recognized him. He hadn't been gone that long. So she tried to talk to him instead of giving the panic signal that would tell the Secret Service agent in the foyer to shoot him dead.

"Zach," she said. "Wait, he's in conference. Zach!"

There was no conference, no matter what the president's schedule said. Everyone in Samuel Curtis's inner circle—a group that once included Zach—knew that 11:15 to 11:25 A.M. every day was sacrosanct. Never bother him for those ten minutes. The one exception was nuclear war, or a terrorist attack. "And it had better be one of the major cities in a swing state," someone had once joked. It was the one rule that was inviolate, if you wanted to keep working for Curtis: you *do not* mess with the president's smoke break.

He'd told the media and his wife that he'd quit, and in truth, he'd made a valiant effort. But it was a stressful job, and he had practically no other vices to blow off steam. He didn't diddle the interns or pop pills like some of the previous occupants of the office. He'd managed to cut back to one cigarette a day. For his sanity, he needed that quiet space. He just didn't need a picture on CNN (or, God forbid, Fox) of him lighting up in the White House.

Zach slammed the door open. The president jumped a bit in his chair, startled. Not even the Secret Service was allowed in the room while he smoked. He hastily stubbed out the butt in an old ashtray—a commemorative glass dish from Nixon's 1960 campaign, a private joke. Technically, the White House, like all government buildings, was a nonsmoking area, but there were some rules the big man was allowed to break.

He realized it wasn't his wife or a reporter. His face darkened with rage when he saw Zach.

Zach was in no mood. He held up a warning finger. "You don't get to be pissed. Trust me on this."

The Secret Service man outside the door heard the tone and poked his head inside the office. The president considered Zach for a moment, then waved him away. "It's all right, Patrick," he said. "Close the door, please."

Zach noticed, for the first time, *The Washington Post* on the desk: WHITE HOUSE CHIEF OF STAFF FOUND DEAD IN APPARENT SUICIDE. The inside pages were full of analysis about how this might relate to the midterm elections, now only a day away.

"Did I interrupt your mourning period?" Zach asked.

The president glanced at the paper, then back at Zach. "He decided that pills would be easier than facing Cade."

"He got off easy."

The president shrugged. "He wasn't the first to spare Cade the work. And he won't be the last. Why are you here, Zach?" Curtis gave Zach his most withering stare, but Zach didn't flinch.

"A lot of people could have died because you trusted the wrong man. Of more immediate concern to me, *I* almost died because of the choice you made."

"Again, it wasn't the first time, and it won't be the last. It goes with the job, Zach. I thought you understood that. Some people said I made a mistake when I chose you for the position you currently fill."

Zach almost smiled. It was a subtle deflection. President Curtis really was untouchable as a politician. But Zach wasn't about to be distracted.

"I'm not playing those games any longer, Mr. President. I am doing the job. I showed up to work. The question is, have you?"

For the first time Zach could remember, the president looked confused. "I'm not sure I follow you."

"Prador was able to get away with as much as he did because he controlled access to you. I had to work through channels. You never knew the threat existed because I couldn't get the information to you. That's no longer acceptable to me."

"It's not?" The president's voice was flat.

"No. You've been handling me—handling all of this—as if it's just another problem to be managed. You should know better. And frankly, neither I nor the country can afford that anymore."

"You're not thinking this through, Zach. There's the matter of secrecy. Deniability. These protocols are in place for a reason—"

Zach cut him off. "I could give a damn, sir. I'm no longer interested in providing you with deniability. I have risked my life for you, and I'll keep doing it. But not to preserve your poll numbers. You are in the loop on all of this whether you like it or not."

For a moment, Curtis simply remained stone-faced. "What do you want?"

"I want the priority line," Zach said. "The one that's not supposed to exist. The little phone in your pocket that nobody else is supposed to be able to call. From now on, that's my line to you. It rings, you pick up. No matter what."

"That's it?"

"No, sir," Zach plunged ahead. "If I ask for anything—from a brief-case full of cash to a nuclear strike—I expect to get it. I cannot keep fighting these things without your full support."

Zach waited as the president considered the angles. "You know, of course," he said, finally, "that one reason I picked you was because you understand politics. You and Cade are never supposed to be connected to this office. That the entire point of all our secrecy is to protect not only the White House, but your operations? Not to mention protecting the American public from the knowledge you and I already have? You're asking a lot, Zach."

Zach clenched his teeth and chose his next words carefully. "You've already given me access to the biggest secrets in American history, sir. Whitewater and Watergate would look like butterfly kisses compared to the shitstorm you'd face if even a few of them got out."

Curtis smiled. "Yes, but most of those sound like the rantings of a lunatic. Deniability is built in. Who would believe someone who claimed that there was a vampire working for the president?"

"I don't know about that, sir. Just think how the *Post* would have played it if they found out Prador was under investigation for treason."

The president leaned forward. The look in his eyes could have scalded paint off the wall. "Are you suggesting someone might tell them such a thing?"

Zach held his ground. "No, sir. I'm speaking hypothetically, of course."

The president leaned back in his chair again. "Of course. So this is an ultimatum? You get this, or you quit?"

Zach felt his anger and frustration about to break, like waves on the shore. He was tired. "No. No, sir. I can't quit. And neither can you. Damn it, *you* picked *me*. You honestly think I'd bother you in the middle of the night to order a pizza? Griff might have been happy to say, 'Ours is not to reason why.' But I'm not him. For one thing, I'm not fighting this as a holding action anymore. I want to win. Someday, I want to put my feet up and celebrate the day we killed every last one of the damned things on the Other Side. This is where it starts. It's that simple. I'm saying I'm done screwing around. I need to know you are, too."

The president kept staring. Zach swallowed. "Sir," he added.

Finally, he reached for a pen and scribbled a number on a small slip of paper.

"I trust you, Zach," he said.

Zach took the paper.

"Anything else?" the president asked.

"Just one more thing."

"I was joking, Zach."

"I'm not, sir." He took a folded sheet of paper from his coat pocket and slid it across the desk.

The president read it, then raised his eyebrows at Zach. "You want me to sign this?"

"It's not a nuclear strike, sir."

"It's not exactly a pizza, either." But with a quick flourish, he signed the document and handed it back.

He reached for another cigarette and his lighter. "Two in one day?" Zach asked.

The president gave him a dangerous look. "Some days are longer than others."

Zach took the hint and headed for the door. As he left, he heard the president exhale heavily as he muttered to himself: "How quickly they grow up."

GRAVES STACKED THE LAST of his papers into his briefcase. He never thought retirement would be so much goddamn work.

When he'd woken up a couple of weeks ago and learned he was still in the old world, he'd felt the inevitable disappointment. He'd failed. The Snakeheads were not tearing through America's heartland. Everything was pretty much the same as it was the day before. He imagined this must be how a lot of people felt on the morning of January 1, 2000.

The Site itself: total loss. The DNA necessary to create the Snakeheads burned to nothing. The Company was looking for new branches of the Marsh family tree, but no one was optimistic about that.

Despite his failure, the Company had no hard feelings. At least, not enough to send a hit squad after him. As a gold watch, Graves was elevated to CEO of Archer/Andrews. He'd spend the rest of his days in comfort, secure in the respect and admiration of his peers.

He'd earned it. Other men, younger men, would carry on the battle for the new world now. He'd help where he could. Until it arrived, he intended to enjoy himself.

Unfortunately, the executive flights to Dubai and steak dinners were put on hold as every federal agency in town stormed the gates.

Within days of Graves's return from Iowa, congressional subpoenas hit the offices. The IRS began an audit. FBI agents were talking to A/A clients, and there were rumors of a federal grand jury. Now even the reporters smelled blood and were circling.

He knew where this was coming from, of course: the White House. He never thought that little bastard Barrows could generate so many problems in such a short amount of time.

He'd just spent another long day calming the fears of the board members while overseeing damage control. The lawyers called every twenty

minutes. The shredders in the basement were running full-time, and Graves had a tech team wiping hard drives in every office.

Graves looked at his watch—past nine P.M. At least he'd get out before midnight, for a change.

Then he noticed the figure standing at the door of his office. He pursed his lips in disgust.

Cade.

Great. That was all he needed.

Graves sighed. "I don't suppose you're here for a job."

"Not exactly."

"Do we really have to do this again? You cannot touch me. Ever. And I will never fear you again. Learn to accept defeat. Or don't. Either way, I have a busy schedule this week."

"You're an important man. I know that," Cade said as he entered the room, closing the door behind him. "I promise, this won't take long."

He slid a single sheet of paper across the desk.

Graves recognized the form. An order for *Indefinite Preventive Detention*.

The signature under "authorization" was crisp and clear: the President of the United States.

And in the line at the top, Graves saw his own name. The one he'd left behind when he joined the Company. His real name: PETER SINCLAIR.

True names have power. He remembered telling someone that.

He broke out in a cold sweat. Cade's mouth twitched in amusement. Bell's last gift.

She really was a genius at research.

Colonel Graves was the recipient of a presidential pardon. Immune from all prosecution or sanction. Untouchable.

Peter Sinclair, on the other hand . . .

"You have been designated as an enemy combatant, Colonel," Cade said.

"No," Graves said. "You can't do this."

Cade took a step closer to the desk.

Graves's voice rose to a scream. "No. *You can't do this! I have rights!*"

Cade smiled. "Not anymore."

There was more after that, but Cade hadn't been lying. It didn't take long. For him.

For Graves, it lasted the rest of his life.

ACKNOWLEDGMENTS

I've been lucky enough to have the help and support of many people in writing this book. Many thanks are due:

Alexandra Machinist, peerless agent; Rachel Kahan, fearless editor; Ivan Held; Justin Manask; Lucas Foster; William Heisel, for his relentless enthusiasm; Bryon Farnsworth; Amanda Rocque; Megan Underwood Beatie; Lynn Goldberg; Britt McCombs, for sparing the world my sadistic abuse of the comma; Tom Alfaro; the legendary Beau Smith; Lauren Kaplan; Victoria Comella; Eric Almendral; John Whalen and Jonathan Vankin, for their generous permission to quote from *The 80 Greatest Conspiracies of All Time*; Patrick Fitch; Dr. Rachel Lynn; and Dr. Laura Seay.

I'm unbelievably blessed to have Jean Roosevelt Farnsworth as my first reader and our daughter, Caroline, for moral support and all-purpose motivation.

For the real-life stories of the black world, I recommend Trevor Paglen's remarkable *Blank Spots on the Map: The Dark Geography of the Pentagon's Secret World* and Tim Weiner's *Legacy of Ashes: The History of the CIA*.